The Unwanted

David Lee Corley

DEDICATION

Table of Contents

Quote

"No one wants a warrior, until the enemy is at the gate."

\- Unknown

Prologue

Most of us have forgotten those that we owe much. It's normal. Life takes our time and our thoughts. Life is not easy. But we should take a moment… just a moment to remember… to be grateful for the shoulders we stand on. Guardians that have given all to secure our forthcoming. They did it without hope for reward, without even our acknowledgement. They didn't know us. It was selfless love. Knowing that their sacrifice would be our future. Soldiers, police, firemen, nurses, the unseen, and more. Heroes often find themselves cast aside, shunned by a society that cannot comprehend the depths of their sacrifice.

This is the story of the unwanted, until we needed them. Those that work in the shadows. Those that know wrong from right. Those that follow their heart. They continue to fight, not on the battlefield, but in the shadows of a world that has forgotten them. They battle against the demons that haunt their dreams, the memories that threaten to consume them. They cling to the hope that their sacrifices were not in vain, that the future they fought for is still worth defending. In the depths of their being, they know that their service, their bravery, and their dedication have made a difference.

The Egg

Snow fell thick on Moscow's streets, the flakes dissolving in puddles of yellow lamplight. Inside Café Pushkin, candlelight flickered across marble tables where the city's wealthy dined on beluga caviar and gold-rimmed china. Waiters in black moved between gilt-framed mirrors that multiplied the crystal chandeliers into infinity. The air carried hints of saffron, truffle and old money.

Lev Mikhailovich Andreev sat alone at his usual table, the best in the restaurant, positioned to see every entrance and exit. His manicured fingers rested near a lacquered box small enough to hold in one palm. The box gleamed with the deep shine of generations of careful polishing, its surface adorned with intricate inlays of mother-of-pearl and gold.

Viktor Nikolaevich Petrov entered with four men, their expensive suits cut wide to hide shoulder holsters and ceramic plate armor. His face bore the weathered creases of Siberian oil fields, of empire built in cold and mud and blood. His security team spread through the dining room with practiced efficiency, eyes scanning corners and doorways, hands never far from concealed weapons. Their polished shoes left wet prints on Persian carpets.

Petrov paused at the table's edge. His security chief leaned in to whisper something, but Petrov waved him off. The room had grown quieter, other diners suddenly very interested in their meals.

"Sit," Andreev said, gesturing to the empty chair. "Please. The chef has prepared something special - golden osetra, perfectly aged."

"Lev Mikhailovich." Petrov's voice carried careful respect despite his clenched jaw. "I did not expect to find you in Moscow."

"Business brings me home. Sit. We should discuss your company's future like civilized men."

Petrov remained standing for a moment longer, weighing pride against prudence. Andreev's reputation hung in the air between them - the stories of rivals who disappeared, of families who vanished, of empires that crumbled overnight. Finally, Petrov settled into the chair.

Andreev slid the lacquered box across fine linen. "A gift. To begin our conversation properly."

Distrust flickered in Petrov's eyes, but curiosity won. His fingers found the box's brass catch, aged to a deep patina. The lid opened on silent hinges. Inside, light caught a gold and platinum Fabergé Egg, crystal carved to look like frost. The Winter Egg of 1913, lost since the Revolution when the Bolsheviks seized the Imperial collection. Petrov's breath caught at its perfection.

"Beautiful, isn't it?" Andreev said softly. "Like holding history in your hands."

"How did you acquire this?" Petrov's voice was barely a whisper.

"The same way I acquire everything - with patience and resources." Andreev sipped his wine. "I'm doubling my previous offer for your company."

"The company is worth ten times that amount. The Asian contracts alone—"

"Perhaps it's time to retire, Viktor Nikolaevich. Enjoy your remaining years. Travel. Spend time with your family."

"My son will run the company when I step down. He has the education, the vision. Harvard Business School, five years at Goldman Sachs—"

"Sons can be a weakness." Andreev's voice carried neither threat nor emotion. Just cold fact. "They make us vulnerable in ways we don't see until it's too late."

Petrov's hand trembled slightly as he closed the box. The click of the latch seemed very loud. "The egg is exquisite, Lev Mikhailovich. A generous gift. But my answer remains no." He tucked the box under his arm and stood, inclining his head with careful politeness. His security team materialized around him as he walked away.

Andreev watched him go, pale eyes unblinking. Outside, snow still fell, erasing footprints, covering all traces of what had been. The sommelier appeared at his elbow with another bottle of Bordeaux. Andreev's glass had gone empty without him noticing. The wine poured red as blood against white linen.

Viktor Petrov's mansion rose from Moscow's outskirts, its limestone facade bright against gathering storm clouds. Inside the grand living room, crystal chandeliers cast warm light across marble floors. His wife Marina adjusted a brass pedestal centered on an antique mahogany table, while their children watched - Mikhail, twenty-eight, fresh from his Goldman Sachs trading desk, Dmitri, sixteen, and Anya, twelve.

"We should have a proper display case," Mikhail said, straightening his Italian silk tie, "Something more secure for a treasure so precious."

Petrov lifted the Winter Egg and its golden stand from its lacquered box with reverent hands. "This belonged to the Romanovs," he said, placing it on the pedestal. Light caught the crystal and platinum, throwing patterns across the walls. "Now it belongs to our family. Something to pass down through generations."

Marina touched his arm. "It's beautiful, Viktor."

Three hundred meters away, behind the wheels of a parked delivery van, Andreev's man watched through a Leupold spotting scope. His breath fogged the eyepiece as he studied the family tableau. The egg sat exactly where it needed to be. The detonator lay in his lap, its red LED steady.

Anya stepped closer to the egg, finger reaching out to touch the delicate metalwork. "Careful," Petrov warned with a smile. The girl pulled her hand back, grinning at her father.

Mikhail moved closer, examining the egg with a banker's eye. "The insurance value alone—"

The assassin's finger found the detonator's button. He pressed it without hesitation.

The explosion tore through the room's center, the blast consuming the Petrovs in a single violent instant. The mansion's windows shattered outward as fire roared through its heart. The force knocked the van's side mirror askew. Through the scope, the assassin watched flames climb into iron-grey sky. No one emerged from the inferno.

He started the van's engine, then paused to send a single text: Complete.

Snow began to fall, white flakes turning black as they spiraled into the flames.

Andreev sat in his private study, the room lit only by three wall-mounted screens. The largest showed a Russian news anchor, her face grave as she reported the Petrov family tragedy. Images of the burning mansion filled the screen. The second monitor tracked Petrov Oil's stock price in real time, numbers falling like drops of blood. The third displayed trading volumes, each spike marking another institutional investor fleeing the company.

He poured himself a glass of Macallan 25, the amber liquid catching blue light from the screens. The news anchor's voice filled the silence: "Sources say the explosion may have been caused by a gas leak, though investigators have yet to make an official statement. Viktor Petrov, along with his wife Marina and their three children..."

The stock price fell through another support level. Hedge funds were dumping shares in blocks of millions. Without Petrov or his Harvard-educated heir to guide the company, the market's verdict was swift and brutal.

Andreev lifted his phone, pressed a single number. "Begin purchasing at forty-five dollars," he said. "Use the shell companies we discussed. Keep the individual orders small enough to avoid scrutiny." He sipped his scotch, watching the price continue its plunge. "Yes, all of them. Buy until we have fifty-one percent."

He set the phone down and turned up the news volume. They were showing photos of the family now - vacation shots, charity events, graduation ceremonies. Mikhail in his Goldman Sachs ID photo. Anya at her ballet recital. The anchor's voice cracked slightly as she read the children's ages.

Andreev muted the television. The second screen showed the stock touching forty-six dollars. Soon the buying would begin, carefully orchestrated to look like multiple independent investors seeing value in the panic. By morning, he would own the company.

He finished his scotch, ice cubes clicking against crystal. On screen, flames still consumed the Petrov mansion, erasing all trace of the family that had once lived there.

The Lighthouse

The sky darkened as the Nor'easter gathered strength, its ominous presence looming over the churning sea. Slate-gray clouds, heavy with moisture, rolled in from the horizon, blotting out the last remnants of daylight. The wind picked up, carrying with it the scent of brine and impending fury. Whitecaps formed on the waves, growing larger and more violent with each passing moment. The storm's approach was relentless, a force of nature bent on reshaping the coastline.

Standing defiant against the encroaching darkness, a weathered lighthouse rose from a small, rocky island. Its paint peeled and faded from years of harsh coastal elements. The structure creaked and groaned under the assault of the strengthening gale, but still, it endured. From its crown, a beam of light cut through the gloom, sweeping across the turbulent waters in a steady rhythm—a last bastion of hope for those caught in the tempest's path.

As the storm's first raindrops began to fall, a massive silhouette emerged atop the lighthouse. The figure stood motionless, a dark shape etched against the angry sky. Lightning flashed, illuminating for a brief moment the sheer scale of the man—a giant among mortals. His shoulders, impossibly broad, stretched the fabric of his worn jacket to its limits. His stance was that of an immovable object, unfazed by the wind that whipped around him or the rain that now fell in sheets.

As the storm raged, monstrous waves hurled themselves against the breakwater. Water exploded skyward in violent plumes, easily reaching the height of the lighthouse itself. The impact resonated through the island, a deep, thunderous boom that seemed to shake the very bedrock.

As night fully descended, the tempest showed no signs of abating. The Nor'easter had laid siege to the coast, and in its unrelenting fury, it seemed determined to reshape the very land itself. Yet the lighthouse stood, its light a defiant beacon, and atop it, the keeper maintained his vigilant watch, as immovable as the stone upon which the tower was built. Then, without warning, he let out a howl against the night. A hellish roar that would chill any sane person's blood. Pain. Remorse. Rage. A mortal man with the soul of a beast. His name was Frank Kane.

Dawn broke over a transformed coastline. The fury of the Nor'easter had passed, leaving behind a world scrubbed clean and eerily still. Sunlight glinted off puddles and wet stones, casting a golden sheen over the battered landscape. The air hung heavy with the scent of salt and wet earth.

Frank emerged from the lighthouse, his massive frame filling the doorway. He paused, squinting against the morning light. The calm felt alien after the night's chaos. Only the gentle lapping of waves against the shore and the occasional cry of a gull broke the silence.

Sunlight revealed a man reshaped by violence. Scars crisscrossed Frank's once-handsome face—a jagged knife wound from temple to jaw, mottled burn marks pulling his lips into a permanent half-grimace. His Roman nose, broken and poorly reset, spoke of countless brawls. Deep-set eyes, still sharp and alert, peered out from beneath a heavy brow, having seen more than most could bear.

Frank's bare arms told their own stories: bullet wounds puckered his left bicep, while shrapnel scars dotted his right forearm. A recent gash across the back of his hand suggested violence remained a constant companion. His broad chest and back bore a mix of precise surgical scars and chaotic marks of desperate struggles.

Despite this canvas of violence, Frank carried himself with quiet dignity. His movements were controlled and purposeful, unbowed by the weight of his experiences. Without a word, he began inspecting the storm's aftermath, moving with surprising grace for a man his size. His eyes scanned every inch of the lighthouse's exterior. Debris littered the ground— broken windows, twisted metal, splintered wood. Frank's expression remained impassive as he cataloged each piece of damage in a small notepad.

At the base of the tower, he stopped. Three stones, each as big as a man's torso, were broken. The mortar around them had crumbled, leaving a gap in the lighthouse's foundation. Frank knelt, his scarred hands hovering over the fractured rocks. He traced the new edges, feeling the rough texture beneath his calloused fingers.

Standing, Frank took a step back to assess the full extent of the damage. The broken stones stood out like a wound against the weathered surface of the lighthouse. Maintaining a New England lighthouse was a constant battle against nature and nature often won.

Without a word, he moved towards the boat dock shielded by the massive boulders forming the island's breakwater. There was work to be done, and Frank Kane was not a man to leave a task unfinished. The lighthouse had weathered the storm. Now it was time to ensure it would stand against the next one.

Frank's world was contained within the circular walls of the lighthouse keeper's quarters. The small, sparse room at the base of the tower held little more than necessities. A narrow bed, its springs creaking under his bulk, occupied one corner. A battered desk faced the single window, its surface clean save for a logbook and a chipped mug. A hot plate and a few dented pans served as a kitchen.

His days were consumed by the monumental task of restoring the dilapidated lighthouse. Frank attacked the work with silent resolve, his powerful hands moving from one repair to the next. He repointed crumbling mortar, replaced rotted timbers, and painstakingly scraped decades of salt-caked paint from metal railings. Each completed task was a step toward the lighthouse's rebirth—and toward Frank's own departure.

The irony wasn't lost on him. Once restored, the lighthouse would be upgraded with an automated system, rendering the keeper obsolete. Frank worked towards his own redundancy with the same stoic acceptance he applied to all aspects of his life. This place, like all others before it, was merely a temporary stop. No place had ever truly been home since he was a child.

His routine remained predictable. Each morning, Frank rose before dawn, his movements economical as he dressed and checked the light. He took his coffee black, the bitter liquid a stark counterpoint to the sweetness of the salt air. Maintenance and restoration tasks filled his daylight hours. Each evening, he logged the day's events in terse, efficient sentences.

The feral cat appeared months ago, a ragged ball of fur and fury that jumped in the lighthouse boat without warning or permission. Frank never named it. The cat crept around the lighthouse grounds, a ghost with matted gray fur and piss-yellow eyes full of distrust. Twice daily, Frank set out food and water, his movements slow and deliberate. The cat watched from a distance, hissing if Frank lingered too long.

Their interactions were a study in mutual wariness. The cat's ears flattened when Frank approached, claws digging into weathered wood. Frank's eyes narrowed, his massive hands flexing at his sides. Neither sought the other's company, yet both seemed to find comfort in the other's presence. It was an arrangement built on tolerance rather than affection.

At night, with the beacon sweeping over dark waters, Frank sometimes spotted the cat perched on the windowsill. Its silhouette stark against the glass, as vigilant in its watch as Frank himself. In these moments, a flicker of understanding passed between man and beast—two solitary creatures united in their temporary shelter.

Frank recognized in the animal a kindred spirit— fierce, independent, scarred by life. Neither needed companionship, yet each acknowledges the other's right to exist in the shared space.

As weeks bled into months, their routine remained unchanged. Frank restored the lighthouse piece by piece, the cat patrolled its territory pissing on everything to mark its ownership. They coexisted in a silence broken only by the occasional hiss or the constant moan of the wind. It wasn't friendship, not even cohabitation. It's simply life as Frank knew it—solitary, predictable, unburdened by the complexities of human interaction. And like all things in Frank's life, it was temporary, a fleeting moment before he moved on, as rootless as the tides.

Nestled along the craggy coastline, the village of Stormhaven clung to the edge of the continent like a barnacle to a ship's hull. Weather-beaten clapboard houses in faded shades of gray and blue lined narrow, winding streets that meandered down to the harbor. Salt-encrusted fishing boats, some seaworthy, others long abandoned, bobbed gently in the protected cove.

The heart of the town beat in the working harbor. The air was thick with the smell of brine, diesel, and fresh catch. Weathered fishermen in oil-stained slickers mended nets and swapped tales on creaking docks. The processing plant at the end of the pier hummed with activity, the only stable employer in a place where fortunes rose and fell with the tides.

Main Street boasted a handful of stalwart businesses—a general store with warped floorboards and perpetually fogged windows, a diner serving the same menu since 1952, and a bait and tackle shop doubling as the town's unofficial gossip hub. The Rusty Anchor, a bar as old as the town itself, stood sentinel at the street's end, its neon sign flickered weakly against the perpetual sea mist.

Beyond the town center, empty summer cottages dotted the shoreline, their windows dark and shuttered against the harsh winter winds. On the hill overlooking it all, the town's small cemetery told the story of generations lost to the sea, white headstones standing in solemn rows like breakers against the grass.

The village wore its isolation like a badge of honor. The nearest city was hours away, connected by a single winding road that hugged the coastline. Strangers were rare and viewed with a mix of curiosity and suspicion. Family names carried weight, and grudges were measured in decades.

The old truck's engine wheezed as Frank approached Millstone Quarry. Rust had long ago claimed dominion over the vehicle's once-blue paint, and the passenger-side mirror dangled precariously, held in place by fraying duct tape and stubborn hope.

As Frank pulled into the quarry's gravel lot, a fine mist of stone dust settled on the truck's hood, adding another layer to its patina of age and neglect. He stepped out, his heavy boots crunching on the loose stones. The truck's door shrieked in protest as he slammed it shut. He made his way towards the neatly stacked slabs of granite.

Gus, the wiry quarry owner, emerged from a corrugated metal shack that served as an office. He watched as the imposing figure of the lighthouse keeper moved among the stone slabs, studying each with a critical eye. Gus ignored Frank's disfigured face and arms. Gus had seen plenty of scarred soldiers during his time in Vietnam. Besides, the lighthouse keeper was a customer. That was all that mattered.

Frank's scarred hands ran over the rough surfaces, testing for imperfections. He moved between the stacks until he found what he was looking for. With a nod of satisfaction, he turned his attention to three particular slabs.

Gus approached, clipboard in hand. "Good eye," he remarked, glancing at Frank's selections. "Those are some of my best cuts. Just got them in yesterday. You want me to get the forklift?"

Before Gus could finish his offer, Frank was already in motion. He bent at the knees, his massive hands finding purchase on the stone's edges. Muscles rippled across his back and arms as he lifted, veins standing out like cords beneath his skin.

The slab of granite, easily weighing 600 pounds, rose from the ground. Gus's jaw dropped as he watched Frank carry the massive stone to his truck with deliberate, measured steps.

The vehicle's suspension groaned in protest as Frank lowered the first slab into the truck bed. Without pausing for rest, he returned for the second, then the third. Each time, Gus's eyes grew wider, his weathered face a mask of disbelief.

Other quarry workers stopped their tasks, watching in awe as this solitary giant single-handedly moved stones that typically required a team and heavy equipment.

With the granite loaded, Frank turned his attention to the stacked bags of mortar. He hefted two onto his shoulder, dropping them into the truck bed, which now sat perilously close to the wheel wells.

Gus approached cautiously, clutching an invoice. "That's quite a feat," he said, his voice a mix of admiration and unease. "Never seen anything like it."

Frank took the invoice, eyes scanning it briefly before pulling a worn wallet from his back pocket. He counted out the cash with thick fingers, handing it over to Gus.

As Frank climbed back into the driver's seat, the truck sank even lower, its springs pushed to their limit. The engine coughed to life, sputtering a plume of blue smoke. He eased the overloaded vehicle out of the lot, leaving behind a group of stunned quarrymen and a swirling cloud of stone dust.

Gus watched the truck disappear down the road, its rear end nearly scraping the ground. The quarry seemed unusually quiet in the wake of Frank's departure, as if the very stones were still in awe of what they'd witnessed.

Frank's weathered truck rumbled to a stop outside the Seaside Diner, its suspension groaning under the weight of the massive granite slabs in the bed. Through the smudged windshield, he saw the place was bustling, nearly every table occupied. His shoulders tensed, a frown deepening the lines on his scarred face. The thought of driving away crossed his mind, his stomach growling in protest.

For a long moment, Frank sat motionless, his large hands gripping the steering wheel. Options were scarce in this small coastal village, and hunger was a persistent adversary. With a resigned grunt, he heaved himself out of the truck, the vehicle lifting noticeably as it shed his considerable weight.

As Frank's boots hit the pavement, a little girl walking by with her mother as they left the diner pointed at him. Her eyes were wide with a mix of fear and curiosity. "Mommy, look at the marks on that man's—"

The mother's hand clamped over her daughter's mouth, muffling the rest of the words. She pulled the child close, quickening her pace as they hurried past.

Frank gave no other sign that he'd heard the little girl's comments. But he had. He just didn't care. He moved towards the diner entrance, his massive frame casting a shadow over the pavement.

The bell above the diner's door chimed as Frank entered, the sound almost comically delicate compared to his imposing presence. Conversations dimmed momentarily as heads turned, a ripple of unease passing through the crowded space. Frank kept his eyes straight ahead, navigating through the maze of tables and patrons who seemed to shrink in on themselves as he passed.

He made his way to the far corner, sliding into a booth that faced the wall. It was his usual spot, offering a modicum of privacy in the crowded diner. The vinyl seat groaned under his bulk as he settled in, his broad back a barrier between himself and the curious glances of other diners.

Maggie, a veteran waitress with graying hair and eyes that had seen it all, approached without hesitation. She carried a glass of Coke—no ice. Setting it down, she spoke with the familiarity of acquaintance.

"Double-meatloaf sandwich, smothered in gravy," Maggie announced, her voice carrying a hint of affection beneath its matter-of-fact tone. "Side of fries and coleslaw. That do you, Frank?"

Frank's response was a slight nod with no eye contact. Maggie, long accustomed to his ways, took no offense. She turned back to the kitchen, her departure releasing some of the tension in Frank's broad shoulders.

Frank's gaze fell to his hands resting on the worn Formica tabletop. A fine layer of stone dust from the quarry coated his skin, settling into the deep lines and scars that crisscrossed his palms. Without a word, he reached for the glass of water Maggie had left on the table.

With slow, deliberate movements, Frank dipped his fingers in the glass, then poured water on his hands. The water turned cloudy as he rubbed his palms together, the grit from the granite sloughing off. He paid no mind to the other patrons, some of whom watched this impromptu washing with a mix of fascination and disgust.

When he was satisfied, Frank pulled out a wad of napkins from the dispenser and wiped his hands dry. He set the now-murky glass aside and drank half the coke.

The diner's usual chatter slowly resumed, though muted whispers and furtive glances in Frank's direction persisted. He remained still, a solitary island in the sea of lunchtime commotion.

When Maggie returned, she carried a plate piled high with food. The double-meatloaf sandwich was a behemoth, thick slices of bread barely visible beneath a flood of rich, brown gravy. A mound of golden fries teetered on the edge of the plate, while a generous scoop of coleslaw completed the meal.

As the plate landed before him, Frank's demeanor shifted subtly. His massive hands took up knife and fork with surprising deftness. He attacked the meal with the single-minded focus of a bear emerging from hibernation.

Forkfuls of meatloaf and gravy-soaked bread disappeared in rapid succession. Fries vanished by the handful. The coleslaw provided brief, crunchy interludes in the steady rhythm of his eating.

Around the diner, conversations faltered as patrons watched as Frank devoured his meal. Some of the locals, more accustomed to the sight, returned to their own lunches with knowing smiles. Newcomers and tourists stared openly, their own meals forgotten.

In three minutes, the plate was clean. Frank used the last piece of bread to mop up the remaining gravy, leaving no morsel behind. He washed it all down with long gulps of Coke, the glass emptying as quickly as the plate.

As if to punctuate the end of his meal, Frank let out a thunderous belch that echoed through the diner, causing nearby patrons to flinch and stare in horrified silence, while he remained utterly undisturbed by their reactions.

Maggie appeared as if summoned, placing the bill on the table and whisking away the empty dishes. "Ya know, Frank. You might want to work on your social skills a bit seeing how you look like a chewed-dog toy and have the manners of a bull. Who knows? You might even make a friend."

Frank grunted his lack of interest.

"Anything else?" she asked, knowing the answer but asking all the same.

Frank shook his head, already reaching for his wallet. He left cash on the table—exact change plus a reasonable tip—and rose to leave. The diner fell quiet once more as he made his way to the door, patrons instinctively leaning away from his path.

The bell chimed again as Frank stepped out into the sunlight. Inside, the diner exhaled collectively, conversations slowly bubbling back to life. Outside, Frank climbed into his truck, the vehicle dipping under his weight. The engine roared to life, and he pulled away, leaving behind a diner full of people with a story to tell about the giant who ate lunch.

The small boat's motor chugged steadily as Frank guided it through the choppy waters towards the lighthouse island. Salt spray misted his face, mingling with the sweat on his brow. The craft rode dangerously low, its gunwales mere inches above the water's surface, weighed down by one of the three massive granite slabs and the bags of mortar. Frank's huge frame seemed to fill half the boat, his calloused hands gripping the engine's throttle with practiced ease.

As he approached the weather-beaten dock, Frank cut the engine, allowing the boat to drift the last few feet. The old wood creaked as he secured the vessel. Barnacles crunched under his boots as he rose, eyeing the precarious load.

Frank's muscles strained as he lifted the first granite slab. It was roughly four feet long and two feet wide. Yet in Frank's grip, it seemed almost manageable. He transferred it from boat to dock with a grunt, the entire structure shuddering under the sudden weight. Next, he unloaded the bags of mortar. Two more boat trips brought over the additional two slabs.

With the boat emptied, Frank headed for the lighthouse keeper's quarters. The lighthouse door creaked open, revealing a spiral staircase consumed by rust and decay. The once-proud helix now sagged dangerously, its metal treads eaten through by decades of salt air. Scaffolding embraced the failing structure, a modern steel skeleton supporting history's bones.

Wooden beams, rough and unfinished, braced against the weakest sections. Near the base, steps hung precariously, more memory than metal. Higher up, entire sections were missing, replaced by swaying wooden platforms that bridged yawning gaps.

As Frank's gaze traveled upward, the enormity of the task ahead became clear. Each step towards restoration would be a battle against time and the relentless sea.

Frank turned to his battered toolbox near the doorway for easy access. It was a heavy-duty metal affair, scarred and dented from years of use. He selected his tools with careful deliberation: a Stanley tape measurer, its yellow casing scuffed but the markings precise; a twenty-pound sledgehammer, its hickory handle shortened and polished smooth by years of use; a stonemason's hammer with its long chisel-shaped blade; a piece of soapstone; a Marshalltown cement trowel, its stainless steel blade honed to a keen edge; and a carbide-tipped drove chisel, its business end scarred from countless strikes against unyielding stone.

At the lighthouse's base, Frank knelt before the first damaged stone. His fingers, thick as sausages yet surprisingly sensitive, probed the cracks. Decades of salt air, freezing winters, and baking summers had taken their toll. Hairline fractures spiderwebbed across the granite's face, deepening towards the edges where mortar had crumbled away.

Frank positioned the long-blade of the stonemason's hammer with precision born of years of experience. The sledgehammer swung in a controlled arc, striking the smaller hammer's head with a resounding crack. Fragments of stone and mortar showered down as he worked, methodically loosening the damaged block. After several minutes of calculated strikes, Frank set aside his tools and gripped the stone with both hands. Veins bulged on his forearms as he exerted pressure, slowly working the block free from its centuries-old bed.

With the stone removed, Frank meticulously cleaned the recess, scraping away old mortar with the trowel. He then turned his attention to measurement, the tape measurer extending as he scribbled the dimensions on a pocket notepad. Each measurement was double-checked, his eyes squinting in concentration.

Moving to the first new slab, Frank marked it with soapstone, creating a precise outline. The drove chisel sang against the granite as he began to shape it, each strike of the hammer deliberate and controlled. Chips of stone flew as he worked, the rough slab gradually taking on the exact dimensions needed to fill the gap in the lighthouse wall.

In a large bucket, Frank mixed the mortar. He added water slowly to the dry mix, his massive hands kneading the mixture like dough. He tested the consistency repeatedly, adding small amounts of water or dry mortar until it was perfect – not too wet, not too dry, just sticky enough to bond stone to stone for another hundred years.

Using the trowel, Frank spread an even layer of mortar along the edges of the shaped stone and within the recess in the wall, ensuring complete coverage without excess.

With a deep breath, Frank lifted the new stone. Despite its weight, he maneuvered it with remarkable precision, easing it into place. It slid home with a satisfying squelch, fitting so perfectly that the seams were barely visible. Frank used the trowel to clean away excess mortar, then stepped back to survey his work with a critical eye.

As the sun began to set, casting long shadows across the island, the repaired section stood out slightly from its weathered neighbors. But Frank knew that in time, wind and water would blur the distinction, making his work indistinguishable from the original construction.

The feral cat appeared silently, watching Frank with wary yellow eyes. The cat crept along the edge of the wall, its body low and tense. Its gaze never left Frank, a mixture of curiosity and hostility evident in its unblinking stare. As Frank lifted another stone, muscles straining with the effort, the cat's ears flattened against its skull.

The sudden movement seemed to trigger something in the feline. It let out a hair-raising yowl, the sound echoing off the lighthouse walls. The cat's back arched, fur standing on end, making it appear twice its size. It hissed viciously, baring yellowed fangs as if Frank were an intruder in its domain.

Frank paused, the massive stone suspended in his grip. His eyes, as hard and unyielding as the granite he worked with, locked onto the cat. For a moment, man and beast engaged in a silent battle of wills, neither willing to back down.

Then, with a deliberateness that seemed to vibrate the very air, Frank spoke. "Piss off," he said, his voice a harsh croak, like stones grinding together. The words seemed to scrape their way out of his throat, a reminder of old wounds and a life lived hard.

The cat, startled by the unexpected sound, took a step back. Its yellow eyes widened, reflecting a mix of surprise and grudging respect. For a heartbeat, it held its ground, tail lashing back and forth. Then, as if deciding this battle wasn't worth the effort, it turned and slunk away, disappearing into the growing shadows with the same silence with which it had appeared.

Frank watched it go, his face an unreadable mask. Then, without further acknowledgment of the interruption, he turned back to his work. The stone slid into place with a soft grinding sound, another piece of the puzzle slotting perfectly into the lighthouse's weathered facade.

As night began to fall in earnest, Frank's silhouette stood out against the darkening sky, a solitary figure engaged in his endless task of holding back the ravages of time and tide.

The lighthouse creaked in the night wind. Frank lay on his narrow bed, his massive body overflowing the metal frame and mattress. His eyes moved rapidly beneath closed lids as the dream took hold of him.

Congo. Wet heat and cordite. The mining facility sprawled across red earth, chainlink topped with razor wire. Frank moved through shadows, leading his team of mercenaries toward the perimeter. Gunfire erupted from the guard towers. Child soldiers, their small silhouettes visible against flickering work lights. The local warlord had armed them with AKs, drugged them with brown-brown, turned them into fearless killers. They had overrun the mine killing the local security force. Frank and his team were being paid well to take it back.

Frank's team returned fire, suppressing the towers as they advanced. Bullets cracked past his head. He dove behind a dilapidated wall, concrete crumbling from impacts. His breath caught.

On the wall's opposite side, a boy crouched, perhaps ten, AK-47 trained on Frank's chest. Their eyes met across the gun barrels. The boy's pupils were huge, black holes from the cocaine-gunpowder mix. But something else lived in those eyes. Pure rage. Cold. Absolute.

Frank lowered his weapon slowly. "Easy," he said. "You don't have to die here." The boy's finger stayed on the trigger, but confusion crossed his face. No adult had ever shown him mercy. The AK's barrel dipped slightly.

Radio static crackled. "Moving to your position," a voice said. The rest of Frank's team was coming. The boy heard them too. His eyes went wild, drug-rage returning. The AK's barrel started to rise.

They fired simultaneously. The boy's rounds punched into Frank's armored vest, walking up his chest as the barrel rose under full auto. Fire tore through Frank's throat. His own shots caught the boy center mass. Small hands released the AK. The boy looked surprised, touching the blood spreading across his shirt before falling.

Frank's blood poured between his fingers as he clutched his neck and fell backward. Williams, the team medic, skidded to his side. "Christ, Frank. Hold on." The medic's hands moved fast, packing the wound. Frank's vision dimmed. He turned his head, found the boy's empty eyes staring at clouds. No rage now. No mercy. Just another child who'd never had a choice.

Frank woke, sweat soaking his sheets despite the cold. His hand found the scar where the bullet had torn through flesh. The lighthouse light swept across his room, regular as a metronome. But he saw only the boy's eyes, and the moment when protecting his men meant killing a child who'd never had a chance at innocence.

Grace

Willow Crest, an exclusive enclave nestled in Connecticut's Gold Coast, sat within an easy commute to Wall Street, its manicured streets a showcase of new money masquerading as old. Gated driveways lined Magnolia Avenue, each guarding a mansion more ostentatious than the last. Victorian-style homes with suspiciously pristine gingerbread trim stood alongside neo-Georgian manors, their columns gleaming white against red brick.

The community boasted all the trappings of old-money respectability: a members-only country club with a golf course designed by a famous architect, tennis courts perpetually occupied by tanned players in crisp whites, and a yacht club where sleek vessels bobbed in their slips, many rarely touched open water. On weekends, the streets buzzed with luxury cars as residents made their social rounds, air-kissing at charity galas held in oversized ballrooms.

Streets bore lofty names like "Astor Place" and "Vanderbilt Lane," invoking images of Gilded Age tycoons. Gardeners meticulously trimmed hedges into fanciful shapes, while sprinkler systems ensured lawns remained an unnatural shade of green year-round.

Amidst this landscape of curated grandeur, the Kane estate dominated Willow Crest. The modernized château sprawled across three acres, its limestone facade and Welsh slate roof a testament to opulence. A wrought-iron gate, curled into an ornate "K," marked the entrance to a winding driveway. Inside, antiques mingled with bespoke pieces, each room a stage set designed to impress. Crystal chandeliers hung from coffered ceilings, while oil paintings of vaguely aristocratic "ancestors" gazed down from silk-papered walls.

The mansion stood as a monument to aspiration, a golden cage both beautiful and suffocating, much like the life it contained—a perfect embodiment of Willow Crest itself, where appearance was everything and old money dreams were bought at new money prices.

Grace "Gracie" Kane leaned close to the bathroom mirror, her breath fogging the glass as she carefully applied a thin line of black eyeliner below each eye. Her parents called her "Gracie" while her friends called her "G." At thirteen, her face was losing its childish roundness, cheekbones beginning to emerge like the first hints of dawn. She stepped back, critically examining her handiwork. The eyeliner was subtle – hopefully not enough to raise suspicion, but just enough to make her feel older, bolder.

She smoothed down her school uniform, the pleated skirt and blazer a stark contrast to the rebellion brewing beneath. Her fingers lingered on the hem of the skirt, tempted to pin it up, push just a little further. But not today. Small steps, she reminded herself.

Back in her bedroom, Grace's gaze swept over the conflicting decor. Fairytale castles and unicorn figurines shared space with posters of Joan Jett's fierce grin and David Bowie's otherworldly stare. Miley Cyrus and Zendaya gazed down from the walls, embodiments of the woman Grace yearned to become – confident, successful, free.

The intercom crackled to life, the family chef's voice filling the room. "Breakfast is ready, Miss Grace."

Grace's jaw clenched. The formality, the routine, the expectations – it all felt suffocating suddenly. Her eyes fell on her childhood teddy bear, propped against her pillows. Yesterday, she'd hugged it for comfort. Today, it looked like a mockery of the woman she was trying to be.

A surge of emotion – anger, frustration, fear – welled up inside her. With a choked cry, Grace grabbed the bear and hurled it across the room. It hit her bookshelf, sending a cascade of fairytale books tumbling to the floor.

The sight of her childhood littered across the carpet broke something loose inside her. Grace moved through her room like a whirlwind, tearing down posters of cartoon princesses, sweeping stuffed animals off shelves, and yanking childish trinkets from her vanity.

She dumped armfuls into her trash can, which quickly overflowed. Glitter pens, friendship bracelets, and a tiara from her princess phase spilled onto the floor. Grace stomped on the tiara, feeling a vicious satisfaction as the plastic gems popped free.

Breathing hard, she surveyed the carnage. Her room looked like a battlefield where childhood had lost to adolescence. A glint of gold caught her eye – a locket her mother had given her for her tenth birthday. Grace's hand trembled as she picked it up.

For a moment, she stood frozen, torn between the comfort of the past and the allure of the future. Then, with a sharp intake of breath she considered her options.

The intercom crackled again. "Miss Grace? Your breakfast is getting cold."

In response, Grace let the locket slip from her hand and fall into the trashcan. There would be no retreat. No going back.

Grace squared her shoulders, pushing down the ache in her chest. She glanced in the mirror, taking in her thin eyeliner and flushed cheeks.

With a final glance at the wreckage of her childhood, Grace strode out of her room. She was done with being caught in between. From now on, she was moving forward – no matter how much it hurt.

As Grace descended the grand staircase, her parents' voices drifted up from the patio.

"Jesus, Richard, two bodyguards each? Plus two for the house? It's overkill," her mother's voice snapped.

"It's necessary, Vivian. You know the shit I deal with," her father's tone was clipped. "The more money I make, the more dangerous our lives become. We are just lucky we have the resources to afford the very best protection money can buy… to keep Grace and you safe."

Grace peered around a marble column. Her mother, Vivian, stood with her arms crossed, still strikingly beautiful despite the scowl on her face. Years of international modeling had left her with an instinct for poise, even in anger. She wore yoga pants and a fitted top – a studied casualness.

Richard Kane, Frank's identical twin, cut an imposing figure in his tailored suit. He shared Frank's impressive build and chiseled features, but where Frank's face was a tragedy, Richard's was smooth and refined. His education was evident in every calculated word.

The Kane twins had once been indistinguishable, their matching faces exhibited their shared DNA. But life had carved separate paths for the brothers; while Richard's visage remained unmarred, a billboard of a Harvard education and a Wall Street success, Frank's had become a rugged topography of scars and hardship, each line and mark a record of a life lived in the shadows of violence and solitude.

"We're living in a goddamned fortress, Richard. Is that what you want for Gracie?" said Vivian.

At the mention of her name, Grace stepped onto the patio. Both parents turned, their argument dying abruptly.

"Morning," Grace mumbled, sliding into her seat.

She noticed two figures standing near the patio railing, their backs to the family as their trained eyes scanned the manicured grounds. These weren't the rent-a-cop types found in shopping malls; these men were clearly professionals and heavily armed.

The one on the left, a tall Black man with shoulders like a linebacker, stood perfectly still, his hands clasped behind his back. A sleek earpiece curled around his ear, occasionally emitting a soft crackle of communication. His partner, a wiry white guy with a military-style crew cut, slowly panned his gaze across the property, one hand resting casually near his hip where his pistol was hidden.

Grace knew from overheard conversations that they carried more than just sidearms. Concealed knives, tasers, and who knew what else were part of their everyday gear. Their jackets were specially designed to hide the bulletproof vests underneath, a constant reminder of the perceived threats surrounding the Kane family.

Despite their imposing presence, the bodyguards might as well have been statues for all the attention Vivian and Richard paid them. To Grace's parents, they were just another part of the landscape, like the expensive patio furniture or the meticulously pruned topiaries. But to Grace, they were yet another symbol of the gilded cage she lived in.

The security team leader, Ken Davis, moved along the perimeter wall. Two of his men swept the grounds with German shepherds. The dogs' ears pricked toward movement in the boxwood hedge. A rabbit darted out. The lead dog's muscles tensed but a sharp command from his handler kept him in check.

Inside the command center, monitors displayed thermal images of every approach to the mansion. A delivery truck appeared at the main gate. Davis's team intercepted it, mirrors checking under the chassis, dogs circling the vehicle. The driver's credentials were verified before they allowed him through.

The morning sun rose higher as his men rotated positions with practiced efficiency, the illusion of safety maintained through force and vigilance.

Richard's eyes narrowed as he scrutinized his daughter's face. The family chef served breakfast in tense silence.

"What's with the eyeliner, Gracie?" Richard asked suddenly.

Grace's fork clattered against her plate. "Dad, come on. It's barely there."

"Barely there is still there," Richard said. "Take it off before school."

"Richard," Vivian interjected, "it's just a little makeup. All the girls—"

"All the girls aren't on thin ice with their headmaster," Richard cut in. He turned back to Grace. "You've already been suspended once. You want to make it twice?"

Grace slumped in her chair. She glanced at her mother, hoping for support, but Vivian had already turned away, suddenly fascinated by her coffee.

"Whatever," Grace muttered, stabbing at her free-range eggs.

Richard stood, straightening his tie. "I'm heading out. Busy day." He pecked Vivian's cheek and squeezed Grace's shoulder as he passed and whispered a reminder, "Lose the eyeliner."

As Richard's shoes clicked on the marble floor, Grace caught her mother's eye. For a moment, she thought she saw a flicker of understanding. But then Vivian's face smoothed into its usual mask.

"You heard your father," she said softly.

Grace nodded, suddenly feeling very small. She ate mechanically, already planning to reapply her eyeliner in the school bathroom. A tiny rebellion against her gilded cage.

Eyeliner free, Grace slid into the backseat of the family's latest acquisition - a matte black, bullet and bomb-proof SUV that looked more appropriate for a war zone than a Connecticut suburb. The vehicle's weight settled noticeably as her two bodyguards took their positions.

"All clear, moving out." said Kovacs, the driver. He was a stocky Eastern European with close-cropped salt-and-pepper hair and hands that looked like they could bend steel. His partner, Martinez, a wiry ex-Marine with watchful eyes, sat in the passenger seat, his gaze constantly scanning their surroundings.

Both men wore crisp suits that barely concealed their muscular builds, with telltale bulges hinting at concealed sidearms. Coiled wires ran from their earpieces down into their collars. Between them, within easy reach, sat two Heckler & Koch MP5 submachine guns, their presence a reminder of the threats lurking in the world outside.

As they pulled away from the Kane estate, Grace caught snippets of their terse communication.

"Checkpoint Alpha clear," Kovacs muttered.

"Roger that. Eyes on Boulevard approach," Martinez responded, his hand hovering near the MP5.

Grace sank lower in her seat, feeling both embarrassed and oddly detached from the situation. The tinted, reinforced windows separated her from the normal world outside - kids waiting for school buses, joggers on morning runs, all oblivious to the rolling fortress passing by.

As they approached the school, Sinclair Academy, Martinez's posture stiffened. "Approaching drop-off point. Stand by for sweep."

The SUV came to a stop in front of the school's main entrance. Martinez exited first, his eyes darting from point to point, one hand inside his jacket. Only when he gave a curt nod did Kovacs open Grace's door.

"All clear, Miss Kane. Have a good day at school," Kovacs said, his accent thick but his tone professional.

Grace stepped out, acutely aware of the stares from her classmates. Martinez stood nearby, his back to her but his attention clearly focused on potential threats. Kovacs remained by the vehicle, one hand resting casually near the MP5.

As Grace walked towards the entrance, she could feel the weight of their vigilant gazes on her back. She knew they would remain outside, watching, waiting.

The sleek, silver Bentley, armored, purred to a stop at the entrance of La Marina, the most exclusive restaurant on the waterfront. Vivian Kane emerged, a vision in a Chanel tweed suit and Louboutin heels, her blond hair swept into an elegant chignon. She slipped off her Gucci sunglasses, revealing expertly applied makeup that took years off her already youthful face.

One of her bodyguards, a broad-shouldered man named Reeves, stepped out after her, his eyes scanning the area with practiced efficiency.

"That'll be all, Reeves," Vivian said, her tone breezy but brooking no argument. "Take the car and wait out of sight. I won't have my friends thinking I'm some sort of paranoid recluse."

Reeves hesitated, his training warring with Vivian's command. "Mrs. Kane, Mr. Kane insisted—"

Vivian waved a manicured hand dismissively. "I'm quite aware of what my husband insists. I'm also aware that this is a public place in broad daylight, and I refuse to lunch with an audience. You and Dawson can watch from the parking lot."

She turned on her heel, not waiting for a response, and sashayed towards the restaurant's outdoor seating area. Several well-heeled patrons turned to watch her progress, a few offering greetings which Vivian acknowledged with practiced nods and smiles.

As she approached a table where three women sat, their own outfits and jewelry a matched display of wealth and status, Vivian glanced back. Satisfied that the Bentley and her guardians were no longer in sight, she turned her full attention to her waiting friends, slipping effortlessly into the role of carefree socialite.

"Ladies," she greeted, air-kissing cheeks as she sat down. "Shall we start with mimosas? I'm simply dying to hear about Bethany's new weight trainer."

Richard's armored Maybach glided down Vanderbilt Boulevard, past the columned facades of investment banks and brokerage houses that made up Willow Crest's financial district. It was as if the high-stakes financiers built their own mini-Wall Street in Connecticut where they lived with their perfect families. No need to deal with Manhattan traffic and homeless addicts trying to clean your spotless windshield for a tip.

Morning fog rolled in from Mirror Lake, softening the edges of red brick and limestone buildings. Kane Investments rose ahead, commanding the highest ground overlooking the water. The original structure, built in 1888 as the region's first merchant bank, dominated the corner. Its granite columns and ornate cornices spoke of permanence, of wealth earned generations ago and carefully maintained. Behind this Victorian facade, connected by a glass-walled atrium, stood the seven-story office annex where Richard's traders and analysts worked. Though modern, its architect had echoed the main building's proportions and materials, creating harmony rather than contrast. The terraced gardens between buildings cascaded down toward the lake, their fountains creating veils of mist in the morning air.

Richard's palm pressed against the biometric scanner hidden in the brick arch. The garage door rose silently on hydraulic arms. The Maybach turned into the private entrance. Blake and Torres, Richard's bodyguards, exited first, their H&K MP5 submachine guns at the ready. They scanned the area with practiced efficiency, communicating through their headsets in clipped, professional tones.

"Clear," Blake announced after a tense moment.

Only then did Richard emerge, impeccable in a tailored Brioni suit. Yet despite his polished exterior, something was off. A slight furrow in his brow, a tightness around his eyes - subtle tells that most wouldn't notice, but signs of inner turmoil for a man accustomed to making million-dollar decisions without breaking a sweat.

As they neared the elevator, Richard hesitated for a fraction of a second before the retinal scan. Blake and Torres exchanged a quick glance, noting the uncharacteristic pause.

The elevator ascended in silence, its walnut panels reflecting their images. Richard's eyes seemed distant, his mind elsewhere, preoccupied with some unseen concern.

The doors opened directly into his corner office. Nineteenth-century millwork and coffered ceilings spoke of old-world power, while bullet and blast-resistant windows offered views across Mirror Lake and the terraced gardens between buildings. The adjoining modern wing housed his highly-paid employees, visible through the glass-walled atrium that connected the structures.

As Blake and Torres moved efficiently through the space checking for threats, Richard settled behind his desk. Multiple screens flickered to life, integrated seamlessly into the historic woodwork, displaying real-time market data and global news feeds. But for once, the scrolling numbers and breaking headlines failed to capture his full attention.

He took a deep breath, forcing his focus back to the screens before him. Whatever was bothering him, Richard knew he couldn't afford to let it show. In his world, even a moment of weakness could have million-dollar consequences.

Sinclair Academy stood as a bastion of privilege and academic excellence, its Neo-Gothic architecture sprawling across fifty manicured acres. Founded in the late 19th century, the school exuded an air of timeless erudition behind its wrought-iron gates.

Inside, polished hardwood floors and oil paintings of distinguished alumni contrasted with smart boards and holographic displays. The state-of-the-art science laboratories rivaled those of many universities, while the arts center boasted a professional-grade theater and light-filled studios.

Athletic facilities were equally impressive, featuring an Olympic-sized pool, tennis courts, a multi-purpose stadium, and an equestrian arena. The library, a cathedral-like space with towering bookshelves and stained-glass windows, served as the intellectual heart of the campus.

The student body was a carefully curated mix of old money, new tech wealth, and a sprinkling of scholarship students. Uniforms ostensibly leveled the playing field, but designer accessories still served as subtle markers of status.

For Grace, the Academy was both a haven and a prison. Its rigorous academics challenged her mind, while its insular, pressure-cooker environment often felt suffocating. At Sinclair every achievement was a step on the carefully plotted path to the Ivy League and beyond, creating a world of opportunity laden with relentless expectations.

Grace slipped into the second-floor girls' bathroom, her heart pounding. She glanced at her watch – five minutes until the next class. Plenty of time. From her bag, she pulled out the slim black eyeliner pencil, a small act of defiance against her father and the suffocating rules of both home and school.

Leaning close to the mirror, Grace steadied her hand and began to apply the liner with practiced strokes.

Grace rushed into the locker room, late for riding class again. She tried stuffing her American history book into her backpack as she rounded the corner to her locker. Her shoulder slammed into Victoria Ashworth, two years her senior, knocking her sideways. Victoria stumbled, scuffing her Italian leather paddock boots against the metal bench.

Victoria stared at the deep scratch across the toe. "You stupid little—"

"I'm sorry," Grace stammered. "I didn't see—"

"Do you know how much these cost?" Victoria's face reddened. Behind her, three other girls stopped changing into their riding clothes to watch. "More than your entire Walmart wardrobe."

Grace straightened her spine, found her voice. "Maybe you should try being interesting instead of just being mean, Victoria. Mean is easy. Anybody can do mean."

The locker room went quiet. Several girls turned to stare.

Victoria's laugh cut like a whip, but something flickered in her eyes. "Did you hear that? The mouse tries to roar."

"Leave me alone, you bitch!" Grace's hands shook.

"Or what?" Victoria stepped closer. "What exactly will you do?"

Grace's throat closed. She had no answer. Victoria knew it.

"That's what I thought."

In the arena, Thunder, a bay thoroughbred, shifted beneath Grace, sensing her tension.

Mrs. Blackwood stood at the center, her silver hair pulled tight beneath her helmet. "Posting trot, please. Keep your diagonals. Emily, shorten your reins. Victoria, give that gray more leg."

The riders circled, hooves drumming against packed dirt. Grace focused on her position, trying to forget the locker room. Sit, rise, sit, rise. Thunder's stride lengthened.

"Good," Mrs. Blackwood called. "Now canter. One at a time. Sarah, you first."

With the instructor looking in the opposite direction, Victoria reined her dapple gray shoulder close to Grace and Thunder, pushing them toward the rail. Grace dug her heels in, urged Thunder to push back. For a moment, they held their ground.

Victoria's eyes narrowed. She reached over, jabbed Thunder's flank with her riding crop.

Thunder leaped forward. Grace lost her stirrup, felt herself sliding. The arena dirt rushed up to meet her. She hit hard, air rushing from her lungs.

"Guess Daddy's money can't buy balance," Victoria said. She circled once, then trotted away.

Grace stood slowly, brushing sand from her jodhpurs. Her cheeks burned. She'd lost the fight, but at least she'd fought back. As she led Thunder to the mounting block, Grace felt something shift inside her. A hardening. Next time she fell, she'd land better. Next time she'd be ready.

She just had to figure out how.

Leverage

The final bell rang, signaling the end of another meticulously scheduled day at the Academy. Grace emerged from the ornate main entrance, her shoulders sagging slightly under the weight of her backpack and the day's pressures. At the bottom of the stone steps, the familiar black armored SUV waited, a stark contrast to the other luxury vehicles picking up her classmates. Kovacs, stone-faced as always, opened the rear door as Grace approached. "Afternoon, Miss Kane," he mumbled, his eyes continuously scanning the surroundings.

Grace climbed in, sinking into the leather seat. Martinez sat in the front passenger seat.

As they pulled away from the school, Grace noticed her classmates staring. Some with envy, others with a mix of fear and fascination. She slumped lower in her seat, wishing for once she could just take the bus like a normal kid.

The armored SUV drove away from the Academy. Another day over. Kovacs drove silently while

Martinez scanned their surroundings from the passenger seat, the MP5 submachine gun within easy reach.

Five minutes into their usual route, Kovacs suddenly tensed. "Accident ahead," he reported tersely. "Taking alternate route."

The SUV veered off the main road into a maze of narrower streets. Grace frowned, an uneasy feeling settling in her stomach. Something felt off.

Martinez's hand moved to his earpiece. "Say again, Control?" His eyes narrowed. "Understood. Initiating Protocol Echo."

Grace sat up straighter. She'd never heard of "Protocol Echo" before.

Kovacs accelerated. "Martinez, our six."

Martinez twisted in his seat, staring out the rear window. "Black SUV, gaining fast. No plates."

Grace's heart began to race. This wasn't normal. Not at all.

"Another on the left," Kovacs barked, swerving sharply into an alley. "Hang on, Miss Kane." The SUV lurched, and Grace grabbed the seat to steady herself.

Martinez turned to her, his voice urgent but controlled. "Miss Kane, get down on the floor now."

Grace scrambled to comply, releasing her safety belt and sliding onto the floor. The carpet smelled of leather and gun oil.

"What's happening?" she asked, her voice shaky.

"Stay down," was all Martinez said, his attention back on their pursuers.

The SUV accelerated hard, pressing Grace against the backseat. Through the floor, she felt the vibration of the engine straining as Kovacs maneuvered through the narrow streets.

"Two more, converging from the north," Kovacs reported, his usual stoic tone tinged with tension.

Grace's mind raced. Four vehicles boxing them in? This was coordinated. Professional. Her father's warnings about the dangers of his work suddenly felt very, very real.

The SUV swerved again, tires screeching. Grace heard a loud thump – had they hit something?

"Contact rear!" Martinez shouted. Grace heard the unmistakable sound of glass cracking – bulletproof glass, she realized with a jolt.

"Backup ETA?" Kovacs demanded.

"Five minutes out," Martinez replied, his voice tight. "They're pushing us away."

The next minute was a blur of screeching tires, sharp turns, and terse communications between Kovacs and Martinez. Grace curled into a tight ball on the floor, her heart pounding so hard she thought it might burst from her chest.

A black van skidded to a halt in the middle of the street in front of them blocking their escape route.

"Hang a right down that alley!" said Martinez pointing.

The armored SUV turned sharply into a narrow alley, Grace clutching the seat to keep her balance. Suddenly, Kovacs slammed on the brakes. "Shit!" he cursed, breaking his usual stoic demeanor.

Grace popped her head up to see what was happening.

A large garbage truck blocked the exit of the alley ahead, its bulk ominous in the confined space.

Before Grace could process what was happening, two figures wearing balaclavas to hide their faces and hair emerged from either side of the truck. The glint of metal was all the warning they had.

"Down!" Martinez roared, just as the air exploded with the deafening rattle of gunfire.

Grace threw herself to the floor once again, her heart pounding in her ears. The windshield, though bulletproof, starred and cracked under the assault of heavy-caliber rounds.

Kovacs didn't hesitate. He threw the SUV into reverse, the tires screeching as they raced backwards down the alley. Grace felt the impacts as bullets continued to slam into the vehicle.

"Control, we are under attack!" Martinez yelled into his headset, his voice nearly drowned out by the gunfire and the roar of the engine. "Heavy weapons, multiple assailants. Requesting immediate backup!"

The SUV jolted to a stop again. Grace, still on the floor, heard Kovacs swear. "Van behind us. Two more gunmen."

The sound of gunfire doubled as the new attackers opened fire. Grace curled into a tight ball, her hands over her ears, certain that at any moment a bullet would punch through and find her.

But Kovacs wasn't done. The engine roared as he gunned it, and Grace felt the SUV lurch backward.

"Brace for impact!" Kovacs shouted.

The world became a chaos of noise and motion as the SUV raced toward the van. There was a tremendous crash, the shriek of tearing metal, and the pop of airbags deploying. The van tumbled into the street in front of the alley entrance. The SUV spun, tires squealing, before coming to a stop.

"Stay down!" Kovacs roared, throwing the SUV into Drive. Wheels spun.

As they lurched forward, Martinez turned to check on Grace. "Miss Kane, are you—"

The windshield exploded inward from a gunman's Teflon-covered bullet penetrating the glass. A spray of blood and brain matter hit Grace as Martinez slumped backward over the seat, a bullet hole in the back of his head. Grace's scream was lost in gunfire and screeching tires.

His partner dead, Kovacs didn't stop. He kept driving, gunning the engine. "Stay down!" he shouted at Grace, who was frozen in shock, Martinez's blood warm and sticky on her face and clothes.

They shot forward, weaving through traffic. Car horns blared and pedestrians dove for cover as the bullet-riddled SUV careened down the street. In the side mirror, Grace caught glimpses of black vehicles in pursuit.

"They're coming," she said weakly.

Kovacs took a sharp turn, the SUV tilting dangerously. "Call your father," he ordered, tossing his phone to Grace. "Speed dial one."

Grace's blood-slicked fingers fumbled with the phone. The call connected just as another hail of bullets peppered the back of the SUV.

"Daddy," Grace sobbed. "They're trying to kill us. Martinez is dead. There's so much blood—"

"Grace!" Her father's voice was tight with fear. "Where are you?"

Before she could answer, a massive impact rocked the SUV. Grace was thrown against the door as another vehicle T-boned them at an intersection. The world spun, glass shattered, and metal screamed.

When it stopped, the SUV was on its side. Smoke filled the air, and Grace could taste blood in her mouth. Kovacs hung limply in his seat, unmoving.

In the distance, through the broken windshield, Grace saw figures approaching with military precision, weapons raised, balaclavas hiding their identities.

The phone, somehow still intact, crackled with her father's frantic voice. "Grace! Grace, answer me!"

But Grace couldn't speak. She could only stare at the approaching figures, her world collapsing around her in a haze of blood and terror.

One of the gunmen pulled a Sawzall from a duffle bag and went to work cutting open the back door. Sparks flew. Grace backed away as far as she could as the door flew open. A rifle barrel hovered in the open doorway. Two shots killed Kovacs. A gunman reached into the backseat and grabbed Grace. She screamed.

"You motherfuckers! I'll kill you if hurt my daughter!" shouted her father over the phone's speaker.

But there was nobody left alive to hear his threat. Grace and the gunmen were gone.

A large hand on Grace's arm guided her roughly up the stairs, each step uncertain beneath the black hood. Her school uniform clung to her skin, stiff with Martinez's blood. The memory of his death played on endless loop - the bullet punching through bulletproof glass, the spray of red, his body slumping backward. Martinez died trying to protect her. That's what good men did. They died.

Floorboards creaked beneath her feet. A door opened. The hood came off, and Grace blinked in harsh fluorescent light. The room was small but clean, with pale blue walls and simple furniture - a twin bed, desk, dresser. Thick bars covered the windows mounted on the inside. A bathroom door stood open, revealing a basic toilet and shower. The guard - broad-shouldered wearing a balaclava - gestured to a pile of clothes on the bed. "Change." His accent was thick, Eastern European.

Grace searched the room with desperate eyes. The windows were secure. The door was steel, the hinges inaccessible. Even the light fixtures were recessed, offering no possibility of access to wiring or ceiling space. They'd done this before. They knew how to keep someone locked away.

"I need..." Grace's voice cracked. She cleared her throat, tried again. "I need underwear."

"No." said the guard.

"Mine are… wet. I need a clean pair."

The guard's face remained impassive. "Clean yourself. Put on what's there. Nothing else." He gestured to the bathroom. "Go. Wash off blood."

Grace hugged herself, fighting back tears. "Please. Just underwear. I'm cold."

"You don't make rules here." He stepped toward the door. "Ten minutes. Then I check on you. Be changed by then." The door closed. The lock engaged with a heavy click.

Grace stared at the sweatpants and hoodie on the bed. Standard grey, no markings. Like prison clothes. She touched her skirt, stiff with Martinez's blood and bits of tissue. A sob caught in her throat. But crying wouldn't help. Not now. Not here.

She went to clean herself up. To wash away the evidence of how quickly her gilded life could turn to horror.

She looked in the bathroom mirror at her face covered in blood and rivulets of eyeliner. She washed the black streams from under her eyes first like somehow this was all her fault for being rebellious. She considered for a moment, staring into the mirror. For the time being, she was all alone. Her expression hardened. "No more crying, G," she said to herself. "Don't give those bastards the satisfaction."

Yellow police tape fluttered in the late afternoon breeze, creating a rough rectangle around the intersection of Maple and Cedar. The armored SUV lay on its side like a wounded animal, its dark windows shattered, armor plating scarred from bullets and the savage cuts around the back door.

Officer Chen walked slowly along the skid marks, measuring them with a contractor's tape measure. He called out numbers to Officer Reynolds, who jotted them in his notepad.

Officer Rio circled the overturned vehicle, taking photos with his iPhone, documenting anything he thought might be important. The low-hanging sun caught the brass shell casings near the driver's door, two lonely evidence markers beside them. Dark blood had pooled beneath the driver's side window, staining the suburban street's pristine blacktop.

A growing crowd of onlookers gathered behind the police tape - mothers in yoga pants clutching coffee cups, landscapers pausing their routes, kids on bikes on their way home from school. All watching, all filming with their phones, as their quiet community's illusion of safety crumbled in the dying light.

Police Captain James Reeves stood beside the overturned SUV, struggling to process the violence that had erupted in his quiet suburb. In fifteen years as head of the Willow Crest Police Department, the worst he'd dealt with was domestic disputes, traffic accidents, and the occasional shoplifter. Nothing like this.

Officer Reynolds approached, notepad in hand. At twenty-six, he was one of the department's youngest officers, but this day had aged him considerably.

"Captain, we've pieced together what we think happened according to the evidence and witnesses," Reynolds said. "It started in the alley behind Main Street. Multiple shooters ambushed the SUV using a garbage truck as a barricade. They pursued the vehicle through town - we've got brass casings and bullet holes all along Cedar Drive, Maple Street, and ending here at the intersection."

Reeves studied the two bodies still in the front seats of the armored vehicle. "These boys were professionals," he said, noting their tactical gear and builds. "Private security, maybe military background. When is the county medical examiner arriving?"

"It's still going to be a while. A kid on a bike got hit by the commuter train. Once he's done with that, he'll head our way."

"Kid on a bike? Sad, but no real mystery there. This on the other hand…"

"I'll check on his progress and see if I can't hurry him along."

"You do that."

"Those rounds that went through the windshield? Probably .50 caliber. That's anti-material rifle territory."

"Jesus," Reeves muttered. "What's the story on the backdoor?"

"The backdoor was cut open with some kind of power saw," Reynolds continued. "Same as the fire department uses."

"Any luck IDing the victims?"

"We've got their names from their drivers' licenses and one of them had a business card from a security company."

"Could be their employer."

"That's what I was thinking. I have Hazel checking on it. Oh, and one more thing… An FBI guy stopped by about thirty minutes ago. He was looking for you. I got his card."

"FBI? Don't you think you should have led with that?"

"Sorry, Boss. I guess I should have."

"Where is he now?"

"He was heading toward the alley where the shootout started."

"Where's his card?"

Reynolds handed him a card. Reeves studied it for a moment then moved toward his car. "You boys, stay here and wait for the medical examiner. It's probably gonna be dark by the time his arrives, so go to Henry's hardware and buy some floodlights and extension cords. Set 'em up and use local power from the businesses. I'll be back when I'm done."

Reeves parked his car next to the alley and stepped out. He stood at the alley's entrance, staring at the violence etched into the familiar walls. Every morning for ten years, he'd walked past this alley on his way to his favorite coffee shop. Now it looked like something from a war zone.

The narrow alley ran behind Main Street's row of small businesses - a nail salon, a coffee shop, and Lucy's Boutique. Dumpsters lined one wall, their afternoon pickup missed amid the chaos. At the alley's entrance, someone had dragged the abandoned garbage truck sideways, its massive bulk leaving black skid marks on the pavement.

Officer Peterson worked his way down the alley, placing yellow evidence markers next to each shell casing. He'd run out of numbers at fifty and started using sticky notes torn from his ticket book. Spent brass littered the ground like fallen leaves, mixing with the usual alley debris of cigarette butts and discarded receipts.

High-caliber rounds had chewed into the brick walls on both sides, leaving circles of pulverized red dust. Some shots had punched clean through the rear wall of Lucy's Boutique, peppering the back-room's dress racks with holes. A plate glass window, fifteen feet up, had shattered, leaving a glittering carpet of glass shards below.

Bullet holes traced a path along both walls, telling a story of intense crossfire in the confined space. Some rounds had struck the dumpsters, leaving deep craters in the metal. Others had torn chunks from the wooden utility poles. The height of the impacts varied wildly - shots fired from multiple angles.

"Found another cluster, Captain," Peterson called out, placing a sticky note beside three more shell casings. "That's ninety-two so far, just in the alley."

Behind the police tape, the owner of the coffee shop watched in dismay as Peterson photographed bullet holes in his back door with an iPhone. The fresh-baked muffins grew stale inside, forgotten in the chaos of cordite and brass.

FBI Agent Cooper stood in the middle of the alley, hands in his pockets, studying the pattern of bullet holes in the brick. He'd removed his suit jacket in the afternoon heat, his shoulder holster visible against his wrinkled dress shirt. His eyes moved from impact to impact, reconstructing the gunfight in his mind.

"Agent Cooper? I'm James Reeves, Police Captain here in Willow Crest."

Cooper turned, offering his hand. "John Cooper, FBI field office in Manhattan. I hope you don't mind me taking a look around?"

"Please. We could use another set of eyes on this."

Cooper nodded, turning back to the bullet holes. "Your shooters were military-trained. Look at these groupings. Three-round bursts, consistent spacing. And here..." He pointed to a series of impacts. "He maintained fire discipline while moving to cover. Not street thugs. Not mob guys either."

"Started here?"

"Probably. Garbage truck blocks the exit. They knew the route, knew the vehicle would turn down this alley. Probably had blocker vehicles herding the SUV into the alley." He walked a few paces, studying the opposite wall. "Your security team was good too. See how they kept buttoned up and let the vehicle's armor do its job as they tried to push through the Killzone. Smart."

Reeves hesitated before asking, "You think it might be terrorists?"

"I doubt it. If it were terrorists you'd have a lot more civilian casualties. No, whatever these guys wanted was in the backseat of that SUV. They came prepared to cut an armored vehicle open."

"So, what was it?"

Cooper turned to face Reeves. "...or who was it? No idea at this point. We need a lot more data to figure that one out." He crouched, picking up a bent piece of brass with his pen. "Getting a lot of pressure from upstairs to take this case. Our regional director lives in the area."

"I suppose that's to our advantage."

"Maybe. But without a clear federal nexus, my hands are tied." Cooper stood, letting the casing fall. "For now, anyway."

"If it's a robbery?"

"With this level of violence? Could be federal."

"And a kidnapping?"

"Minors are always federal. Some adults too. But if it was a kidnapping, how come the family hasn't reported it yet?"

"Good question."

"Look, I seriously doubt any of these gunmen are local. They probably came out of New York or New Jersey. In other words, they crossed state lines to commit a felony and that makes the investigation federal. I think there's a strong chance we're gonna be working together on this, Captain. I just need to confirm a few things."

"I hope that's true. People in these parts don't like the government poking their nose into their business. But in this case, we're a bit over our heads. We could sure use the help."

"Then keep digging and keep me in the loop," said Cooper handing him a card.

"Thanks, but I already got one," said Reeves patting his suit jacket.

Cooper nodded, then walked away, leaving Reeves in the alley with its pockmarked walls and scattered brass, each piece of evidence suggesting something far more dangerous than a simple robbery gone wrong.

Brothers

Gray clouds scudded across the sky, casting shifting shadows over the lighthouse as waves crashed against the rocky shore, the rhythmic roar punctuated by the mournful cry of distant gulls.

Metal groaned as Frank wrenched free another section of rusted railing from the lighthouse cupola. He tossed it down with a clang, adding to the pile of corroded iron at the base of the tower. Sweat glistened on his forearms as he measured and cut a length of new steel bar already bent to match the railing's curve, his movements precise and economical.

The screech of power tools cut through the air as Frank secured the new section in place. He paused, running a calloused hand along the smooth metal, testing its stability. Without much ado, he reached for the next piece. Frank didn't need a pat on the back for doing his job. It was work and work was good.

A glint of sunlight on metal caught Frank's eye. He straightened, squinting against the glare. A black SUV pulled into the gravel parking lot on shore. The vehicle's new appearance stood out starkly against the faded paint of his old pickup truck.

Even at a distance, Frank could see the SUV's reinforced bumpers and grill. Thick windows… bullet and blast-proof. He knew the look of civilian armor.

Frank's hands stilled on the railing. His eyes narrowed as two men in suits emerged, their vigilant postures and roving gazes marking them as professional security. They surveyed the area with practiced efficiency before one nodded towards the vehicle.

The back door opened. A man stepped out, his build and posture a mirror image of Frank's own. Richard.

For a long moment, Frank stood motionless, staring down at his twin brother.

Richard turned, looking up towards the lighthouse. Even at this distance, the brothers' eyes met. A flash of recognition, a moment of tension that seemed to stretch across the years and miles that had separated them.

Frank steered his boat to the dock on shore where his brother was waiting. The two bodyguards stood nearby, eyes continually scanning for threats in the surrounding treeline.

Richard said nothing as Frank tied up his boat to a cleat and stepped onto the dock. Then…

"Hello, Frank," said Richard. "It's been a while."

"Hello, Dick," said Frank.

"It's not Dick anymore, Frank. It's Richard."

"Right… Dick."

Richard controlled his anger… barely.

"You're a hard man to find. I suppose that's the way you like it," said Richard, then… "Is there someplace we can talk?"

Richard and Frank sat in Frank's truck. Doors shut, windows up. "That's quite a scent you got going in here," said Richard. "Fish… and sweat."

Frank was unamused and said nothing.

"Okay, I'll get to the point," said Richard. "I need your help."

Frank turned his brother, surprised. Richard pulled out a photo of Grace from his jacket pocket and placed it on the dashboard next to Frank.

"I have a daughter… Gracie. You didn't know you had a niece, did you?" said Richard, then continued not expecting a response. "She's thirteen. Quite a handful."

Richard choked back his emotions as he said, "She's been kidnapped. I can't go to the police or FBI. They'll kill her if I do. I want you to get her back. I'll pay you anything you want. Just bring my little girl back home. Safe."

Frank was deep in thought, still said nothing. His fists tightened on the steering wheel. For a moment, it seemed he would break the steering wheel. Then, he released it, calming himself.

"It's a lot to take in. I know," said Richard. "It's not the way I wanted us to meet again after all this time… and what I said. I wouldn't ask if there was some other way. But I have no choice. I need you."

There was a long silence before Frank simply said, "No." in his raspy voice.

"What do you mean 'no'?"

"I don't do that anymore."

Richard studied his brother for a long moment, then said, "While I appreciate your effort to change, this is not the time to be noble. I need you. Gracie needs you. She needs the old Frank."

"It's not me anymore. The life I live, it's—"

"Different than before. I can see that. But this is family, Frank."

"I don't have a family," said Frank. The more he spoke the raspier he voice sounded.

"Is this about what I said? I told you… I'm sorry for that. I had no right to tell you how to live your life. I was a judgmental prick back then. Christ, half the time I was coked out of my mind. But I've changed, Frank. Being a husband and a father, it changed me. I'm far more tolerant and understanding now. I have to be… for my family's sake."

"I can't go back to who I was."

"Yes, you can, Frank. I know you. No matter how hard you try to bury it, it's still in you deep down inside. You can't get rid of something like that… the fury. The rage. These bastards are killers. They deserve whatever justice you choose to mete out. Unleash the beast one more time… for Gracie's sake."

Richard stopped talking. He knew it was time to shut up and let Frank think. And that's what Frank did for several long minutes.

So much of what Frank had done in the past was bad. Really bad. It had taken years to put it to rest. To finally find some peace. Now, a brother that he hadn't seen in years was asking him to give up that peace. To bring back the evil that had entombed him for so long. That had turned him into something that he was ashamed of, something to be feared. The life he had rebuilt wasn't normal. It would never be normal. But nobody was getting hurt. Nobody was dying by his hands. That was something. How could he give that up?

Was it a worthy cause? Of course. But it wasn't his fight. Frank looked down at the photo on the cracked dashboard. He didn't know the girl in her school uniform, but there was something about her… her eyes. She had the eyes of his mother. There was no denying it no matter how hard he tried. Her blood was his blood. She was family. How could he let harm come to his niece and still be human? Dammit.

Richard watched Frank's face. He could see his slow surrender, his massive shoulders lowering, his hands releasing their vise-like grip on the steering wheel, his head bowing. Then…"Okay. I'll bring her back."

Richard's eyes welled, but he said nothing. They were twins. He didn't need to.

Frank entered the lighthouse with Richard following. Richard looked up at the scaffolding around the weather-damaged stairwell. "This is one helluva project you've got going."

Ignoring his brother, Frank turned, his eyes narrowing as he scanned the room. In the shadowy corner near the door, a pair of yellow eyes gleamed. The feral cat crouched there, its matted gray fur bristling slightly as it watched Frank with a mixture of wariness and expectation.

For a long moment, man and beast regarded each other in silence. Frank's face remained impassive, but something flickered in his eyes - a hint of recognition, perhaps even understanding.

"What in God's name is that thing?" said Richard noticing the yellow eyes in the shadow.

With a barely audible grunt, Frank reached for the worn KA-BAR knife sheathed at his hip. The cat tensed, ready to bolt, but Frank paid it no mind. Instead, he knelt beside the unopened sack of dried cat food leaning against the wall.

In one swift, practiced motion, he sliced a clean gash along the bottom edge of the sack. Pellets of food spilled out, forming a small mound on the concrete floor.

The cat's ears perked forward, its nose twitching at the scent of food. Still, it didn't move from its corner, eyes fixed on Frank.

Rising to his full height, Frank moved to the bathroom. He lifted the toilet lid with his boot, the hinges creaking in protest. The bowl was full of clear water, a contrast to the salt-encrusted fixtures surrounding it.

As Frank turned back to the main room, he found the cat had inched closer to the food pile, though it still kept a cautious distance. Their eyes met again, and Frank gave a short, almost imperceptible nod.

Frank pulled a well-worn metal footlocker from underneath his bed in the lighthouse. He didn't open it. Richard helped him carry it to the boat. "What in the hell do you have in here, gold bricks?" said Richard.

Frank grunted in response.

The armored SUV's tires rolled over the tarmac of the single-runway airfield, coming to a stop near a sleek executive jet. The aircraft's engines hummed, a low, persistent drone that spoke of imminent departure.

Heat waves shimmered above the jet's wings, distorting the view of the clear sky beyond.

Frank emerged from the SUV first, his worn boots hitting the ground with a solid thud. He squinted against the sun, taking in the jet with a quick, assessing glance. Richard followed, his polished shoes gleaming in the bright light, a stark contrast to the scuffed tarmac.

Frank and Richard strode toward the jet's lowered passenger stairs, their gaits eerily similar despite their different attire. They ascended and disappeared into the aircraft's interior.

At the rear of the SUV, the two bodyguards maneuvered Frank's massive footlocker out of the vehicle. The metal case scraped against the SUV's interior before landing on the ground with a heavy clank. Without pause, they lifted it between them and headed for the jet, struggling with the container's weight.

A crew member approached, directing the bodyguards to the jet's cargo compartment. With practiced efficiency, she opened the compartment's door, revealing a spacious hold. The bodyguards carefully slid the footlocker into the cargo area, securing it with straps.

As the cargo compartment door sealed shut, one of the bodyguards broke away, heading back to the SUV. He slid into the driver's seat. The remaining guard climbed the passenger stairs, disappearing into the jet.

The jet's main door sealed with a pneumatic hiss. On the tarmac, the SUV's engine roared to life, its retreat marked by the crunch of gravel. The aircraft's engines increased in pitch, drowning out all other sounds as it prepared for takeoff, carrying the brothers towards an uncertain confrontation.

Inside the jet, an attractive flight attendant brought over a bourbon on the rocks with a twist of lime to Richard. "May I get you something? Drink perhaps?" she said to Frank.

He shook his head and she moved off to attend to Richard's bodyguard. Richard moved closer to the seat across from Frank. "I bet you have a lot of questions," said Richard. "Let me give you the backstory of what happened. That might help."

Frank nodded. "Shortly after Gracie was kidnapped, the kidnappers sent me an email from an anonymous server that couldn't be traced. There was a photo of Gracie and a copy of the New York Times to verify the date… plus the ransom demand of $157 million."

Richard saw that Frank looked puzzled. "I know… weird amount. The only reason I could figure was that they must be foreigners that are going to transfer the money into another currency that is more of an even number."

"Can you pay?" said Frank.

"Normally, yes. But things have gotten a bit more complicated recently with my access to funds."

Richard continued, "Last year some of the traders in my firm started dealing with several overseas investment companies based in tax havens. We did our due diligence and checked them out. They were clean. Not too long after that, the United States Treasury Department froze all of my firm's bank accounts claiming we were laundering money. It didn't matter that we were innocent and they had no real evidence.

The Treasury Department has a bad policy of freezing bank accounts first and asking questions later. My lawyers assured me that they will be able to unfreeze the accounts, but it would take time to get a federal court order. In the meantime, I am using my overseas accounts to pay my employees and company expenses. But I can't bring any money into the United States without the Treasury Depart freezing the funds until this thing is cleaned up. I am attempting to raise cash by selling my personal assets and taking out a mortgage on my house and other real estate that Vivian and I own, but it takes time and besides it's not going to be nearly enough to meet their demands. There is no way to contact them, so I can't negotiate a lower amount. I have to wait until they contact me."

Frank grunted.

"Frank, I will do whatever I have to do to get Gracie back safety, but everything I can think of takes time and I don't think Gracie has a lot of time before they do something horrible to her."

Frank nodded knowingly and said, "I'll get her back before that happens."

Richard nodded and said, "I know you will, brother. You're the meanest, cruelest son of a bitch I know."

Frank smiled slightly like it was a compliment.

Grace, the scratches on her face and arms starting to heal, sat on the edge of a twin bed, her eyes fixed on the digital clock on the nightstand. Six hours since her last meal. Six hours of cataloging every inch of her prison.

The room was clean and comfortable, but far from luxurious. A small bookshelf was filled with an eclectic mix of novels. A window, barred on the inside, teased the possibility of the outside world. Grace had already discovered it was securely locked and the glass had been replaced with unbreakable plexiglass. She imagined the tinting on the outside of the window was some sort of mirror finish so as not to draw attention and making it impossible for her to signal for help.

A soft knock interrupted her thoughts. Grace tensed, backing away from the door.

"Dinner," a voice called, young and uncertain.

The lock clicked, and the door swung open. A kidnapper wearing a balaclava over his head entered. He carried a tray with what smelled like a home-cooked meal. Grace studied her captor. There was something in his movements… less confident than a man. She could tell he was quite a bit younger than the others, more her age, a teenager.

"I'll be looking after you this evening," he said, his voice low as he set the tray on the small table in the corner.

Grace watched as he lifted the cover, revealing a plate of roasted chicken, vegetables, and mashed potatoes.

"I need to cut the chicken. You're not allowed to have a knife," he mumbled, producing a knife from his pocket and opening it.

"Do all of you wear those things on your heads?" said Grace.

"Balaclavas? Yeah. Boss's orders."

"Boss?"

"Sorry. I'm not supposed to talk with you."

"Right. I get it. Rules. Everyone's got rules."

"Yeah, rules." He considered for a moment, then added, "They're more about protecting you than us."

"The masks?"

"Yeah. When all this is over, if you can't identify us we have nothing to worry about and we can just let you go."

"And if I can… identify you?"

"That wouldn't be good."

"Oh."

He quickly sliced the meat into bite-sized pieces, then pocketed the knife again.

"Go ahead and eat. I need to stay until you are done."

"You can sit," Grace said, gesturing to the chair opposite her.

The young man hesitated before sitting down.

Grace nodded, taking a bite of chicken. "So," she began casually, "do you guys draw straws for who gets dinner duty, or what?"

He shifted uncomfortably. "We're not supposed to talk about that."

"Right, of course," Grace said, her tone light. "Well, we don't have to talk about that. But we could talk about something. It gets pretty quiet in here."

The kidnapper remained silent, but Grace noticed his fingers tapping nervously on his knee.

"How about your name?" she pressed gently. "I'm Grace, but I guess you already knew that. You can call me 'G.' My friends do."

He hesitated, conflict clear in his eyes. "I… I'm not supposed to…"

Grace shrugged, taking another bite. "Okay, no name. Maybe I'll just call you 'Chef' since you prepared this meal so nicely."

A small smile tugged at his lips before he could stop it. "I didn't cook it," he admitted. "Just reheated and served."

"Still," Grace persisted, "it's nice to have a name with the face. Even if it's not your real one."

He was quiet for a long moment. "Alex," he finally said, so softly Grace almost missed it. "My name is Alex."

Grace smiled warmly. "Nice to meet you, Alex. So, since we're stuck here together, how about a little conversation? Nothing about... all this," she gestured vaguely around the room. "Just normal stuff. Like... do you like books? I've been working my way through that shelf over there."

Alex glanced at the bookshelf, surprise flickering across his face. "You've been reading?"

"Well, yeah," Grace shrugged. "Not much else to do in here. Have you read any of them?"

"I... uh, I liked *The Outsiders* when I was in school," Alex admitted, then looked like he regretted sharing the information.

Grace's eyes lit up. "That's a good one. 'Stay gold, Ponyboy,' right?"

"Yeah, right."

"I always wondered what happened to those characters after the book ended. Do you think Ponyboy made it out okay?"

Alex seemed to relax slightly. "I hope so. He seemed smart, you know? Like he could make something of himself if he got the chance."

"Yeah," Grace nodded, her voice thoughtful. "Sometimes all it takes is one person believing in you, giving you a chance." She looked directly at Alex as she said this, holding his gaze for a moment before he looked away.

"What about you, Alex?" Grace asked softly. "Did you have someone believing in you growing up?"

Alex's face clouded. "I... we shouldn't be talking about personal stuff."

Grace backpedaled smoothly. "You're right, I'm sorry. Let's stick to books. Have you read anything good lately?"

As Grace continued eating, she kept the conversation flowing, asking Alex about other books, movies, music – anything to keep him talking. With each response, Alex seemed to relax slightly, his answers becoming less guarded.

When Grace finished her meal, Alex stood to collect the tray. As he reached for it, Grace touched his hand gently and said, "Thanks, Alex. For the conversation, I mean. It gets... lonely in here."

Alex paused, conflict clear in his eyes. He pulled his hand away. "I shouldn't... I'm sorry."

Before Grace could respond, Alex hurried out with the tray, the lock clicking behind him.

As she lay back on the bed, Grace allowed herself a small smile. Everyone underestimated her because of her age. That was their mistake.

The massive front door of the Kane mansion swung open, revealing Vivian Kane, her eyes puffy and red from crying. For the first time in many years, she had not bothered to put on makeup. It didn't seem important. She was still beautiful.

Frank stood on the threshold, a living ghost of her husband, yet utterly alien. Imagining for a brief moment that he was Richard, she gasped slightly at seeing his scared face before catching herself. Behind him, Richard placed a hand on his brother's shoulder, guiding him inside.

"Vivian, this is my brother Frank," Richard said, his voice strained with forced casualness.

Vivian's manicured hand trembled slightly as she extended her hand to shake Frank's massive hand. "Of course. It's a pleasure to meet you, Frank. I wish it could have been under better circumstances. Please, come in."

Frank stepped into the foyer, his heavy boots leaving faint smudges on the polished marble. Vivian flinched at the sound, so unlike Richard's usual quiet tread. Richard followed, closing the door behind them with a soft click that seemed to echo in the tense silence.

"Make yourself at home," Vivian said, her voice tight. Her eyes darted over Frank's scarred arms, down to his calloused hands, then quickly away. "Can I get you something to drink? You must be parched after the flight."

Frank shook his head.

"I'm sure Richard has told you about... about our situation and how anxious we both are to have it resolved as soon as possible," said Vivian.

Frank nodded once, his silence filling the spacious foyer, making it feel claustrophobic. Richard cleared his throat. "Frank's here to help, Viv. He's our best chance."

Vivian wrung her hands, her composure cracking. "Yes, of course. We're grateful you're here, Frank. Gracie, she's..." A choked sob escaped her.

Frank turned toward her, his expression unreadable. Vivian struggled to meet his eyes, so familiar yet so foreign.

Richard stepped in, his arm going around Vivian's shoulders. "We've prepared a place for you to stay,

Frank. We thought you might be more comfortable in the pool house. It'll give you some privacy. I had Vivian rent you a BMW to get around in. It's parked out front, just outside the gate."

Vivian nodded quickly and handed Frank the car keys. "Yes, and don't worry about meals. The refrigerators are fully stocked, both here and in the pool house. And our chef, Marcus, he's always available if you need anything specific. You only need to ask."

Heavy boots dented the grass as Vivian led Frank across the manicured lawn towards the pool house. The structure, a modernist blend of glass and stone, stood in stark contrast to the main mansion's traditional architecture.

"Here we are," Vivian said, her voice carrying a forced cheerfulness as she unlocked the door. "I hope you'll be comfortable."

Frank stepped inside, his eyes methodically scanning the space. The open-plan interior dwarfed his lighthouse keeper's quarters. Floor-to-ceiling windows offered a panoramic view of the Olympic-sized pool and meticulously landscaped grounds beyond.

Vivian moved through the space, pointing out features with the practiced ease of a Realtor. "The bedroom's through there, with an ensuite bathroom. Kitchen's fully stocked, and here's the living area."

She paused at a gleaming wet bar that dominated one corner of the room. "The bar's fully stocked too. Richard wasn't sure what you might prefer, so there's a bit of everything."

Frank nodded silently, his scarred hands running over the polished surface of the bar. The bottles glinted in the afternoon sun, their labels speaking of expense that could fund a month's worth of lighthouse repairs.

Vivian watched him, her composure slipping slightly. "Is it... Will this be alright?"

Frank nodded his approval. An uncomfortable silence stretched between them. Vivian fidgeted with her wedding ring, her eyes darting between Frank and the door.

Finally, she spoke, her voice barely above a whisper. "Can you do it? Can you really find her?"

Frank turned to face her fully. For a moment, Vivian saw a flicker of her husband in his features, a ghost of familiarity that made her heart ache.

"I'll try," Frank said simply.

The words hung in the air, heavy with its brutal honesty. Vivian flinched as if struck, the uncertainty clearly difficult to bear.

"I... I see," she managed, her voice trembling. "It's funny, a mother never really understands what she has until it's gone. Gracie is everything. Sure, I have Richard, but he is usually tied up in his own world of high finance and golfing with his buddies. Gracie is my world. I'll do anything I need to get her back safely. Anything. We're counting on you, Frank. Our lives… Gracie's life are in your hands."

Frank nodded.

"Well, if you need anything, anything at all, just ask."

She moved towards the door, pausing with her hand on the knob. "Thank you for coming, Frank. I know it can't be easy for you either."

Frank said nothing, but gave a slight nod. Vivian slipped out, the door closing behind her with a soft click.

Left alone, Frank stood motionless in the center of the luxurious space, a scarred sentinel in a world of opulence, preparing for a battle that was all too familiar.

Frank eased open the door to Grace's bedroom, his scarred hand contrasting sharply with the polished brass knob. His eyes, accustomed to scanning horizons for approaching storms, now methodically swept the room.

Sunlight filtered through gauzy curtains, illuminating a space that defied easy categorization. Frank moved silently, his presence as out of place here as in the mansion's opulent halls.

A bookshelf caught his attention. Among the expected young adult titles, Frank's calloused fingers paused on a book about survivalism, then another on lockpicking. The corner of his mouth twitched, almost imperceptibly.

Posters plastered the walls, a gallery of rebels and outcasts. Jodie Foster's intense gaze from *The Silence of the Lambs* seemed to follow Frank as he moved. David Bowie in full Ziggy Stardust regalia, Joan Jett's leather-clad form, the defiant poses of Pussy Riot – each image a challenge to the status quo.

At Grace's desk, he riffled through papers with practiced efficiency. Straight-A report cards lay beside detention slips for "disruptive behavior." Frank paused at a half-finished sketch – a girl breaking free from chains. He studied it, his own hands flexing unconsciously.

The closet revealed school uniforms hiding band t-shirts and ripped jeans. A studded leather jacket hung at the far end.

Kneeling, Frank found a hidden compartment in the baseboard. Inside, joints and ecstasy pills spoke of secret rebellion.

The bedroom door creaked open. Frank froze, his hand hovering over the secret stash of joints and pills.

"Oh!" Vivian's startled gasp broke the silence. "I... I didn't realize you were in here."

Frank rose slowly, his body angled to block Vivian's view of the open compartment. He faced her, expression unreadable.

Vivian's eyes darted around the room, a mix of discomfort and curiosity on her face. "I was just..." she trailed off, gaze settling on the posters. A frown creased her brow. "I've been meaning to redecorate. Make it more suitable for a young lady."

Frank's jaw tightened subtly. He discretely shoved the compartment closed with his boot as he shut the closet doors, then moved towards the bedroom door, effectively steering Vivian back into the hallway.

"Did you... find anything helpful?" Vivian asked, her voice tinged with hope and fear.

Frank paused in the doorway. He gave a single, short nod, then pulled the door shut behind him. The soft click of the latch seemed to echo in the silence.

Vivian opened her mouth as if to say more, then closed it. She watched as Frank strode down the hallway, his silence leaving her questions unanswered. As he disappeared down the stairs, Vivian's hand reached for the doorknob, hesitated, then dropped away. She stood there for a moment, torn between curiosity and respect for her daughter's privacy, before finally turning and walking in the opposite direction.

Inside the room, the faces on the posters seemed to watch the closed door, guardians of Grace's secrets.

The hidden compartment remained safe from prying eyes.

Richard was waiting at the bottom of the stairs as Frank descended. A man in a crisp suit approached, his hand hovering near a concealed weapon. "Frank, this is Ken Davis. He's our head of security," said Richard.

Offering his hand, Davis said, "Nice to meet you, Frank."

Frank looked down at Davis' hand, but didn't shake it. Frank's gaze swept the room, noting exits, potential weapons. Davis tensed, recognizing the assessment of a fellow professional. After a moment, Davis withdrew his hand, doing his best to ignore the slight.

Richard seemed unsure of what to say or do. "Davis is here to help, Frank. He'll brief you on what we know so far," Richard explained. "He's been coordinating our investigation."

"Perhaps we should move this to the study," Davis suggested, his tone clipped.

As they moved toward the study, Richard explained, "We've kept it quiet, Frank. No police, no FBI. Any hint of law enforcement involvement, and they could..." He trailed off, unable to finish the thought.

"Just us, Vivian, and a small team Davis trusts," Richard clarified. "We've told the school Grace is ill."

Vivian remained in the foyer, surrounded by the trappings of a life suddenly turned upside down. She watched the three men disappear into the study, the door closing behind them with a finality that sent a shiver down her spine. In that moment, standing alone in the vast, empty space, Vivian had never felt more isolated in her own home.

The study door clicked shut. Davis moved to a large touchscreen mounted on the wall, while Richard sank into a leather armchair, his face drawn with exhaustion. Frank remained standing, eyes fixed on Davis. Davis cleared his throat as he pulled a stack of folders from his briefcase. "We've been monitoring known players who might have a grudge against your brother. So far, nothing concrete. I have prepared dossiers on the key suspects for your review."

Frank seemed uninterested in the folders.

"Let me get you up to speed, Frank. Grace Kane was taken two days ago," Davis began. "Last seen leaving Thornfield Academy at 3:45 PM." He tapped the screen, bringing up a grainy security camera image of Grace climbing into the family's armored SUV.

Frank stepped closer, studying the image intently.

Davis continued, "Vehicle was found abandoned five miles from the school. Driver, Sam Kovacs, and security specialist, Ed Martinez, were found dead from gunshot wounds in the vehicle. The gunmen used large caliber Teflon bullets to penetrate the bullet-proof windshield and kill Martinez." Another tap, another image – a black SUV, its windshield spider-webbed with bullet holes.

Richard inhaled sharply. Frank's expression remained impassive.

"Attack was well-coordinated. Multiple vehicles, professional gunmen. They disabled the SUV before we could reach it. Grace was gone when we arrived."

The image on the touchscreen changed to video. Grace appeared, seated in a metal folding chair against bare concrete. She wore the same clothes from the day she was taken, her face pale but composed.

Frank stood motionless, watching his niece on the screen. Richard sat behind his desk, head bowed, unable to watch it again.

"Tell them," a voice commanded off-camera.

Grace swallowed hard. "Mom, Dad... I'm okay. They're..." She glanced to the side, then continued. "They're treating me alright. They say if you do what they want, they'll let me go."

A gloved hand appeared, holding today's Wall Street Journal. Grace read the date aloud.

The camera shifted. A man in a black ski mask filled the frame. When he spoke, his accent was Eastern European, his voice digitally distorted.

"Mr. Kane. One hundred fifty-seven million dollars. That is the exact amount. No negotiation. No police. No FBI." He paused.

Richard's jaw clenched. Davis caught the tension but said nothing.

"Transfer instructions will follow." The masked man moved aside, showing Grace again. "Failure to comply... we send her back in pieces."

The video ended.

Davis glanced between the Kane brothers. "Two things stand out here. First is the amount - $157 million exactly. Not 150, not 160. That specific number. Why?" He looked directly at Richard. "It's enough money that it can't be delivered physically. Has to be a bank transfer. And they'd have to know any transfer that size needs to go to a jurisdiction where U.S. authorities can't reach it." Davis leaned back, studying Frank's reaction. "These aren't street thugs asking for cash in a duffle bag."

Frank's eyes never left the screen.

"Second odd thing," Davis continued, his tone carefully professional. "No deadline. Every kidnapping I've dealt during my tenure at the FBI, they gave us a tight window. Create pressure. But these guys... nothing. Almost like they understand accessing this kind of money takes time."

Frank's gaze shifted briefly to his brother, who still hadn't looked up.

"That accent could be fake," Davis added. "But it's definitely Eastern European. Either way, these guys are professionals. Military training, based on how they took down my security team." He closed the laptop. "Any thoughts on who might have connections to that part of the world, Richard?"

Richard finally looked up, his face carefully blank. "No. None. So, what do we do?"

"We wait. Let it play out and look for an opportunity. That's all we can do."

"You're a fool," said Frank in his raspy voice.

"Hang on a minute…" said Davis. "I don't know who you are except you're Richard's long-lost brother. You've offered no references or credentials from your past experience. As far as I am concerned, you could have been a trash collector and that doesn't qualify you to tell me my business."

"That's not necessary," said Richard. "I vouch for my brother. He's more than qualified."

Frank remained quiet as he always did, keeping his own counsel. Then… "She was your responsibility."

There was a long silence before Davis responded.

"Yeah, she was. And I lost two of my best men trying to protect her," said Davis.

"They failed," said Frank.

"I don't have to listen to this bullshit. You claim to be a professional. Then you know that with enough determination and resources an experienced assailant can get to anyone. Even the President of the United States." Davis turned to Richard, "My men did their job and they gave their lives trying to save your daughter."

"Yes, they did," said Richard. "But Frank's not wrong, Davis. Gracie was your responsibility. You and your men failed."

"More bullshit. If I wasn't a professional, I'd pull my team and leave you and your pretty little wife on your own."

"You know, maybe you should…"

"Should what? Pull my team out? Who's gonna protect you? And who is going to rescue Grace once we find her? Frank? You'd have better luck with rent-a-cops."

"Maybe. But Frank didn't lose my daughter. You did. I can't trust you anymore."

"Okay. Have it your way. My men and I are out of here. I'll mail you our final bill. You're on your own," said Davis storming out of the room.

Vivian came rushing in and said, "What's going on? Where are Davis and his men going?"

"Leaving. I fired them."

"Well, that was stupid, Richard. Who is going to protect us?"

"There is nothing to worry about. I'll have a new security team by tomorrow."

"And how about until then?"

"We've got Frank."

"Great. That's just great."

Aggravated, Vivian stormed off hoping to convince Davis and his men not to leave. It was too late. They were gone.

Richard moved to his study's closet and used a key to open the locked door. He pulled out a Steyr AUG 3 submachine gun that looked like it belonged in the latest Tom Cruise movie. "I hope those motherfuckers are stupid enough to try something," said Richard chambering a round. Frank sighed at his weekend-Rambo brother. He was in no mood to babysit.

Frank entered the pool house, his heavy boots echoing on the polished floor. Every time Frank entered any room, his eyes surveyed the surroundings for hidden intruders or potential threats. It was a habit, one that he had no intention of breaking. He moved to the bedroom where the massive footlocker waited.

The lock clicked open under his practiced touch. Frank lifted the lid, revealing a series of neatly arranged trays. His scarred hands moved with practiced efficiency as he began to inventory his arsenal.

The top tray came into view. Two Ruger Super Redhawk revolvers with 7.5-inch barrels lay nestled in custom-fit foam, their stainless-steel frames gleaming dully in the soft light. The trigger guard of each pistol had been expanded to fit Frank's fingers and the pistols' grips had been lengthened to make room for his enormous hands. Beside them, a compact Remington Model 95 derringer rested, a stark contrast to its larger counterparts. The derringer easily fit in a small, hidden holster inside his left boot. Six speed loaders, each filled with large caliber rounds for the revolvers, completed the tray's contents.

Frank lifted this tray out, setting it carefully on the bed. The second tray revealed a deadlier cache. Boxes of ammunition were meticulously organized, including a section of illegal Teflon-coated rounds. Frank's expression remained impassive as his fingers brushed over an assortment of grenades. Fragmentation, smoke, and the particularly lethal thermite variants were all present, a grim rainbow of destructive potential. There were also multiple blocks of high-explosive C-4 with blasting caps.

The third tray held a different kind of weaponry. Electronic devices - signal jammers, tracking beacons, and communication equipment - shared space with an array of knives. From tactical folders to wicked-looking fixed blades, each weapon was honed to razor sharpness. Collapsible batons, their compact forms belying their striking power, rounded out the tray's inventory.

As Frank removed another tray, the true foundation of his arsenal was revealed. A well-worn bulletproof vest lay at the bottom of the locker. Its fabric bore the scars of numerous conflicts - bullet holes and shrapnel tears meticulously stitched closed. Ballistic plate inserts to the level of protection Frank deemed necessary. In a custom-made holster pocket sat a Colt Cobra .38, one of the few small revolvers that had a trigger guard that fit Frank's fingers. It was his weapon of last resort. When all else failed, he could count on the six rounds in the Colt.

Beside the vest, two shoulder holsters for the twin Redhawk revolvers waited. The leather was supple from years of use, molded perfectly to Frank's broad frame.

Frank stood motionless for a moment, surveying the tools of his trade. Each item represented a potential lifeline, a means of completing the mission and returning his niece safely.

In the moment, surrounded by the implements of violence, the disparity between the luxurious pool house and the grim reality of his world was thrown into sharp relief. Frank slid the derringer into his boot and the Colt into his jacket pocket. No need to overdo it. He doubted the kidnappers would show up on the doorstep. That would be too easy. But just in case…

Frank's calloused hand paused on the ornate doorknob of Richard's study. The muffled sounds of a heated argument seeped through the heavy door. He stood motionless, his face impassive as the voices inside grew louder.

"How could you, Richard?" Vivian's voice cracked with a mixture of fury and despair. "How could you bring him here? You hardly know this man."

Something crashed inside the room – likely a glass hitting the wall. Frank's muscles tensed imperceptibly.

"What would you have me do, Viv?" Richard's voice was strained, teetering on the edge of control. "Sit here and wait while our daughter—" His voice broke.

"Of course not!" Vivian shouted back. "But this? Your brother? A man you haven't seen in seventeen years? A man who—"

"Who what, Vivian?" Richard's tone turned dangerous. "Go ahead, say it."

A tense silence followed, broken only by Vivian's ragged breathing.

"I can't believe you're doing this," Vivian finally continued, her voice trembling. "You're just handing him our daughter's life? Our Grace?"

"What choice do we have?" Richard's reply was low, intense. "The police can't help us. Davis and his team have gotten us nowhere. Every second we waste, Grace is in more danger."

"But Frank?" Vivian's laugh was bitter, bordering on hysterical. "You don't even know who he is anymore! The way you talk about him..."

Frank leaned closer to the door, his ear almost touching the wood.

"You made him sound like some kind of demon," Vivian continued, her voice breaking.

"No," Richard's response was immediate, firm. "He's the man demons fear."

"And that's the type of man you want to entrust with our daughter's life?"

"Yes." Richard's answer was unflinching. "Whoever took Grace is evil, Vivian. Pure evil."

"So, you want to fight evil with evil?" Vivian's voice rose, hysteria fully taking hold. "Have you lost your mind, Richard? What happened to the man I married? The man who believed in law and order?"

"That man's daughter was kidnapped!" Richard roared, causing Frank to stiffen outside the door. The sound of a fist slamming on a desk echoed through the room.

Several heartbeats of silence passed before Richard spoke again, his voice now eerily calm.

"Frank's not evil, Vivian. He has a strong sense of right and wrong. But once he chooses sides, he'll stop at nothing under Heaven to win. That's who we need to rescue Grace from the bastards that took her."

The sound of muffled sobbing filled the air.

"He's one man, Richard," Vivian finally said, her voice small and defeated. "One man against God knows how many kidnappers. How can you be so sure?"

"Because I know my brother," Richard's tone was unwavering. "Yeah, he's one man. But he's the right man for the job. I'll make sure he has whatever he needs to get our daughter back safely."

"And what if he can't?" Vivian whispered, fear evident in every syllable. "What if we never see Grace again? What if your brother is as much a monster as the men who took our baby?"

"Then God help us all," Richard replied, his voice hollow.

The sound of approaching footsteps caused Frank to step back from the door, melting into the shadows of the hallway. The study door flew open, slamming against the wall.

Vivian stormed out, tears streaming down her cheeks. She paused for a moment, her red-rimmed eyes scanning the dim hallway. For a split second, her gaze seemed to lock with Frank's hidden form. A shudder ran through her body, and she hurried away, her sobs echoing down the corridor.

Richard appeared in the doorway, looking like a man who had aged a decade in a single evening. His eyes, so similar to Frank's yet worlds apart, searched the shadows. For a moment, it seemed he might call out. Instead, he sagged against the doorframe, running a trembling hand through his hair.

"Find her, Frank," he whispered. "For God's sakes... find her."

With a final, haunted look, Richard retreated into his study, the door closing with a soft click that seemed to echo in the tension-filled air.

Just outside the mansion's gates, Frank stared at the BMW 3-Series Vivian had rented. His massive frame made the sleek German sedan look like a child's toy.

He pulled the driver's seat all the way back, but it changed nothing. The car wasn't built for men six-seven and nearly four hundred pounds. He tried to fold himself in anyway, his knees pressed against the steering wheel, his head bent sideways against the roof. The seat groaned under his weight.

More adjustments. The seat back reclined until it almost touched the rear cushion. The steering wheel tilted up as far as it would go. Frank's hands too big for the delicate controls.

A jogger slowed to watch the giant wrestle with the tiny car. Frank ignored him, concentrating on getting his right leg under the steering wheel without snapping anything expensive. The BMW's leather creaked in protest.

Finally situated, sort of, Frank reached for the key fob. His elbow hit the gearshift. His knee knocked the turn signal. Everything was too small, too close. Like trying to wear a child's clothes.

The engine started with a refined purr that seemed to apologize for the car's dimensions. Frank managed to get it in gear, though his knees made it difficult to reach the pedals properly. The car moved forward, its suspension sagging noticeably to the left.

He caught his reflection in the side mirror - a face twisted sideways, massive shoulders hunched like a bear trying to fit in a cardboard box. The jogger had stopped completely now, phone raised to capture the absurd sight.

Frank drove away, his body contorted into spaces it was never meant to occupy. The BMW handled beautifully, but that hardly mattered. He looked like a gorilla in a telephone booth.

Streetlights cast sodium-yellow pools across the crime scene. Frank moved through them like a spectre, his boots testing the ground where Grace's armored SUV had made its turn down the alley. Shell casings still littered the alley entrance, overlooked by the crime scene techs or deemed unimportant. He picked one up. Military grade. The brass was clean, no oxidation. Professional weapons, well maintained.

In his mind, he traced the SUV's path through empty streets. The vehicle moved with professional precision, her security team scanning for threats.

His boots followed the skid marks. Here - the SUV had braked hard, trying to avoid the vehicle that pulled out suddenly and blocked its path. Another set of marks showed a second vehicle closing from behind. Classic military trap. Force the target to turn where you want it.

The garbage truck used to trap the SUV had left deep skid marks. Frank measured them with his eyes, calculating the angle. The truck had been positioned beforehand, waiting. Which meant surveillance. Planning. He found marks on the loading dock where someone had waited, watching this route day after day. Cigarette butts - Turkish brand, expensive. A patient hunter with expensive taste.

The gunmen were too experienced not to know that their submachine gun ammunition, even with Tefloncoating, would not penetrate the armored vehicle. Instead, they used their weapons like bullwhips to herd the SUV where they wanted it. Where larger caliber weapons waited.

The chase burned through his mind. Grace's SUV had taken the only route left open - the narrow alley that seemed to promise escape. The high walls channeled sound, limited escape routes. Grace's SUV had been like a rat in a maze, every turn leading to another dead end. But why a blocked alley?

Leaving the alley, Frank studied the skid marks. The SUV had skidded to a stop in the intersection to turn around. *That's why*, he thought. *A sniper had been waiting to take out the bodyguard in the SUV*. Frank studied the surrounding buildings outside the alley and determined which one he would use if he were the sniper.

Frank moved between buildings, calculating angles, studying sight lines. Each step measured, each position evaluated through a sniper's eyes. The old warehouse caught his attention - perfect elevation, unobstructed view of the kill zone. He climbed the fire escape, rust flaking beneath his boots.

The roof access door had been picked, not forced. Professional work. Inside, his boots found broken glass and bird droppings, except for one clean area near the edge. Someone had swept a shooting position, made it workable.

Frank knelt where the sniper had waited. A perfect hide. The warehouse's height matched the exact distance needed for a .50 caliber round to punch through reinforced glass. The shooter had known his ballistics, understood the physics of killing through armor.

Scuff marks on the floor showed where a bipod had been set up. Frank lay prone, his massive frame settling into the shooter's position. Through an imaginary scope, he traced the SUV's final approach. The lane below created a natural funnel, concrete walls channeling the target exactly where the sniper wanted it.

No brass casings. The shooter had policed his area meticulously, leaving nothing to chance. But Frank found other signs - the faint impression of an equipment case in the dust, a scrape where a spotter's elbow had rested. The hidden traces that only another professional would recognize.

A cigarette burn marked the edge of the rooftop - not from a domestic brand. Russian. Made for Arctic conditions, the kind Spetsnaz used because they burned even in Siberian cold. The sniper had waited patiently, smoking to pass time until his shot came.

Frank's finger touched where the rifle had rested. The position was perfect - accounting for wind, elevation, even the afternoon sun's position. This wasn't just skill. This was art. The kind taught only in the world's most elite military units.

Then he saw it - near the roof's edge where summer heat had softened the tar. A partial boot print, pressed deep into the surface. Frank knew the pattern - Russian military issue, but not standard infantry. The distinctive tread belonged to boots made specifically for Spetsnaz mountain units. He'd seen similar prints in Afghanistan, in places where only ghosts and killers ventured.

He stood, understanding his enemy better now. These weren't just local hired guns. The sniper's craft, his patience, his attention to detail - this was a supreme professional. Someone who lived in the spaces between nations, who killed with mathematical precision.

Frank's scarred hands clenched. He'd faced men like this before, in places where violence had no rules and death had no protocol. Now one had come here, brought his lethal art to these quiet streets.

Good. Frank preferred hunting professionals. They died just as easily as amateurs, but they made it more interesting.

Frank examined the ground where the rifle's bipod had dug into the tar when it fired. It was a Barret M82 Sniper Rifle. He knew it well. He had used it many times himself and still owned one. It was a heavy beast weighing almost thirty pounds, even more with a full magazine of .50 Caliber shells.

Leaving the warehouse, Frank walked along the path that the SUV had taken after Martinez was killed. The driver, Kovacs, was skilled. He kept moving, never letting his vehicle get out of his control. The gunmen had tried to take out the tires. It didn't work. No-flat tires held up even during the chase.

Shell casings marked each shooter's position. They'd organized in teams, maintaining interlocking fields of fire. No wasted shots, no crossed lanes. Everything precise, rehearsed. These men had trained together, knew each other's movements.

Frank came upon the intersection where Grace had been taken. Police tape cordoned off the wrecked SUV. There was nobody around. He slipped under the tape and approached the SUV still on its side. He studied the damaged armored panels and the skid marks.

Another vehicle had sped into the intersection as the SUV crossed through. It had T-boned the SUV with incredible force. The SUV had rolled onto its side, incapacitated, defenseless. The gunmen would have closed in cautiously.

Then the cutting began. Frank found traces of metal shavings where they'd used the powered saw. The cuts were exact, showing intimate knowledge of the SUV's armor specifications. They'd known exactly where to breach, how to defeat the security features. Someone had inside information.

Frank looked inside to complete the story. The bodies had been removed. Blood spray patterns and bits of skull sticking to the headliner and seats revealed the death of the passenger, Martinez. It was like Frank thought. A single high-caliber shot through the windshield had taken a portion of the man's head off.

Later, a gunman had shot the driver, Kovacs, twice in the head. Kovacs was a professional and therefore a threat while alive. They left nothing to chance.

Even the timing was precise. Four minutes from first contact to extraction. Long enough to ensure no immediate response from other security teams, short enough to avoid police response. Professional work. The kind that required serious resources and training.

Frank's hand touched another shell casing. Russian-made. The brass felt cold, deadly. High-end ammunition, match grade. Even their weapons showed extensive preparation. No random gunfire, no stray shots. Every round had a purpose.

Frank wanted to look at the security footage from surrounding businesses. It would help complete the story, but he knew the police would have already collected them and would not be in the mood to share with an out-of-town stranger.

In his mind, Frank saw Grace being pulled from the vehicle. Tactically trained men moving her to a waiting van - no windows, stolen plates. They'd vanish into traffic before anyone could respond. Every contingency planned, every angle covered.

These weren't ordinary criminals. The precision, the equipment, the tactics - this was a military operation disguised as a crime. Someone with serious resources had planned this for weeks, maybe months. They'd known the route, the security protocols, everything.

Headlights swept the scene. A patrol car rolled up, its engine idling. Officer Chen stepped out, coffee in one hand, Danish in the other. He nearly dropped both when he saw the massive figure examining the overturned SUV.

"Hey! This is a crime scene. You can't—" The words died in Chen's throat as Frank straightened to his full height, turning to face him. The streetlight caught his face, threw shadows across features twisted by old violence.

Chen's hand twitched toward his holster, then stopped. He was alone on patrol in a quiet suburb. Whatever this giant was - whatever had marked him so terribly - wasn't worth dying over.

Frank made no move toward his concealed weapons. He kept his hand open, where the police officer could see that he wasn't a threat. He had no interest in killing a cop, especially one just doing his job.

"Just... just move along, okay?" Chen's voice cracked slightly. "I don't want any trouble."

Frank's eyes met his for a moment. Chen took an involuntary step back. Then the disfigured giant simply walked away, disappearing into darkness like he'd never existed.

Chen waited until he was sure Frank was gone before letting out the breath he'd been holding. His coffee had gone cold. Suddenly he wasn't hungry for the Danish either.

The shell casings Frank had collected rode in his pocket like cold promises. These men were trained, equipped, experienced. But experience meant patterns. Patterns meant predictability. And predictability meant death.

They'd shown him how they worked. Now he would show them how he hunted.

Crypto

The BMW's suspension groaned with relief as Frank extracted himself from the driver's seat. His massive frame unfolded in stages, like a piece of heavy machinery deploying. A shoulder caught the seat belt. His knee banged the steering wheel. The door barely opened wide enough to accommodate his chest.

Getting out was worse than getting in. The driveway gravel crunched under his weight as he finally freed himself, his body straightening to its full intimidating height. Joints popped back into proper alignment.

Inside, Richard waited in the study. He stood at the window, drink in hand.

"Did you find anything?" Richard asked as Frank entered.

"Mercenaries."

"The kidnappers?"

Frank nodded. "Well-trained. Expensive."

"Davis thought they could be from organized crime." Richard's fingers tightened around his glass.

"Wrong." Frank's voice was gravel. "Ex-military."

"So, where does that leave us?"

"Your clients. I need their files." Frank turned to his brother. Richard's drink froze halfway to his lips.

Silence filled the study. Even the ice in Richard's glass seemed to stop clinking. The implications hung in the air like smoke - someone with resources, with military connections, with a reason to strike at Richard Kane through his daughter.

Someone from Richard's carefully guarded client list.

Richard's eyes widened, a flicker of panic crossing his face. "My client files? Frank, those are highly confidential. The SEC would have my head if—"

Frank cut him off with a sharp look. "Do you want Grace back?"

"Of course."

Richard ran a hand through his hair, conflict clear on his face. He paced the room, muttering about legal implications and breach of trust. Frank waited silently, his steady gaze never leaving his brother.

Finally, Richard stopped. He turned to Frank, his decision visible in the set of his shoulders. "Alright," he said quietly. "We'll need to go to my office. My computer is the only way to access them. But Frank, this has to stay between us. No one else can know."

Frank nodded once, understanding the weight of what Richard was offering.

"What about protecting Vivian?" said Richard.

"They have Grace. They don't need Vivian."

"I suppose you're right. Still, I'll see if Captain Reeves can send an officer for the day. I donated big time for his last campaign. He owes me."

Frank grunted, then turned back to the window. The morning rays of sunlight glinted off the pool, a deceptively peaceful scene. He knew that somewhere in those confidential files lay the key to finding Grace. And he was prepared to sift through every last page to find it.

The Kane Investments building loomed silently against the morning sky. It was still early before the employees started to arrive.

Frank watched as Richard pressed his palm against a biometric scanner at the building's entrance. A soft blue light pulsed, followed by a quiet beep of confirmation. As the reinforced glass doors slid open, he guided Frank to a private elevator. The elevator, equipped with sensors and internal cameras, whisked them silently to the top floor, where Richard's office suite awaited behind another layer of biometric locks.

Richard's office occupied a corner suite with floor-to-ceiling windows offering a panoramic view of the city. The lights automatically flicked on as he and Frank entered. Frank stood motionless, taking in the trappings of his brother's success - the sleek modern furniture, the abstract art on the walls, the array of financial awards displayed prominently on a shelf. Richard poured himself a glass of bourbon on the rocks.

Frank's eyes swept Richard's office, noting details others would miss. In the sitting area, a pedestal held a single item - a Fabergé egg on a gold stand. The workmanship was unmistakable. The Winter Egg of 1913, one of the lost seven. Last seen in St. Petersburg before the Revolution, when the Bolsheviks seized the Imperial collection.

Frank moved closer. Spotlights illuminated the treasure. The egg was magnificent - rock crystal carved to resemble frost, platinum and diamond snowflakes across its surface. Millions wouldn't touch its true value. This was history, stolen and rewrapped as a "gift." Its presence in Richard's office said more about his business associates than any financial record could.

He touched the small card beside it. The Cyrillic script had been done by hand, the ink still relatively fresh. A gift then, received recently. Frank's fingertips brushed across the pedestal. No dust. The cleaning staff kept it immaculate, like everything else in Richard's world of wealth and power.

"Beautiful, isn't it?" Richard stood at his desk. His voice carried forced casualness. "A token of appreciation from a business associate."

Frank turned, his massive frame casting a shadow over the priceless egg. "Lost in 1917."

"It's a reproduction." Richard's words came too quickly. "Very good work, but—"

"No, Dick." Frank's voice was granite. They both knew what sat in that case - a piece of imperial history that had vanished into the black markets of post-Soviet Russia. The kind of gift that came from men who dealt in more than money.

Richard looked away first. "I have documentation. Papers showing—"

"When?"

"Three months ago." Richard drained his glass. "Before all this started."

Frank turned back to the egg. In its crystalline surface, he saw his own reflection distorted - a scarred giant in a world of delicate things. But he also saw what Richard couldn't. The egg wasn't just a gift. It was a message, written in platinum and diamonds. Someone marking their territory with stolen history. Some gifts came with strings attached. And some strings were made to strangle.

Richard approached a painting on the wall - an abstract piece that seemed out of place among the other décor - and swung it aside to reveal a state-of-the-art wall safe. After entering a complex combination and submitting to another fingerprint scan, he retrieved a small, nondescript USB drive - the hard key necessary to decrypt his most sensitive client files.

Richard inserted the USB hard key into a port on his computer, causing a prompt to appear on the screen. His fingers flew across the keyboard, entering a long, complex passphrase. A progress bar appeared, filling slowly as multiple encryption layers were peeled away. Finally, a new window popped up, displaying a grid of innocuous-looking folder icons. Richard's shoulders tensed as he navigated through the digital labyrinth of his most classified files. He glanced at Frank, his expression a mix of shame and determination. "It's all here," he said quietly, gesturing to the screen. "Every client, every transaction, everything."

Richard hesitated for a moment, then stepped aside. Frank nodded once, then settled into Richard's ergonomic chair. The hydraulic pedestal holding the chair sank. Without a word, he began navigating through the files, his hands moving efficiently over the keyboard and mouse.

Richard paced nervously behind him. "Frank, I can't stress enough how sensitive this information is. If anyone found out-"

Frank silenced him with a look. Richard nodded, understanding the unspoken message. He moved to the small bar in the corner of the office, pouring himself another generous measure of bourbon. It was still early morning, but he needed to calm himself.

The Willow Crest Police Station smelled of coffee and floor polish. Vivian Kane stood at the front desk, her Hermès bag clutched tight against her cashmere sweater. Even distressed, she carried herself with the precise posture that years of modeling had ingrained. Her hands trembled slightly as she signed the visitor log, her perfect script faltering.

The desk sergeant recognized her - everyone in Willow Crest knew Richard Kane's wife. But something was wrong. The carefully curated image had fractures, like expensive porcelain beginning to crack.

Captain James Reeves was finishing paperwork when the sergeant knocked. "Sir? Vivian Kane is here. Says it's urgent."

Reeves found her standing in the lobby, straight-backed but somehow fragile. She looked out of place among the wanted posters and plastic chairs, like a rare bird that had strayed into unfamiliar territory.

"Mrs. Kane?"

"My daughter..." Her voice caught. She steadied herself, started again. "Grace has been kidnapped. Three days ago."

"I think you had better come in my office and sit down, Mrs. Kane."

Reeves led her to his office, away from curious eyes. She sat with practiced grace, but her fingers wouldn't stop moving - straightening her skirt, adjusting her sleeve, small nervous movements that betrayed her distress.

"Where is your husband, Mrs. Kane?" said Reeves.

"He's at work. He doesn't know that I'm here," she said avoiding eyes contact.

"Three days?" Reeves kept his voice gentle. "Why wait so long to report it?"

"Richard said..." She twisted her wedding ring. "The kidnappers were very clear. No police. They said they would hurt her." A tear slid down her cheek, cutting through perfect makeup. "They made us watch a video. Grace was so scared, but trying to be brave. She's always trying to be brave."

"Mrs. Kane - Vivian - what changed your mind about coming here?"

Her laugh held no humor. "My husband is a very successful businessman. He is full of confidence and believes there is nothing he can't negotiate." Her voice hardened. "But things changed. Richard fired our head of security and his team. He said they were incompetent. He brought in his brother Frank and said he would find Gracie and bring her home."

"Frank?"

"Yes. He's Richard's twin brother."

"Big guy with scars on his face and arms?"

"Yes, that's Frank."

"One of my officers met him snooping around the wreckage of the SUV. The officer said he was intimidating."

"He is. I didn't even know he existed until a few days ago. I know nothing about him. Now, Richard has put the life of our daughter in his hands. I lost faith that Richard could keep Gracie safe. I had no choice."

"Has there been a ransom demand?"

"Yes." She opened her bag, removed a DVD disc with shaking hands. "They want money. A specific amount."

"How much?"

"One hundred fifty-seven million dollars." She spoke the number carefully, precisely.

Reeves felt his eyebrows rise. Not a random figure. Specific amounts usually meant specific reasons.

"The kidnappers - have you heard their voices? Accents maybe?"

"Eastern European. Russian, I think." She dabbed at her eyes with a monogrammed handkerchief. "Richard says he can handle it. Says he knows people who can help. But I've seen his face when he thinks I'm not looking. He's terrified."

"How old is Gracie?"

"Thirteen." Her composure cracked. "She's just thirteen. Still sleeps with her old teddy bear even though she pretends she's too grown up for it. She's missing her riding lessons, her math tests. She's missing everything and I just want my baby back."

Reeves felt his stomach tighten. A child. In danger. While they'd wasted three days. "Excuse me a moment."

Outside his office, he closed his door and dialed a number on the receptionist's phone.

"Agent Cooper, it's Sheriff Reeves. I think I have your nexus." Reeves watched through the window as Vivian sat perfectly straight, every inch the society wife. But her hands kept twisting that wedding ring, around and around, like a rosary for the desperate.

"What have you got?"

"Thirteen-year-old girl, kidnapped three days ago. Father kept it quiet. Russian-speaking kidnappers demanding specific ransom - one hundred fifty-seven million."

A sharp intake of breath on the line. "Name?"

"Grace Kane. Father is Richard Kane, the investment banker."

"Kane Investments? The cryptocurrency guy?"

"That's him."

Silence for a moment. Then: "Don't let the mother leave. I'm on my way. And Reeves? If Richard Kane shows up, detain him. Man that wealthy, with those kinds of connections, keeping a kidnapping quiet for three days? He knows something he isn't telling."

Through the window, Reeves watched Vivian dab at fresh tears. Society women didn't come to small-town police stations unless they were desperate. Whatever game Richard Kane was playing, his wife had just changed the rules.

And somehow, Reeves knew, thirteen-year-old Grace was caught in the middle.

Hours passed. The sun set. Frank methodically combed through years of financial records. His face remained impassive, betraying nothing of his thoughts as he absorbed the complex web of transactions, investments, and client relationships.

Richard alternated between anxious pacing and slumping in a chair, nursing his drink. Every so often, he'd glance at Frank, hoping for some sign of progress. But Frank remained focused on the screen, barely moving except to click through to the next file or make an occasional note.

After several glasses of bourbon, Richard dozed off on the couch, his empty glass slipping from his hand and landing on a Persian rug.

Frank considered his snoring brother for a moment. He knew Richard was exhausted, but how could he possibly sleep when his daughter's fate hung in the balance? Richard had always been a narcissist, but Frank thought starting family might have changed that. It hadn't. The world still revolved around Richard Kane. He went back to reviewing the file while his brother slept.

As dawn began to break, painting the sky in hues of pink and gold, Frank suddenly stilled. His eyes narrowed as he focused on a particular set of transactions all by a company named "Falcon Bridge Financial Group." The transactions were for large purchases of Rubicoins, a cyber currency.

After a few minutes of further examination of the transactions, Frank rose from the desk and left Richard's office quietly.

Frank moved into a work area and sat down in an empty cubicle. He picked up the phone's receiver and dialed a number from memory. After a few moments, Frank said, "It's Frank. What do you know about Falcon Bridge Financial Group LLC and who owns it?"

Frank listened.

Richard woke slowly, hungover and with a crick in his neck from sleeping upright on the couch. As he opened his eyes, he saw Frank's giant silhouette looming in front of him, backlit by the morning sun.

Richard looked up, startled. Dark circles under his eyes betrayed his exhaustion. "What is it?"

"Lev Andreeva," said Frank in a no-nonsense tone.

Richard's face paled. "What about him?"

Frank's piercing gaze bore into his brother. He didn't need to say anything; his expression clearly demanded answers.

Richard slumped in his chair, the weight of his secrets finally crushing down on him. "I can explain," he began weakly.

Frank, massive arms crossed, waited.

"I need some coffee and aspirin to clear my head," said Richard.

"After," said Frank.

Richard looked up, like a hurt child.

"Everything," Frank demanded, his voice low but intense. "From the beginning."

Richard took a deep breath and began his story, his voice barely above a whisper. "Five years ago, Bitcoin and other cyber currencies were all the rage. Everyone was talking about decentralized finance, blockchain technology, the future of money. My investment firm was no different. We wanted in on the game, so I created a cyber currency for my firm. I called it 'Rubicoin.'"

Frank listened intently, his expression unreadable as Richard detailed the initial success of Rubicoin. The excitement in Richard's voice was palpable as he described the early days, the rush of creating something new, the thrill of watching value materialize seemingly out of thin air.

"We sold our cyber currency to investors, then invested a percentage of the money in highly leveraged commercial real estate transactions as collateral for Rubicoins," Richard continued. "Things were going great until a casino development project in Las Vegas ran into trouble and the city pulled their building permit. We lost $90 million."

Richard paused, considering. "Which, in retrospect, was not that big of a deal. But it raised questions with our investors, some of which pulled their money out by selling their Rubicoins at a discount. The value of the currency fell. The more it fell, the more investors wanted out. Our money was invested in long-term real estate transactions, so we couldn't get hands on the cash to shore up the currency."

Frank's eyes narrowed. He could see where this was going, the desperate moves of a man watching his empire crumble.

"So, I needed a new group of investors to buy the Rubicoins that the current batch of investors wanted to sell," Richard said, his voice dropping even lower. "That's when I met Lev Andreeva."

Frank leaned in slightly, his interest piqued.

"He was a Russian oligarch that had been banned from investing in the United States and allied countries after Russia invaded Ukraine," Richard explained. "I came up with a simple idea that would hide his investments – Lev would purchase Rubicoins in another country such as Hungary or Egypt under a holding company set up in that country. Any of our investors that wanted to sell their Rubicoins were introduced to Lev's holding company as a potential buyer."

Richard's voice took on a note of pride, despite the circumstances. "Within a short time, the bleeding stopped and the value of Rubicoins was shored up. In fact, the value actually started climbing again. We invested in more real estate deals and started making money hand over fist."

Frank remained silent, his face impassive, but his mind was racing, connecting dots, seeing the bigger picture forming.

"Other oligarchs started buying Rubicoins," Richard continued. "Money was pouring in. Everything was fine until somebody got pissed off and ratted us out to the US Treasury Department."

Richard's face fell, the memory of that moment clearly painful. "They froze most of our bank accounts until we could show them that none of our investors were on the sanctions list. Of course, we couldn't do that. We were holding $157 million of Lev's money in escrow after a block sale of Rubicoins he had been holding. Lev wanted it back. Lev's not the kind of guy you disappoint. All my money was frozen by the US government. I couldn't pay him."

A heavy silence fell over the room. Frank's gaze bore into Richard, who squirmed under the intensity.

"So, he took Grace?" Frank finally asked, though it wasn't really a question.

Richard nodded, tears welling in his eyes. "Yeah... the bastard took my Gracie. I swear, Frank, I don't care about the money. I just want my daughter back safely."

Frank processed the information. The weight of the situation settled over them like a heavy shroud.

Richard couldn't meet Frank's eyes. "I know I should have told you this from the beginning. I was ashamed. I really fucked up. What happened was not Gracie's fault. It was mine. I know that. I'll pay whatever penalty I need to get her back. I don't care what happens to me." Richard took a minute to regain his composure. "So, now you know everything, Frank. Can I still count on you? Will you bring Grace home?"

Frank's expression remained impassive, but a dangerous glint appeared in his eyes. "I'll get her back," he said simply. "Where is Andreeva now?"

"He has a place near Hudson Yards. It's a fortress but I doubt she's there. He's too smart for that."

"I need the car."

"Why? What are you gonna do?"

"Talk to Andreev."

"I don't think that's a good idea, Frank. Lev's one mean son of a bitch."

"So am I."

In an internet provider utility van parked in the adjacent building's lot, a technician adjusted his headphones. The van's interior bristled with surveillance equipment, screens showing audio wavelengths dancing in blue light. Through the front windshield, Richard Kane's office windows glowed.

His fingers moved across the keyboard, transcribing every word coming through the Fabergé egg's hidden transmitter. Frank's deep rasp barely registered on the sensors, but the mic caught his few words - each one heavy with threat. The technician typed faster as Richard revealed Andreev's location at Hudson Yards.

The transcription software flagged key phrases in red: "get her back," "talk to Andreev," "fortress."

The technician encrypted the file and sent it through a secure channel. Within seconds, his phone buzzed. A text from Andreev: Maintain surveillance.

He settled deeper into his chair, headphones pressed tight against his ears, listening as the Kane brothers planned their next move.

Richard's car turned onto the long driveway leading to the Kane estate. Frank, sitting in the passenger seat, noticed it first - the flashing lights, the dark vehicles parked haphazardly on the manicured lawn. His body tensed, years of training kicking in instinctively.

"Richard," he said, his gravelly voice breaking the tense silence.

Richard looked up from the road, his face draining of color as he took in the scene before them. FBI agents swarmed the property, their jackets emblazoned with bold yellow letters standing out.

"Oh God," Richard whispered, "What has she done?"

They pulled up to the house and were immediately surrounded by stern-faced agents. Richard exited the car, his initial shock quickly replaced by a mask of controlled anger. Frank followed, his eyes constantly scanning, assessing.

Inside, they found the foyer transformed into a command center. Agents worked at laptops, phones rang, radios crackled. Vivian stood amidst the chaos, tear-streaked but resolute.

"What have you done?" Richard's voice was quiet, dangerous.

"What you wouldn't do," Vivian shot back. "Our daughter is out there, Richard. I couldn't wait anymore while you played detective with your brother."

"They specifically said no FBI—"

"I don't care what they said!" Vivian's composure cracked. "Grace needs help. Real help."

Agent Cooper approached them, his face tight with controlled anger. "Mr. Kane. I'm Special Agent Cooper, FBI. We need to talk about why you waited nearly seventy-two hours to report your daughter's kidnapping."

"I can explain—" Richard started.

"Two men murdered in broad daylight. A firefight through a business district. And you kept it quiet." Cooper's voice was cold. "We've lost critical time, Mr. Kane. The first forty-eight hours are crucial in kidnapping cases. And now they're gone."

"They said no police, no FBI," Richard said weakly.

"They always say that," Cooper replied. "And we always find ways to work around it. But now we're playing catch-up." Cooper turned to Frank. "You must be Frank."

"My brother," Richard said quickly. "He's been helping—"

"Helping conduct a private investigation that's compromised evidence and potential leads," Cooper cut in. He addressed Frank directly. "Frank, I understand you want to help find your niece. But this is now a federal investigation. I need you to step back and let us do our jobs. Are we clear?"

Frank gave a single nod.

"Good." Cooper turned back to Richard. "My team needs access to everything - phone records, emails, security footage, financial records. Everything. No more secrets, Mr. Kane. Grace's life depends on it."

Richard's face went pale. "Of course. Whatever you need."

"Agent Sheridan will take your statement." Cooper gestured to a female agent. "I want every detail about the ransom demand, the contact methods, everything you've done since Grace was taken."

As Richard followed Sheridan to another room, he shot one last desperate look at Frank. Cooper stopped

Frank before he could leave. "Frank." His voice was quieter now. "If you learn anything that might help find your niece, my door's open. But no cowboy stuff. These kidnappers are professionals. We've seen their handiwork at the crime scenes where Grace was taken."

Frank met his gaze but said nothing.

Cooper handed him a card. "Keep this line open." He moved away to direct his team, leaving Frank standing in the foyer, watching the federal machine grind into motion.

Agents moved through the mansion with focused efficiency. Everything the Kanes had tried to keep quiet was now laid bare for federal scrutiny.

Frank slipped the card into his pocket and walked out. He had work to do, and it wouldn't involve the FBI.

Agent Sheridan found Cooper in the foyer. She pulled him aside, lowering her voice.

"Sir, Kane's being selective about what he'll give us. Says we can have everything personal - phone records, emails, security footage from the house. But he's refusing access to his company files. Claims it's privileged client information."

Cooper's jaw tightened. "Investment firm records?"

"He quoted federal securities laws and attorney-client privilege. Says we'll need a warrant."

"He's stonewalling us," Cooper said, watching Richard through the study doorway. "Two hours ago his wife was begging us to help find their daughter. Now he's throwing up roadblocks about company records?"

"Want me to start on the warrant?"

"No yet. Let me talk to him."

Cooper entered the study, closing the door behind him. Richard sat behind his desk, his usual commanding presence diminished by exhaustion and fear.

"Mr. Kane, let's be clear about something," Cooper said. "Every minute we spend fighting over access to records is one more minute your daughter spends with with those bastards and something could go terribly wrong."

"You don't understand," Richard said. "I have a fiduciary responsibility to protect my clients' confidential information. The SEC—"

"Your daughter's life is at stake."

"And I could go to prison for violating federal securities laws." Richard leaned forward. "I'm not being difficult, Agent Cooper. I literally cannot give you those files without proper authorization. A warrant releases me from liability. Without it, I'd be breaking multiple federal laws and any evidence you collect from my company's records could be thrown out of court because it was obtained illegally."

Cooper studied him for a long moment. Richard was right, and they both knew it.

"How long have you worked white collar crime, Agent Cooper?" Richard asked quietly.

"Fifteen years."

"Then you understand what I'm telling you. Get a warrant. I'll give you everything you need. But I have to do this by the book."

Cooper nodded once, then turned and walked out into the foyer where Sheridan was coordinating with other agents.

"Sheridan," he called. "Drop everything else. I need that warrant. Call Judge Matthews - she'll be up by now. Focus on financial records, phone records, security footage, surveillance cameras, entry logs. Anything showing who's been watching Kane's routine. And mark it urgent."

"On it," Sheridan replied, already reaching for her phone.

Cooper glanced back at the study. Richard's explanation was perfectly reasonable, completely legal, and somehow still felt wrong. The question was - would they get the warrant in time to save Grace?

Pressure

Alex brought in the breakfast tray - cereal bowl, sliced bananas on top, glass of orange juice. The morning sun through the barred window cast prison-bar shadows across the sparse room. Grace sat on her bed, arms crossed, watching him set down the tray.

"What's this supposed to be?"

"Breakfast. Cheerios with banana."

"Seriously? I don't like cold cereal." She poked at the cereal with her spoon. "At home, our chef makes eggs Benedict on Sundays. Or I get that amazing rice soup from the Thai place near school. You know the one on Madison?"

"This isn't a restaurant." Alex's voice had an edge to it. "It's what we have."

"Whatever." Grace pushed the tray away. "I'm not eating this."

"Spoiled brat," Alex muttered, turning to leave.

Grace's face crumpled. Tears welled in her eyes. Not the angry tears of their previous arguments - these seemed to come from somewhere deeper, more broken.

"I'm sorry," Alex said quickly. "I shouldn't have—"

"You think I'm spoiled?" Her voice cracked. "I'm trapped in this room. These men... the way they look at me when they walk by..." She wrapped her arms around herself, making herself smaller. "I hear them talking sometimes, when they think I'm asleep. I know what they want to do."

Alex shifted uncomfortably. "Nobody's going to hurt you."

"You can't promise that." Grace wiped her eyes. "I'm thirteen. Do you know what that's like? To be thirteen and know you're probably going to die? I haven't even had my first kiss. Never will now."

"Don't say that. You'll get out of here."

"Will I?" She looked up at him, vulnerability replacing her usual defiance. "You're the only one who's nice to me, Alex. The only one who sees me as a person, not just... not just something to use."

She stood slowly, moved closer. Alex backed away.

"Grace..."

"I see how you protect me. Bringing my meals, keeping the others away." Her voice was soft, calculated. "You're not like them."

"Yes. I am."

She threw her arms around his neck and kissed him, quick and clumsy. Alex jerked back like he'd been burned, knocking over the orange juice. It spread across the floor.

"What are you doing?"

"I thought..." Her face flushed red. "I just wanted to know what it felt like. Before..." She let the sentence hang.

"No." Alex's voice was hard. "Don't ever do that again. I'm not... this isn't..." He struggled to find words. "You're a kid."

"I won't be a kid much longer. Not in here."

"Stop it." He grabbed the breakfast tray, orange juice still dripping. "Just stop."

He left, slamming the door. Grace sat back on her bed, tears gone. Through the door, she heard Alex's footsteps stop, then continue down the hall, slower now. She touched her lips, thinking.

She'd seen something in his eyes when she kissed him. Not desire - that she could have handled. What she'd seen was better: pity, protectiveness, guilt. Perfect.

Seeds planted.

She lay back on the bed, staring at the ceiling. The breakfast would come again tomorrow. And Alex would be thinking about that kiss, about her vulnerability, about his role as her protector. They had underestimated her because of her age. Men were predictable that way. Even the good ones.

Especially the good ones.

Alex found his associates in the kitchen - Burke, Wolfe, and Decker drinking beer and playing poker at nine in the morning. He was putting the breakfast tray in the kitchen when he heard them laughing.

"Rich little bitch thinks she's tough," Burke said, tossing chips in the pot. Built like a tank, prison tattoos crawling up his thick neck.

"Saw her giving you the eye yesterday, Wolfe," Decker said. "Think she likes you."

Wolfe spat chewing tobacco into his empty beer can. "Give her something to like."

"Shut up." The words were out of Alex's mouth before he could stop them.

The kitchen went quiet. Burke looked up slowly, his eyes dead. "The fuck did you say?"

Alex's heart hammered in his chest, but he didn't back down. "She's just a kid."

"Well, shit." Burke stood, beer can crunched in his fist. "Baby boy's got himself a crush."

"I said shut up." Alex's voice cracked, betraying him.

Burke moved fast for his size. The first punch doubled Alex over, dropping him to his knees. A boot caught him in the ribs, flipping him onto his back.

"Hold this little prick up," Burke growled.

Decker and Wolfe hauled Alex to his feet. Burke's meaty fist smashed into his face. Stunned by the power of the blow, blood filled Alex's mouth.

"Think you're gonna play hero?" Another punch. "Fucking teenager with a hard-on trying to act tough?"

When they finished, Alex lay curled on the floor, spitting blood onto the linoleum. Burke grabbed a handful of his hair, yanking his head back.

"Listen good, you little shit. You're here to feed her and keep her quiet. That's it. Try this hero crap again, I'll put you in the ground. Got it?"

Alex managed a nod.

"Clean your face. Don't need her screaming."

Alex pulled himself up using the counter, ribs screaming. In the window's reflection, his face was already swelling, blood dripping from his nose and split lip.

He'd tried to help her. But in the end, he was just a scared kid pretending to be something he wasn't.

Lev Andreev built his fortune in the chaos following the Soviet Union's collapse, starting with human trafficking. He recruited desperate young women from small villages with promises of modeling contracts in Western Europe. Instead, they disappeared into a network of brothels. Those who resisted were found in shallow graves.

When the Russian mob wars erupted in the mid-90s, Andreev expanded into arms dealing, selling Soviet military hardware to anyone with cash. He shipped weapons to both sides of various African conflicts, profiting from endless civil wars. The United Nations linked him to multiple genocides, but nothing stuck.

By 2000, he had legitimized his operation enough to move into the energy sector, using violence and extortion to acquire oil and gas assets from their rightful owners. Families who wouldn't sell simply vanished. Their properties were acquired through "legal" transfers, the documents signed by people who were never seen again.

He parlayed his energy holdings into banking and real estate, building a facade of legitimacy while maintaining his connections to the criminal underworld. His reputation for brutality kept competitors at bay - everyone remembered what happened to the last oligarch who challenged him. They found pieces of the man's family for weeks.

When sanctions cut him off from Western banks, he simply shifted to cryptocurrency and cyber crime. His technical teams, a mix of former Russian military hackers and recruited criminal prodigies, became legendary in the dark web community. They didn't just ransom corporate networks - they emptied bank accounts, manipulated stock trades, and destroyed companies that refused to pay.

Andreev's hackers were suspected in some of the largest financial crimes in history, but they never left traces. They hijacked power grids in Eastern Europe to mine cryptocurrency. They emptied ATMs across Asia without triggering alarms. Swift Bank lost billions in a series of transfers that seemed legitimate until the money vanished into digital wallets controlled by Andreev.

When the NSA finally breached one of his servers, they found evidence linking him to attacks on hospitals, power plants, and defense contractors. But Andreev's technical teams had buried the operations under so many layers of proxy servers and false flags that nothing could be proven.

The official investigation files contained a single quote from a former associate: "Andreev doesn't solve problems with money. He solves them with blood. The money is just a scorecard."

Andreev chose America, and specifically Manhattan, for the same reason many predators choose to hunt near populated areas - it provided the best cover. In Russia, he was too visible, too much of a target. Every move he made was watched by rivals, police, and intelligence services. His enemies knew his habits, his weaknesses, his daily routine.

But in Manhattan, he became just another wealthy foreigner living the high life. His neighbors were Saudi princes, Chinese industrialists, and tech billionaires - all with their own security, all with their own secrets. No one questioned the armed guards or the armored cars. Such things were expected. Privacy was respected, questions weren't asked.

The city's financial infrastructure was perfect for his needs. Billions in transactions flowed through Manhattan's banks every day. His own movements of money, properly obscured, became drops in an ocean. Wall Street's constant deal-making provided endless opportunities for his hackers to manipulate markets and exploit insider information.

Most importantly, Manhattan put him close to his targets - the banks, investment firms, and financial institutions that controlled the world's wealth. Why hack a system from across the globe when you could sit in your office and watch your mark through a sniper scope?

The American intelligence services knew he was there, of course. But what truly protected Andreev was America's own legal system. The Justice Department, despite its power and funding, was constrained by constitutional limits, rules of evidence, and due process. They needed probable cause for searches, warrants for surveillance, and evidence that would stand up in court. Suspicion wasn't enough. Intelligence briefs weren't enough.

In Russia, police could kick down doors on a whisper of wrongdoing. In America, even with a mountain of intelligence suggesting his crimes, agencies needed to prove every detail through legally obtained evidence. Andreev understood this better than most - he'd hired teams of lawyers to study American law's constraints and exploit them. His cryptocurrency operations were deliberately structured to create reasonable doubt. His computer systems were designed to make evidence gathering nearly impossible without violating constitutional protections.

The same laws that made America strong also made it the perfect haven for someone who knew how to stay just beyond their reach. Andreev had learned that the most effective shield against American law enforcement wasn't violence or bribery - it was American law itself.

Andreev's Manhattan compound occupied a full block on the Upper East Side, surrounded by a fifteen-foot perimeter wall of smooth granite and steel. Security cameras and motion sensors crowned the wall's top, while ground-penetrating radar monitored the subway tunnels below. A single gate of black steel, wide enough for two vehicles, served as the only entrance, with a guardhouse manned 24/7 by armed security.

Behind the wall stood a modern six-story building of glass and steel, its windows tinted and bulletproof. The structure rose like a dark monolith, its sharp angles and black facade a stark contrast to the traditional brownstones of the neighborhood. A helipad crowned the roof, its edges ringed with anti-drone defenses and electronic broadcast domes and dishes.

The lobby, with its marble floors and modern art, served as a kill zone - beautiful but designed for maximum tactical advantage.

The entire second floor of Andreev's compound functioned as a state-of-the-art digital operations center - a black box of technology and surveillance that rivaled government facilities. The space was kept at a constant sixty-eight degrees to cool the servers and equipment. The only illumination came from the blue glow of monitors and status lights.

The main room stretched the length of the building. Three tiers of workstations faced a wall of screens displaying surveillance feeds, network traffic, and threat assessments. Former Russian military cyber operators worked alongside hired civilian hackers, their keyboards clicking in constant rhythm. They monitored dark web chatter, intercepted communications, and probed for digital threats.

A separate section housed the physical security team's command center. Ex-Spetsnaz operators tracked thermal imaging from the perimeter, drone feeds from the surrounding blocks, and cameras covering every approach to the building. They coordinated with roving security teams through encrypted communications.

The heart of the operation was a sealed room in the center - a Faraday cage that blocked all electronic signals. Inside, Andreev's most elite hackers worked on independent systems, completely isolated from outside networks. They could probe and attack without fear of counter-tracing. When they needed to deploy their tools, data was transferred via isolated hardware to "air-gapped" systems that could safely connect to external networks.

The floor had its own backup generators, independent ventilation, and a separate security team. Access required multiple biometric scans and authorization from at least two senior staff members. Even Andreev himself couldn't enter without following security protocols.

This was where his empire's digital heart beat - monitoring global financial markets, tracking threats, protecting his cryptocurrency operations, and gathering intelligence on targets. The floor never slept. Shifts changed every eight hours, but the work never stopped.

The local FBI field office knew the floor existed - their surveillance vans had never been able to penetrate its electronic defenses. Even the NSA's best efforts to breach its systems had failed. The floor was both Andreev's sword and shield, allowing him to strike at enemies while remaining safely hidden behind layers of digital security.

The third floor housed the security team's living quarters and armory. Their weapons were stored in secured lockers - MP5s, body armor, and enough firepower to hold off a small army.

The fourth and fifth floors contained Andreev's personal living space - a luxury apartment wrapped in floor-to-ceiling bulletproof glass. The walls were reinforced concrete behind wood panels, the doors all steel core. The elevator required biometric access, and the stairwells were equipped with reinforced security doors at each landing.

The sixth floor served as Andreev's office and meeting space, decorated with an oligarch's taste for expensive minimalism. Here, he conducted the business that had made him a billionaire before sanctions cut him off from legitimate banking channels.

The basement levels dropped two stories underground. The first subterranean floor contained the garage, accessed through hydraulic steel doors disguised as part of the perimeter wall. A fleet of armored vehicles waited there - mostly black Mercedes sedans with run-flat tires and ballistic protection.

The lower basement level housed secure rooms with concrete walls and steel doors. No windows, no external access points. The perfect place to hold someone who wasn't meant to leave.

Two blocks away, a second building owned through a shell company served as a backup location, connected to the main compound by a tunnel beneath the street. Every contingency had been considered, every escape route planned.

In the heart of Manhattan's wealthiest neighborhood, Andreev had built himself a fortress that didn't pretend to be anything else. The black glass and steel structure sent a clear message - this was a place designed to keep people out, or in, depending on Andreev's wishes.

Lev Andreev sat behind his massive desk of steel and glass, gazing out through bulletproof glass at Manhattan's skyline. He held a tumbler of vodka but hadn't touched it. Davis sat across from him, his suit jacket draped over a chair, shoulder holster visible.

"Cooper's good," Davis said. "He'll push hard for the warrant. Probably already has Judge Matthews writing it up."

"The warrant concerns you?" Andreev's accent was subtle, years of American life having smoothed its edges.

"No. What concerns me is Cooper's instincts. He knows something's off about the ransom amount."

Andreev's lips curved slightly. "It is what it is. It's not so much the amount of money that concerns me. Honestly, it's a drop in a very big bucket. It's the damage it can do to my business if I let anyone slide. It doesn't matter if his accounts were frozen by the treasury department. That's his problem. Richard Kane owes me. He's going to pay."

"Cooper's already looking into Kane's client list. If he connects you-"

"He won't." Andreev set down his untouched vodka. "The shells within shells, the offshore accounts, the cryptocurrency transactions - how many years did it take you to unravel it all?"

"Three," Davis admitted. "But I was working alone then. The Bureau has resources."

"And constraints. They need probable cause. Warrants. Evidence that will stand up in court. American law enforcement's greatest weakness is American law."

Davis nodded. Having spent fifteen years with the Bureau before Andreev recruited him, he understood the frustration of watching criminals hide behind legal protections.

"There's one more matter we should discuss… His brother, Frank."

"What about him?"

"He's hard to pin down. I used all my resources to uncover his background but found little. Frank Kane is a wild card and I know you dislike wild cards."

"It's not that I dislike them. I just feel they should be eliminated early in the game. Their absence makes the outcome more predictable."

"We should be careful. His disappearance could draw unnecessary attention."

"I agree." Andreev's expression hardened.

"Okay."

"The girl?"

"Safe," Davis confirmed. "Viktor's crew has her at the house in Brighton Beach. Just local muscle. Nothing ties them to you."

Andreev nodded, satisfied. Even if someone found the girl, they'd find only Russian gangsters with no provable connection to him. His hands, as always, were clean.

"Sir," Davis said carefully, "what happens to her when this is over?"

Andreev turned back to the window. "That depends entirely on her father."

In the pool house, Frank methodically stripped off his body armor, each plate bearing the scars of past conflicts. His weapons lay arranged on the bed - the Ruger Super Redhawks, spare magazines, knives. Richard stood in the doorway, watching his brother prepare.

"When the FBI finds the connection between Andreev and me, I'm fucked."

Frank grunted, unconcerned with his brother's legal troubles.

"So, what are you going to do?"

"Talk to Andreev."

"Don't be an idiot, Frank. You can't talk to Andreev. He'll never let you into his compound. It's a waste of time."

"Maybe he's curious."

"He's not going to be afraid of you, Frank."

"He should be."

"Maybe, but he's surrounded by an army of well-armed killers. That makes him fearless."

"…and overconfident. I need a bigger car."

Richard sighed and tossed him the keys to the Maybach. "Take mine."

Frank grunted, displeased. The luxury car wasn't his style. He pocketed the keys and turned back to his weapons, a clear dismissal.

Richard lingered for a moment, watching his brother prepare for what might be a suicide mission. He wanted to say something more, but there was nothing left to say. He closed the door quietly behind him, leaving Frank alone with his arsenal.

Frank left all his weapons on the bed. He didn't want to lose them and he was sure Andreev would have him and his vehicle searched. Going unarmed sent a message – he was unintimidated by Andreev's security teams. It took guts to go unarmed, but guts were one thing Frank had in abundance.

Frank exited the house and walked toward the Maybach. In the driveway, he watched the gardeners pull up in a well-used pickup. A slight smile crept across Frank's lips.

Frank drove the gardener's truck across a bridge entering Manhattan.

The gardener's truck idled at the security gate of Andreev's compound. Frank sat motionless behind the wheel, his scarred hands resting lightly on the steering wheel. The guard studied his ID, then made a call.

On the sixth floor, Andreev's phone buzzed. "Sir, Richard Kane's brother is at the gate. Requesting to see you."

Andreev turned to Davis.

"Shit," Davis said. "He's an oversized pain in the ass. Keep him out."

Andreev watched the security feed. Frank waited in the truck, face impassive, seemingly unconcerned by the armed guards surrounding the vehicle.

"He certainly is a big man."

"…and ugly," added Davis. "There is no advantage in letting him in—"

"I don't agree," Andreev said finally. "I want to meet the man foolish enough to drive up to my front gate." He picked up his phone. "Bring him to my office. Search him first. Thoroughly. Especially for a wire."

Davis shifted uncomfortably. "Sir, this isn't—"

"We'll show him I have nothing to hide, right? Somethings are worth the risk, Davis. Besides, he's only one man… even if he is big."

Down at the gate, the guard returned to Frank's window. "Mr. Andreev will see you. Please step out of the vehicle. We need to search you."

Frank complied, his movements unhurried. As armed men approached to search him, his face remained expressionless. But something in his eyes made the guards check him twice, then three times.

The massive steel gate swung open and Frank was escorted by four guards into the compound.

Davis watched as Frank approached the main building. "I can't be here."

"Why not?" said Andreev. "You're part of my security team."

"They'll know I was part of the kidnapping. That's a connection we don't want them to make."

"Fine. Go hide in your office."

Dismissed, Davis left.

The four guards escorted Frank into Andreev's office. He moved with the careful precision of a predator, his eyes scanning the room - noting exits, calculating distances. A USB hard key protruded from Andreev's computer. Frank's eyes scanned the room for possible locations of a safe that would hold the hard key. Nothing stood out. It was well hidden.

Andreev sat behind his enormous desk. Through the bulletproof windows behind him, Manhattan's skyline stretched into the distance.

"Please, sit." Andreev gestured to a chair. Frank remained standing. "Can I offer you a drink?"

"No."

"Fine. I must admit, I'm curious what brings Richard Kane's brother to my door. Especially in a gardener's truck."

Frank's eyes settled on Andreev. "Grace."

"Ah. Rumors spread fast." Andreev leaned back. "A tragic situation. But I know nothing about your niece's disappearance."

Frank said nothing, his gaze steady.

"Your brother, on the other hand..." Andreev spread his hands. "He owes me money. A considerable sum. One must pay one's debts, Mr. Kane. Bad karma otherwise. You never know what can happen… to anyone."

"Where is she?"

"As I said… I know nothing about the girl. But Richard should pay what he owes. It would be better for everyone."

"Hurt her and I'll kill you... slowly."

The guards stepped forward. Andreev waved them off.

"I believe you would try. You seem quite unshakeable. I admire that. But I think you would find that I'm not an easy man to kill, although many have tried… and died in the process."

Frank grunted, unimpressed. He caught sight of a nearby furniture warehouse overlooking Andreev's building.

"In the future, you should keep your distance, Frank. If I see you again, I will not be as cordial."

"Neither will I," said Frank.

"Go home," Andreev said. "Tell your brother to pay his debts. Sometimes the simplest solution is the best one."

The guards stepped forward. Frank held Andreev's gaze for one more moment, then turned and walked out, his reconnaissance complete. Andreev remained starring at the door, contemplating, calculating.

A minute after Frank left, Davis reentered Andreev's office. "Did you learn anything?"

"Yes. Frank Kane is no pussy like his brother… and you."

Davis ignored the slight, "What are your orders?"

"Make it look like an accident."

Cooper found Richard in his study. "Mr. Kane." He held up the document. "Judge Matthews signed our warrant twenty minutes ago. We need to see those client files. Now."

Richard took the warrant, made a show of reading it carefully. "This warrant is highly irregular. My clients' privacy—"

"Are no longer protected when it comes to this investigation," Cooper cut in. "The warrant covers all communication, financial records, and transactions for the past five years."

"Fine." Richard set the warrant down. "But the files aren't here. They're secured at my office in Manhattan. The system requires biometric access and a security key."

"Then let's go." Cooper checked his watch. "Agent Sheridan, get a second team to Kane Investments. I want their cyber unit ready when we arrive."

"Agent Cooper," Richard said, standing. "This will take time. The files are encrypted. Multiple security protocols—"

"Every minute we waste puts your daughter at greater risk, Mr. Kane." Cooper's voice hardened. "Or is there something in those files you don't want us to find?"

Richard met his gaze. "I'll get my coat."

As Richard left the room, Cooper watched him pull out his phone, fingers moving quickly across the screen. He noted the time: 9:47 AM. Whatever Kane was trying to hide, whatever he was trying to delete or move, they'd find it.

The question was - would they find it in time to save Grace?

Driving the gardeners' truck, Frank watched the black SUV in his rearview mirror. It had been with him for six blocks, keeping three car lengths back. Professional distance, professional drivers. The second SUV came up fast in the left lane, muscled past him, then settled in fifty yards ahead.

They would try to box him soon. Probably at the next red light or somewhere they could control the surrounding traffic. The borrowed gardener's truck had no armor, no weapons. Just basic tools in the back - rake, shovel, leaf blower, plastic garbage bins.

Frank's eyes settled on the metal rake handle, calculating its length and weight. Then to the garbage bins. Back to his mirrors.

The front SUV was slowing gradually. The one behind maintained its disciplined distance. They were forcing his speed down, looking for their moment. Both vehicles would be armored. Trained shooters inside.

Frank's scarred hands remained relaxed on the steering wheel. They thought they were hunting him. That was their first mistake.

Richard and the FBI agents entered his corner office. Cooper and Sheridan watched as Richard approached a Rothko painting on the wall and pressed his palm against a hidden sensor. The painting swung away from the wall, revealing a sleek wall safe.

"Biometric lock," Richard explained, pressing his thumb to the keypad. A soft click, then the safe door opened.

Inside lay a single USB drive and several stacks of cash. Richard retrieved it, closed the vault door, swung the painting back in place, then sat at his desk. The drive slid into his computer with a soft click. His fingers moved across the keyboard, entering a complex passphrase.

"Where would you like to start?" Richard asked, his voice carefully neutral.

"The largest cyber currency transactions first," Cooper said, moving behind the desk to see the screen.

Richard clicked through folders. Banking records filled the monitor, each transaction a potential thread leading to Grace - or to Richard's downfall. Cooper leaned closer, studying the numbers.

Behind them, the FBI's cyber team began setting up their equipment, preparing to copy and analyze every byte of data. Richard watched them from the corner of his eye, wondering if they could trace the carefully hidden path to Andreev.

Richard wanted to find Grace more than anything, but he also didn't want his daughter growing up without her father. The embarrassment of having a father in a federal prison would destroy Grace's social standing. He wondered how long Vivian would last if he was in prison before putting herself back in the dating pool to find a new means of support. *Not long*, he thought. Vivian was the perfect wife as long as she didn't feel threatened. Once that happened, all bets were off. She was a survivor. That was one of things he loved about her. Richard knew very well that his little family was at stake if Cooper found out what he had been hiding. Time seemed to slow as Cooper opened the first file.

The crossing gate lowered with a soft ding. Frank eased the gardener's truck to a stop, watching the distant freight train approach. The SUV behind him closed to within yards, blocking any retreat. The one in front pulled over, waiting across the tracks.

Frank saw the reverse lights illuminate on the lead SUV. In that moment, he understood their plan. The train was doing eighty, maybe more.

He pushed the driver's door open, considering his options. Two men emerged from the rear SUV, MP5s held low but ready. They approached his truck from both sides, using practiced tactical movement. Running meant catching bullets in the back.

Frank closed the door. Clicked his seatbelt into place. Reached across to the passenger side and wrapped that belt around his wrist, creating an anchor point.

The SUV in front began backing up.

Frank didn't wait. He slammed the truck into reverse, stomping the accelerator. Metal crunched as he slammed into the SUV behind him, catching the gunmen off guard.

Drive. Accelerator floored. The truck lurched forward, smashing through the crossing gate. For a moment, escape seemed possible.

Then the front SUV shot backward, crashing into him, shoving the truck back onto the tracks. Tires screamed as Frank fought for traction. Black smoke rose from burning rubber.

Engineer Mike Delaney saw the truck between the crossing gates and yanked the horn lever. Two SUVs near it, something wasn't right. At eighty miles per hour, the freight train's headlight illuminated the scene in stark clarity - someone had pushed that truck onto his tracks.

"Jesus Christ!"

He cut power and slammed the air brakes to emergency. Five million pounds of steel and cargo don't stop quickly. The wheels screamed against the rails. His conductor grabbed for support as the locomotive shuddered.

Through the passenger window, Frank saw the train. Massive. Unstoppable. Yards away.

Time gone.

Frank lay across the seat, tightening his grip on the passenger belt, making himself as small as possible against what was coming.

The impact came like the end of the world. The freight train struck the truck's rear quarter panel at eighty miles per hour, transforming two tons of metal into a toy. Frank's head snapped sideways, but the passenger seatbelt wrapped around his wrist kept him anchored as the cab filled with exploding glass.

The truck spun violently down the tracks, each rotation bringing new destruction. The leaf blower launched through the shattered rear window like a missile. A garbage bin exploded, raining plastic shards. The rake handle became a spear, punching through the windshield inches from Frank's head.

When the truck's tires caught the railroad ties, the real violence began. Metal folded. The undercarriage ripped away. The cab crushed inward like a beer can, the roof dropping so low Frank had to press himself flat against the seat. Each impact threatened to tear away his grip on the seatbelt.

The final flip sent the truck airborne, spinning into the tree line. Impact. Darkness. Silence.

Steam hissed from the ruined engine. The truck lay crushed between two massive oaks, barely recognizable as a vehicle. Fluids dripped onto scattered tools and broken glass.

The two gunmen approached with practiced caution, MP5s at low ready.

"Check the cab," the first ordered. "I'll watch the perimeter."

His partner peered through the spiderwebbed windshield. "Empty. Jesus Christ, nobody could've—"

"Shut up and search. His body is here somewhere."

They moved through the undergrowth methodically, sweeping their sectors. Professional. Thorough. But their eyes kept returning to the mangled truck, their minds refusing to believe anyone could have survived.

Twenty yards away, Frank pressed against a tree trunk, controlling his breathing despite the fire in his chest. Blood ran in dozens of rivulets where glass had sliced his face and arms. His left arm hung useless, shoulder clearly dislocated.

Without a sound, he found a Y-shaped branch at chest height. He lifted his dead arm into the crook, then let his body weight drop. The shoulder popped back with a wet crunch. Frank's face never changed expression.

Nine-tenths of a mile down the track, the train finally shuddered to a stop. Delaney's hands shook as he keyed the radio, reporting the collision to dispatch. Twenty-seven years on the rails, he'd never hit a vehicle that had been deliberately placed in his path.

"We better check," his conductor said quietly. "Might be someone needs help."

They climbed down from the cab, walking back along the tracks with flashlights. Emergency vehicles were already screaming toward the crossing in the distance. The two railroad men moved quickly but cautiously through the scattered debris field.

Neither one wanted to find what they feared they would.

Movement. The first gunman was approaching Frank's position, playing his weapon's light through the undergrowth. Frank became a statue, watching the beam sweep past. Waiting.

The gunman passed his tree. One step. Two. Frank moved like liquid shadow. His hand clamped over the man's mouth, stifling the startled breath. The neck snapped with a sharp crack that seemed deafening in the quiet woods.

Frank eased the body down, took the MP5. Fourteen rounds in the magazine. More than enough.

"Jenkins?" The second gunman's voice carried through the trees. "You find anything?"

Frank moved toward the voice, every movement calculated despite his injuries. Through the leaves, he saw his target standing near the truck, weapon light probing the shadows.

"Jenkins? Report."

Frank circled silently, getting closer. The gunman's tension was visible now, his movements becoming jerky as instinct warned him something was wrong.

"Jenkins, goddammit, answer—"

The man never finished the sentence. Never had time to raise his weapon. Never even knew what hit him. It was Frank's fist. His face fractured. Dead.

Frank disappeared into the deeper woods, leaving two cooling bodies among the scattered gardening tools and truck parts. In the distance, sirens began to wail. He had maybe three minutes before the first responders arrived. More than enough time to vanish.

Frank emerged from the woods, glass cuts still bleeding, shoulder aching. He walked down a suburban street lined with modest homes, staying in the shadows. A faded "FOR SALE" sign caught his eye.

The 1965 Chrysler Imperial sat in a gravel driveway like a sleeping battleship. Eighteen feet of Detroit steel from an era when cars were built to dominate, not survive. Its black paint was oxidized, but the body was straight with little rust. These weren't built with modern crumple zones or safety features - just layers of heavy gauge steel welded together by men who built tanks during World War II.

The frame rails and cross members were 14-gauge steel, thick enough to support a house. The body panels were 18-gauge - twice as thick as modern cars. The front and rear bumpers were mounted directly to the frame, designed to push through anything in their path. The same car had been banned from demolition derbies in the 1970s for being virtually indestructible.

Frank studied the massive engine bay, knowing it housed a 413 cubic inch V8. The hood was long enough to land a small plane on. The trunk could hide several bodies - or an arsenal. Even the door hinges were overbuilt, each one strong enough to support the weight of the entire car.

A piece of paper taped to the window showed "$2,500 OBO."

Frank pulled a folded check from his wallet, then moved toward the front door of the house. For what he had planned, this was exactly the tool he needed.

Frank pulled the Imperial into the circular drive of the Kane estate. Most of the FBI vehicles were gone now, leaving only two surveillance vans parked on the manicured lawn. He noted the reduced security presence - opportunity or complication, depending on what Cooper had found in those files.

He found Vivian in the kitchen, hands wrapped around an untouched cup of coffee. At first, she didn't look up.

"They went to Richard's office," she said. "The FBI needed his client records. Agent Cooper had a warrant." She looked up, eyes red-rimmed from crying, and saw the cuts in Frank's face and arms.

"Jesus, Frank. You look like you walked through a plate glass window. What happened?"

"Gardner needs another truck."

"Okay. Okay. Don't worry about that. We'll take care of it. I'll get my purse and take you to the hospital."

"No."

"Well, at least let me put some hydrogen peroxide on the cuts."

"Okay."

Vivian got up as Frank sat down.

"Did you find anything about Grace?"

Frank shook his head. Vivian brought back a bottle of hydrogen peroxide and cotton balls. She went to work cleaning each wound. Frank didn't flinch.

"Where did you go?"

"To ask questions."

"Did anyone answer them?"

"Not yet. They will."

"How can you be sure?"

Frank gave her slight smile. Vivian studied his face, trying to read something in his scarred features. "You know something, don't you? Something Richard isn't telling me?"

Frank remained silent.

"I'm not stupid, Frank. This isn't a random kidnapping. The amount they're asking for, the way Richard's acting..." Her voice cracked. "What has he done? What has my husband done that put our daughter in danger?"

"Ask him."

"I'm asking you."

Frank met her gaze. "Not my story to tell."

Vivian continued cleaning his wounds

"I don't need to know everything. Just... just bring her home. Please."

Frank nodded.

"Video camera."

"We have several with tripods. Do you need one?"

Frank nodded.

"I'll get the best one as soon as I'm done."

In the pool house, some of the larger cuts on Frank's face and arms had butterfly bandages to close the wounds. Frank opened his footlocker. He removed the trays of weapons and equipment, revealing the false bottom. His fingers found the hidden catch, lifting the panel.

The disassembled Barrett M82 lay in custom-cut foam. Frank assembled the weapon with practiced efficiency - barrel, receiver, scope mount, stock. Each piece locked into place with mechanical precision. The scope settled into its mount with a soft click.

He reached into the hidden compartment again, retrieving a box of ammunition. The Teflon-coated .50 caliber rounds gleamed dully in the light. He loaded ten rounds into the box magazine, each round capable of punching through engine blocks, body armor, or bulletproof glass.

The magazine slapped home beneath the rifle with a solid thunk.

Frank pulled his armored vest back on, checking the ceramic plates. His Redhawk revolvers settled into their shoulder holsters. The Barrett went into a long case designed to look like contractor's equipment.

From another hidden compartment, he retrieved blocks of C4 explosive and shaped them in snake-shaped charges, then rewrapped them carefully and placed them in a worn rucksack along with several electronic detonation devices. Fragmentation grenades and thermite devices followed, disappearing into the rucksack. Each item had a purpose, a specific role in what was to come. Grabbing his gear he headed back to the Imperial.

The tools of his trade weren't subtle, but subtlety wasn't what he needed now. Andreev's compound might be a fortress, but even fortresses could fall. It just took the right combination of skill, timing, and explosives.

The FBI surveillance van sat in the Kane estate's circular drive, its engine idling to keep the AC running. Through the tinted windows, Frank could see Agent Morton's bulky silhouette in the driver's seat, hunched over what looked like a fast-food lunch.

Frank watched Morton waddle from the van toward the mansion's side entrance, probably headed for the bathroom. The agent's XXL windbreaker was draped over the driver's seat, his FBI cap on the dashboard.

A minute later, Frank slipped away from the van, the oversized windbreaker and cap tucked under his arm.

Frank sat the hat and windbreaker on the passenger seat in the Imperial. Even though the agent was a big man, Frank had no hope of the windbreaker fitting his incredibly broad shoulders. He would have to make do when the time came. Climbing behind the wheel, Frank started the sedan and headed for the city.

The corner office had transformed into a mobile FBI command center. A half dozen agents worked at laptops, sifting through financial data. Network cables snaked across the floor, connecting to servers the cyber team had set up. The afternoon sun cast long shadows through the floor-to-ceiling windows.

Special Agent Torres from the cyber unit approached Cooper, tablet in hand. His face showed the kind of concern that made senior agents pay attention.

"Sir? We've got a problem."

Cooper looked up from his own stack of transaction records. "What kind of problem?"

"Treasury Department just sent over their records of Kane Investment's registered foreign transactions. I cross-referenced them against what we pulled from his system." Torres handed over the tablet. "These seven files are missing from Kane's database. All transactions from early 2022, all involving offshore accounts."

"Show me."

Torres swiped through the documents. "Here's the Treasury record showing a series of transactions through a Hungarian bank. Matches the time period we're interested in. But..." He pulled up Kane's database. "Nothing. Like it never existed."

"Same pattern with the other six?"

"Yes sir. All from the same three-month period. All involving Eastern European financial institutions." Torres lowered his voice. "Sir, these aren't small transactions. We're talking nine figures each."

Cooper studied the list, his jaw tightening. He walked over to where Richard sat at his desk, still maintaining his facade of cooperative businessman.

"Mr. Kane," Cooper's voice was carefully controlled. "Want to explain why these Treasury-registered transactions aren't in your files?"

Richard glanced at the tablet. His face remained neutral, but Cooper caught the slight tightening around his eyes. "Ah, those. They're archived. Inactive accounts."

"Archived where?"

"Separate server. Compressed files." Richard gestured vaguely at his computer. "Standard practice for closed accounts."

"Standard practice is maintaining records for regulatory review," Cooper countered. "Not hiding them in archives."

"Nobody's hiding anything, Agent Cooper. Financial institutions generate enormous amounts of data. We have to archive older transactions to maintain system efficiency."

"I need to see them."

"Of course." Richard's fingers moved across the keyboard. "But decompressing archived files takes time. The encryption—"

"How long?"

"Few hours, maybe more." Richard shrugged apologetically. "Can't rush the process."

Cooper leaned in close, his voice low. "Mr. Kane, your daughter's life hangs in the balance. If you're stalling..."

"I understand your suspicion, Agent Cooper. But this is simply technical reality. Financial data has to be archived securely. Retrieval isn't instantaneous." Richard's tone was reasonable, professional. Almost too perfect.

"Sheridan," Cooper called. "Get me Judge Matthews on the phone. I want an expansion of the warrant to include any external storage facilities, backup servers, everything."

Richard's fingers paused on the keyboard for just a fraction of a second.

"Torres, stay with Mr. Kane. Watch the process. I want to know the moment those files are accessible."

Cooper turned back to Richard. "And Mr. Kane? The warrant covers ALL your files - active, archived, or otherwise. If anything's missing when we get in there, that's obstruction of justice. Add that to lying to federal officers about a kidnapping investigation..." He let the threat hang.

"I'm doing everything I can to help find my daughter," Richard said quietly.

"Are you?" Cooper studied him. "Because from where I'm standing, it looks like you're more concerned with protecting those archived files than finding Grace."

Richard's mask slipped, just for a moment. Fear flashed across his face before he could hide it.

Cooper waited until the cyber team took a break, leaving him alone with Richard in the corner office.

"Something interesting came up in those Treasury records," Cooper said, perching on the edge of Richard's desk. "Your company's accounts were frozen last month. All of them."

Richard's fingers stopped moving on the keyboard. Just for a moment.

"Routine audit," Richard said smoothly. "Nothing unusual for a firm our size."

"Routine?" Cooper pulled out his phone, read from the screen. "Quote: 'Immediate freeze of all domestic accounts pending investigation of suspicious international wire transfers.' That doesn't sound routine to me."

Richard leaned back in his chair, maintaining his CEO composure. "The Treasury Department can be overzealous. My lawyers are handling it."

"And Grace's kidnapping? The timing seems... convenient."

"Are you suggesting I had my own daughter kidnapped?" Richard's indignation seemed genuine. Almost.

"I'm suggesting," Cooper said quietly, "that someone might be sending you a message. Someone who lost access to their money when your accounts froze."

"That's absurd."

"Is it? One hundred fifty-seven million dollars. Specific number for a ransom."

Richard met Cooper's gaze steadily. "I don't know what the kidnappers are thinking or why they want that specific amount."

Cooper studied him for a long moment. Richard Kane was good - his face showed just the right mix of concern and confusion. But something in his eyes... a flicker of fear that had nothing to do with the Treasury Department.

"Your archived files should be ready soon," Cooper said, standing. "Better hope they don't tell a different story."

He left Richard alone in the office. Through the glass wall, he watched the man pull out his phone, fingers moving quickly across the screen. Sending a warning, probably.

Cooper smiled grimly. Sometimes the most valuable evidence was in how people reacted when you rattled their cage.

"Sir?" Sheridan called from across the room. "Judge Matthews is on the line."

Reopening the door to Richard's office, Cooper held Richard's gaze for a long moment. "Start the decompression, Mr. Kane. Torres, document everything he does. Every keystroke." He walked away to take the call, leaving Richard staring at his screen.

Torres pulled up a chair, settling in to watch Richard work. The office hummed with activity - agents muttering into phones, keyboards clicking, printers whirring. But all Cooper could hear was the clock ticking away whatever time Grace had left.

He picked up the phone, watching Richard through the glass wall of the conference room. Whatever was in those archived files, Cooper was certain it would lead them to Grace - and to whatever Richard Kane was trying so desperately to hide.

Sharp Steel

Grace sat on the edge of the bed with The Pigman open in her lap when Alex brought breakfast - oatmeal today, with brown sugar. Her face lit up when she saw him, not the food.

"I never liked this book before," she said. "But now I get it."

Alex hesitated at the door, the tray steady in his hands. He wasn't supposed to talk to her. Rules were rules.

"The kids in the story," Grace continued, her voice soft, "they don't mean to hurt anyone. They just make choices, and then things spin out of control." She looked up at him. "Have you ever felt like that?"

Something flickered in Alex's eyes. He set the tray down, taking longer than necessary to arrange it.

"You should eat," he said, but didn't leave.

"Sometimes I wonder what happens to people after they make those choices. If they ever get a chance to fix things." She stirred the oatmeal without eating. "Do you believe in second chances, Alex?"

His name hung between them. He shifted his weight, glanced at the door.

"Everyone does things they regret," Grace said. "Even my dad. He works so hard trying to be perfect, but sometimes at night I hear him crying in his office." This was a lie, but she watched it land, saw Alex's shoulders tense.

"Eat your breakfast," he said, but his voice had lost its edge.

"Will you stay? Just for a minute? It gets so quiet in here. The silence..." She wrapped her arms around herself. "It makes everything worse."

Against his better judgment, Alex sat in the room's single chair. Grace took a small bite of oatmeal, made a show of appreciating it.

"Did you make this?"

"Just heated it up."

"It's good. Better than what my dad's chef makes." Another lie, but it made Alex almost smile. "Do you cook?"

"Sometimes. For my sister."

Grace caught the slip - information freely given. She tucked it away like a precious stone but kept her face neutral, just a lonely girl making conversation.

"Younger or older?"

Alex stood abruptly. "I shouldn't be talking."

"I'm sorry," Grace said quickly. "I just... it helps. Makes me feel less scared. The others..." She let her voice trail off, watched his reaction.

"The others what?"

"Nothing. I shouldn't complain. You've been kind to me."

Alex sat back down, his face troubled. "Did someone..."

"No, no. They just look at me sometimes. Like..." She hugged herself tighter. "I probably imagine it. Being locked up makes you paranoid, I guess."

She saw his fists clench, just slightly. Protective instinct. Good.

"Nobody will hurt you," he said.

"Because you won't let them?"

Their eyes met. Alex looked away first.

"You remind me of her sometimes," he said quietly.

"Your sister?"

He nodded. "She's twelve. Smart like you. Too smart maybe."

Grace's heart raced at this new information, but she kept her voice casual. "You must miss her."

"Yeah." Alex stood again, this time with real purpose. "I need to go."

"Alex?" She made her voice small. "Thank you. For staying. For being nice to me."

He paused at the door. "Just eat your breakfast. Try to sleep maybe."

"Will you bring lunch too?"

"Probably."

"Good," Grace said softly. After he left, she set aside the barely touched oatmeal. A sister, twelve years old. It wasn't much, but it was a thread. And threads, when pulled carefully, could unravel everything. She picked up The Pigman again, but her mind was already working on how to use this new information. Alex's protective instinct toward his sister made him vulnerable. And in this place, vulnerability was currency.

She remembered something her father once said about business deals: "Everyone has a pressure point. Find it, press it gently, and people will do anything to make the pressure stop." Grace hadn't understood then. She did now.

Tomorrow she would tell Alex more about her loneliness, her fear. She would make him see his sister in her eyes. And eventually, when the moment was right, she would use that connection to break free. Because that's what survival looked like - finding weakness and exploiting it, no matter how much it hurt.

She just hoped Alex would forgive her someday.

Alex headed downstairs when he passed Kozlov in the hallway heading toward her room. Something about the man's walk, the look in his eyes - Alex's stomach knotted.

"Hey, Kozlov," Alex called out. "What are you doing?"

Kozlov turned, six feet of prison muscle and bad intentions. "What's it look like?"

"Burke said I'm supposed to handle the girl."

"Burke ain't here." Kozlov's grin showed gold teeth. "Besides, little princess could use some company."

"She's thirteen—"

"Listen, lover boy." Kozlov stepped close, backing Alex against the wall. "You got two options. Fuck off and mind your business, or I knock those pretty teeth down your throat. Choose."

Alex's hands trembled. He watched helplessly as Kozlov entered Grace's room, the door clicking shut behind him.

Alex stood frozen in the hallway. His mind raced. Call Burke? Try to stop Kozlov himself? The memory of his last beating was still fresh, ribs still sore. But Grace...

The sound of something falling came from behind the door, followed by Grace's muffled voice, sharp with fear.

Alex's heart hammered in his chest as he tried to figure out what to do. What he could do. What he had to do.

Through the door, Alex heard Kozlov's voice, sickly sweet. "Come on, princess. Just a little hug. Don't be scared."

"Stay away from me." Grace's voice trembled. She'd backed into a corner.

The door opened silently. Alex's pocketknife was already open, blade glinting in the dim light. His hand shook, but his grip was tight.

Kozlov turned at the sound of footsteps. "Didn't I tell you to fuck off?" His eyes found the knife. "Well, look who grew some balls. Give me that to me so I can stick it up your ass."

Kozlov lunged, meaty hands grabbing Alex's shirt. But Alex was already moving, driving the blade into Kozlov's side. Again. Again. Hot blood poured over his hands.

Kozlov staggered back, looking more surprised than hurt. "You little shit—"

"Grace," Alex said quietly. "Don't look."

The next thrust went between Kozlov's ribs, finding his heart. Kozlov's eyes went wide with disbelief. He opened his mouth, but only blood came out. He collapsed, twitching before finally going still.

Alex stood over the body, knife dripping. His hands wouldn't stop shaking. When he turned to Grace, his face was different - older somehow, harder.

"Don't freak out," he said. "We have to move fast. I'm getting you out of here."

Blood pooled around Kozlov's body. Alex wiped his knife on Kozlov's shirt and pocketed it. His hands were still shaking, but his mind was clear.

"We have maybe five minutes before someone comes looking for him," Alex said. He grabbed a blanket from the bed, dropped it over Kozlov's body. "The night crew is only three guys. Two on perimeter, one watching monitors."

Grace stared at the blood seeping through the blanket. "You killed him."

"He was going to hurt you. I couldn't let that happen." Alex checked the hallway. "Grace, look at me. I need you focused. Can you do that?"

She nodded, pulling her eyes away from the body.

"I've got keys to the back door and the garage. There's a van - black Mercedes Sprinter. But we have to move now, before the next guard rotation."

Grace straightened, fear giving way to determination. "What do you need me to do?"

"Stay close. Stay quiet. If something goes wrong..." He pulled out the knife and opened the blade. "Run. Don't stop."

They slipped into the hallway, leaving Kozlov's cooling body behind. No going back now. For either of them.

Alex led Grace through the hallway to the garage, knife ready. The Mercedes Sprinter sat in darkness, a black ghost among shadows. He slid the key into the driver's door, wincing at the soft click of the lock.

"Stay low," he whispered, helping Grace into the passenger seat. "Below the windows."

The garage door motor hummed as Alex pressed the remote. He could feel his heartbeat in his throat as he turned the key. The diesel engine caught instantly.

Upstairs in the security room, Petrov glanced at the monitor showing the garage feed. The Sprinter's headlights flared to life. "Who the fuck is taking the van?"

The van disappeared through the garage door.

Petrov keyed his radio. "Kozlov? The van is moving. Kozlov?" Static. He ran from the monitor room, taking the stairs two at a time.

He found Grace's door open. Inside, the blanket had slipped off Kozlov's body, revealing glazed eyes and a blood-soaked shirt. "Fuck!"

His radio crackled. "What's wrong?"

"Kozlov's dead! The girl's gone! The kid took her!"

On the street, Alex guided the Sprinter through the quiet neighborhood, trying to drive normally despite the adrenaline pumping through his veins. Grace peered over the seat and out the rear window.

"They'll be coming after us," she said.

Alex checked the mirrors. "I know."

The Sprinter's diesel engine hummed as Alex took another random turn, putting distance between them and the safe house. He kept checking the mirrors, expecting vehicles to appear at any moment.

"We need to ditch this van," he said. "Too easy to spot. Find somewhere to hide, figure out our next move."

"Next move?" Grace leaned forward in her seat. "We call my dad. He'll send people to protect us."

"Your father will protect you. Me? I'll go straight to prison. I was part of the crew that took you."

"No, you don't understand. I'll tell him everything. How you protected me, how you saved me from Kozlov. You're a hero, Alex. My dad will reward you, not punish you."

Alex gave a bitter laugh. "That's not how the world works, Grace. Rich guys like your dad don't reward people like me. Best case scenario, I get a lighter sentence for helping you escape."

"Stop it! I won't let that happen." Her voice cracked with frustration. "Why won't you trust me? My father owns half of Connecticut. He can make anything happen."

"Yeah, and guys like me end up in prison so guys like your dad can sleep better at night. Clean ending. Bad guys caught, good guys win."

"You're not a bad guy."

"Tell that to the FBI. Tell that to your father's lawyers." Alex checked the mirrors again. "I kidnapped you, Grace. Held you captive. Doesn't matter why. Doesn't matter what happened after. That's all they'll see."

"Then what's your plan?" Grace demanded. "Keep running forever?"

Alex was quiet for a long moment. "I don't know. But I know calling your father ends with me in handcuffs."

"That's not fair."

"No," Alex agreed. "It's not. But that's the difference between your world and mine. In your world, the good guys always win. In mine?" He shrugged. "We just try not to lose too badly."

Grace slumped back in her seat, arms crossed. "I hate that you don't trust me."

"This isn't about trust. This is about reality." Alex turned down a side street, pulling over, killing the van's engine. "We need to find somewhere safe. Then we can figure out what's next."

But they both knew what was next. Grace would return to her world of wealth and privilege. And Alex? He'd disappear into the shadows, running from both the kidnappers who would kill him and the law that would cage him.

That was the reality neither of them wanted to face.

Burke's hands were shaking as he dialed Andreev's private number. Kozlov's body wasn't even cold yet.

"This better be important." Andreev's voice was cold, precise.

"We have a situation." Burke paced the blood-stained room. "The girl's gone. The kid, Alex - he killed Kozlov and took her. Stole the Sprinter van about twenty minutes ago."

The silence on the other end was deafening. Burke could almost feel the temperature dropping through the phone.

"Explain to me," Andreev said quietly, "how a teenage boy managed to kill one of your men and escape with my leverage against Richard Kane?"

"Kozlov went to the girl's room. Wasn't supposed to. Kid must have caught him—"

"I don't want excuses." Andreev's voice could have frozen hell. "What assets do you have in pursuit?"

"Two cars following. But they're being careful - don't want to draw attention. Need more men for the search. They couldn't have gone far."

Another long silence. Burke could hear Andreev's measured breathing, could picture him sitting in his modernist office, deciding whether Burke would live through this conversation.

"I'm sending ten men. They're already in the city on another matter. Professional hunters, not thugs like Kozlov." Andreev's tone made it clear what he thought of Burke's crew. "They'll coordinate the search. You will follow their lead. They'll split up and cover likely locations - malls, train stations, bus terminals."

"Yes, sir. Thank you—"

"Burke." Andreev cut him off. "When they find the girl - and they will find her - the boy dies slowly. Make sure my men understand that. And Burke? Don't call me again unless you have them."

The line went dead. Burke stared at his phone, then at Kozlov's body. The kid had seemed so harmless, so scared. That had been their mistake.

Within fifteen minutes, black SUVs began arriving. The hunters moved with military precision, downloading security apps on their phones, coordinating search grids. Andreev was right - these weren't street thugs like Burke's crew. These were professional killers.

The kid didn't stand a chance.

Alex pulled the Sprinter into the crowded mall parking lot, wedging it between two SUVs near Macy's. The van's black paint was already collecting dust, helping it blend in with other service vehicles.

"We need new transportation," Alex said, scanning the lot. "Too many people looking for this van."

Grace's stomach growled audibly.

"Food court first," Alex decided. "Quick bite, then we move."

Inside, the mall's fluorescent lights and piped-in music created an artificial cheerfulness that felt surreal after their violent escape. Shoppers moved in lazy circles, unaware of the blood still dried under Alex's fingernails from Kozlov.

At the food court, Alex handed Grace a corndog on a stick, the smell of fried batter mixing with the cinnamon from the pretzel stand nearby.

"Seriously?" She stared at it like it might bite back.

"Eat it. We don't have time to be picky."

Grace took a small bite, trying not to think about the processed meat. "At least it's hot." Her attempt at bravado was undermined by another hunger-induced stomach growl.

Through the food court crowd, Alex spotted them first - Petrov and Dmitri, Viktor's most vicious crew members, methodically scanning faces. Their phones were out, probably coordinating with others. They must have found the van.

"Don't look," Alex whispered. "But we need to move. Now."

Grace saw them anyway. She dropped her corndog. The men were getting closer, speaking rapidly into their phones. Petrov's jacket bulged slightly where his shoulder holster sat.

"Walk normal," Alex said. "Until we clear the food court."

They made it twenty yards before Dmitri's shout cut through the mall noise. Alex grabbed Grace's hand and they ran.

They weaved through shocked shoppers, knocking over a display of designer handbags. Behind them, heavy footsteps and Russian curses. Alex led them down a service corridor, then back into the main concourse, past a group of teenage girls who screamed as Petrov shoved through them.

"Stop! Security!"

A young mall cop grabbed Grace's arm, yanking her to a halt, almost pulling her off her feet. His badge read "Phillips." "No running in the—"

Alex's knife appeared without warning, sinking into Phillips's side. The guard's eyes went wide with shock. He released Grace, stumbling backward, hand pressing against spreading red.

"Come on!" Alex pulled her away from the fallen guard.

"You stabbed him," Grace gasped as they ran. "He was just doing his job!"

"He was in the way."

They burst through an emergency exit into the parking lot. Car alarms blared. Grace glanced back at the blood on Alex's hand, suddenly unsure who she was really running with.

Alex scanned the parking lot, his eyes settling on a black Tesla Model S, its owner approaching with shopping bags. The man looked young, probably some tech executive.

"There," Alex pointed. "Perfect."

They approached quickly. When the owner reached for his key fob, Alex pressed the knife against his ribs. "Phone. Wallet. Key. Now."

Grace watched in horror as Alex forced the man against the car.

The man complied, trembling. Alex checked the phone's location services were off, then pocketed both items.

"Run," he ordered. The man scrambled away as Alex slid behind the wheel. "Grace, get in!"

Grace hesitated for just a moment before climbing into the passenger seat. Behind them, Petrov and Dmitri burst through the emergency exit. The Tesla's electric motor hummed to life. Alex backed the car out of the parking space, then threw it in drive.

"Hold on," Alex said, a hint of excitement creeping into his voice as he floored the accelerator. The Tesla shot forward with instant torque, pressing them back in their seats. Despite everything, Grace caught Alex's slight grin as they took a corner at speed. For a moment, he looked his age - just a kid stealing a cool car.

Then she saw his blood-stained hands on the steering wheel, and reality came crashing back.

"The guard," Grace said quietly. "Will he...?"

"I didn't cut him deep. He'll live." Alex's voice was flat. "Small price for keeping you alive."

Grace stared out the window at the city blurring past, processing what she'd seen. Alex had saved her life again, but at what cost? The line between protector and predator was becoming increasingly blurred.

"You've done this before," she said. It wasn't a question. "The knife. The carjacking. All of it."

Alex's silence was answer enough. His slight grin from earlier was gone, replaced by the hard look she was starting to recognize - the one that made him seem much older.

The Tesla's screen showed a near-full battery. At least they wouldn't need to stop for gas. Small comfort as Grace wondered what other lines Alex would cross to keep them alive - and whether she could live with the consequences.

Secrets

The abandoned furniture warehouse loomed against the cloud-streaked sky, its red brick facade stained black from decades of city grime. Loading docks lined the building's north side, their rollup doors sealed with heavy padlocks. Faded letters on the wall still read "METROPOLITAN FURNITURE WHOLESALE."

Frank studied the security setup. No cameras. No alarm system visible. Just rust and neglect. He selected the door farthest from the street, working in the shadows. His lock picks made quick work of the ancient padlock. The rollup door protested as he lifted it just enough to slip under, the sound echoing through the empty building.

Inside, darkness and dust. Shafts of light pierced through broken windows, illuminating floating particles. The vast space smelled of mold and pigeons. Steel support columns marched into the gloom. Here and there, forgotten furniture lay scattered - broken chairs, rotting particle board desks, a water-stained mattress where some homeless person had once sheltered.

The elevator was dead, its shaft a black mouth in the wall. Frank found the stairs, checking each step before putting his full weight down. Debris crunched under his boots. On the fourth floor, he caught movement - rats scurrying for cover.

The roof access door had been chained shut, but the hasp was barely attached to the rotting frame. One sharp pull and it came free.

Six stories up, the city opened around him. To the east, the glass and steel of Andreev's compound rose like a black monolith. Frank moved to the building's north edge, where the water tower's skeletal supports provided cover.

He retrieved his equipment from the Imperial. The surveillance gear was heavy, but the stairs were solid enough. He set up behind the water tower's support struts, using them as a natural blind.

A Celestron spotting scope on a heavy tripod, capable of reading text messages off a phone screen at five hundred yards. Next to it, he mounted a Canon video camera with a 600mm lens, recording everything at sixty frames per second.

Frank lay prone behind the spotting scope, adjusting the focus. Through the high-powered optics, Andreev's office filled his view.

The Russian sat at his desk, phone to his ear. Frank could see his lips moving. He could also see that the wall safe was closed and Andreev was inserting a USB hard key into his computer.

Frank switched to the video camera and adjusted the lens so it focused on the keyboard and screen. He pressed record to capture Andreev's keystrokes as he typed.

Switching back to the scope, Frank focused on the telephone's numerical keyboard. He wrote down any phone number Andreev dialed. He also noted any passwords Andreev entered on his phone.

The sun climbed higher. Sweat dripped down Frank's back in the stagnant air, but he remained motionless except for his eyes and the hand recording observations. He'd done surveillance like this before, in other places, on other targets. The patience of a sniper combined with the attention to detail of a safecracker.

Through the lens, he watched Andreev's security patterns emerge. Like all men who thought they were untouchable, he had routines. Habits. Weaknesses.

Pigeons cooed somewhere in the building below. A subway train rumbled deep underground, its vibrations traveling up through the old structure. Frank ignored it all, his focus absolute.

He just had to wait and watch. Everyone makes mistakes eventually.

An hour later, Andreev removed the USB hard key from his computer and moved toward his wall safe. He placed his hand on a scanner, then typed in a long number into a numerical keypad. Moments later, the safe opened. He placed the USB hard key inside in a foam slot and closed the safe's door, then swung the painting over hiding the safe.

Frank considered the biometric locking system. Not easy. He would need Andreev's hand. He smiled slightly at the thought of removing one of Andreev's hands. Unfortunately, it wasn't necessary. There were other methods of dealing with sophisticated safes. Non-conventional methods.

Andreev stood in his sixth-floor office, looking down at the city through bulletproof glass. His phone was on speaker, voice echoing off modernist concrete walls.

"What should we do with the girl when we find her?" asked the team leader.

"Take that girl back to the safe house and keep a guard in her bedroom at all times. No more privacy for little Gracie. She's lost that privilege."

"And the boy?"

"Kill him… slowly. But not in front of the girl. I don't want her traumatized any more than necessary. When all this is done and my money has been returned, I still may need to deal with Richard Kane. Come to think of it… bring the boy here. I will deal with him personally. I don't want anyone to see him enter the compound."

Andreev walked to his desk, pressed a button that brought up blueprints on one of his monitors. "Three blocks east of my compound, there's a brownstone. Looks abandoned. The basement connects to my compound through a tunnel we maintain. Call me when you arrive. My security chief will meet you there with access codes."

He gave them the address, then added, "The entrance is behind a false wall in the mechanical room."

"What if they've split up?"

"The boy won't abandon her. He thinks he's her protector now." Andreev's lip curled slightly. "Use that. Use her."

A pause on the line. "Sir, I examined Kozlov's body. The boy... he wasn't just lucky. He knew where to put the knife."

"You think I don't know that?" Andreev touched his keyboard, bringing up a file. "Alex Petrovin. His father was Spetsnaz before a Lithuanian mob killed him over a gambling debt. The boy learned things, growing up on those streets. But he's still just a boy. Find them."

"Yes, sir."

"One more thing." Andreev's voice hardened. "If the FBI or police get close to catching them, kill them both. Richard Kane is more useful to me grieving than cooperating with federal agents."

He ended the call and stood at his window again, looking toward the brownstone three blocks away. Somewhere out there, a teenager was trying to outrun his organization. The thought almost made him smile.

Almost.

The hunters arrived in three black Suburbans, parking behind the safe house. Eight men in tactical gear emerged, moving with military precision. Their leader, Volkov, stood a head shorter than his men but carried himself with the quiet authority of someone used to dealing death.

Burke watched them gear up. No flashy weapons, just suppressed MP5s and compact radios. They moved like special forces, checking equipment with practiced efficiency.

"Report," Volkov ordered, his accent thick but voice soft.

Burke explained about the Tesla carjacking at the mall. Volkov cut him off with a raised hand.

"Your men are idiots. Making a scene in public." He turned to his team. "Viktor, take three men, work the traffic cams backward from the mall. Monitor police bands and traffic incidents. Find that Tesla."

He pulled out a tablet, fingers moving across the screen. "The boy will avoid highways. Too many cameras. He'll stick to surface streets, industrial areas." A map of the city appeared, gridded into sectors. "We work this systematically. No more mall shootouts."

Burke shifted uncomfortably. "My guys can—"

"Your guys can shut up and follow orders." Volkov never raised his voice. "The boy has training. His father was Spetsnaz. You're chasing him like he's some street punk, and he's making you look foolish."

The hunters moved out in pairs, their vehicles blending into traffic. No sirens, no speeding, nothing to draw attention. Just professionals starting a hunt.

Volkov checked his watch. "The boy will need rest soon. The girl will need food, bathroom. They'll make mistakes." He looked at Burke. "When they do, we'll be ready. Now get your men out of their fucking track suits and into proper clothes. We're not drawing any more attention."

The hunt was on. But this time, the hunters knew their prey.

Volkov pulled his Suburban to the curb near a homeless encampment under the bridge. He approached an old woman wrapped in layers of scavenged clothes, counting out hundred-dollar bills where others could see.

"Looking for two kids," he said, letting the money fan. "Teenagers. Girl's rich - you can tell by how she walks, how she looks at people. Boy's protective, dangerous. Stole a black Tesla."

The old woman's eyes fixed on the cash. "Marvin might know something. He sleeps in the loading dock over on Wilson. Says he saw some kids fitting that description."

More bills appeared. Word spread through the shadows. Soon Volkov had a dozen reports - the Tesla, the way the girl complained about walking, how the boy moved like a soldier despite his age.

"They're staying east," Volkov said into his radio. "The homeless network has eyes on them. Moving block by block."

In Andreev's compound, a hacker sat before six screens, fingers flying across keyboards. "Got them. Tesla's software is calling home, trying to download an update. They're on Davidson Avenue."

Volkov's voice crackled through the speaker. "Can you shut it down?"

"Better. I can lock them inside, then kill the motor. Just need them to slow down or stop."

Alex drove the Tesla through a light traffic, checking his mirrors. Grace had been quiet since they ditched the mall.

Suddenly, the car's screen lit up with warnings. The engine died, brake pedal went stiff.

"What the hell?" Alex pumped the brakes as the car rolled to a stop.

Grace stared at the screen's flashing warnings, her face draining of color. "They hacked the car. They're tracking us through Tesla's network." She was already unbuckling her seatbelt. "We have to run. Now!"

"How do you—"

"Our chef has a Tesla. They can control everything remotely. Alex, we have to move!"

Through the rear window, black Suburbans appeared at both ends of the block, racing toward them.

Alex threw his elbow against the driver's window. The impact sent pain shooting up his arm but the glass held. He tried again, harder. Still nothing.

Grace dug through the glovebox, found the emergency glass breaker. "Here!" Alex snatched it, slammed the pointed metal tip into the window's corner. Spiderweb cracks spread but the glass remained intact. Behind them, car doors opened. Boots hit pavement. "Protect your face," Alex told Grace. He wrapped his jacket around his hand, drew back, and punched the weakened glass with everything he had. The window finally shattered. Grace scrambled through first with Alex's help. Alex right behind her. Glass crunched under their feet as they sprinted down the nearest alley. Shouts and footsteps echoed behind them.

Alex grabbed Grace's hand, pulling her down the alley. Behind them, boots pounded pavement.

"Fire wide," said Volkov. "Whatever you do, don't hit the girl."

Several bullets sparked off brick, sending fragments flying, pelting Alex and Grace, but not stopping them.

"Keep moving," said Alex.

"Chain-link fence," Grace warned, breathing hard.

"Good." Alex boosted her up. "They're too big, too slow. Have to go around." He followed quickly. Below, hunters reached the fence just as they dropped to the other side in a construction site. Alex was wrong. The hunters scaled the fence with brute strength.

Alex led Grace through scaffolding, ducking under tarps. Grace knocked over paint cans. She stomped on one can laying on its side popping off the lid. The lead hunter slipped on the paint, went down hard. Smart girl.

"Through there!" Alex pointed to a half-finished doorway. They squeezed through plastic sheeting. Somewhere above, radios crackled with Russian voices coordinating the pursuit.

A hunter appeared ahead, MP5 raised. Alex pushed Grace behind a dumpster, grabbed a piece of rebar. The man's finger tightened on the trigger, but Alex was already swinging, years of street fighting taking over. The rebar connected with the hunter's wrist. The gun clattered away. Alex followed with an elbow strike, then brought the rebar down again. The hunter collapsed.

"Service entrance," Grace pointed, her voice shaking. "It'll lead through the building."

They burst into a kitchen, startling dishwashers. A cook shouted in Cantonese. Alex grabbed a pot of boiling water, threw it behind them as two hunters appeared. Their screams confirmed his aim.

Through the restaurant, past shocked diners eating dim sum. Tables overturned. A hunter slipped on spilled shrimp dumplings. Out the front into a crowd of tourists photographing the Empire State Building.

"Baseball caps," Alex said, grabbing two from a street vendor's display. Money scattered on the counter. "Walk normal. Blend in."

They merged with the crowd, hearts pounding. Behind them, hunters pushed through, searching faces. One passed within inches, never seeing them behind their caps.

In Andreev's compound, the second floor hummed with technology. Three hackers worked in parallel, their screens showing grids of live surveillance feeds. Traffic cameras, ATMs, shop security systems - all routed through NYPD's network, now compromised.

"Movement on Canal," said Yuri, his fingers flying across keys. "Camera 2247."

On his screen, two figures in baseball caps slipped through a crowd of tourists. The video enhanced, zoomed. Recognition software outlined their faces.

"Seventy percent match," Yuri reported into his headset. "They're heading north toward Chinatown."

"Track them," Volkov's voice crackled back. "Every camera."

Alex pulled Grace into the shadow of a loading dock. Her shoes were soaked from running through puddles, her borrowed clothes already filthy. A police siren wailed somewhere to the east.

"We can't keep running," Grace said. "They'll corner us eventually."

"I know." Alex wiped blood from his split lip from an old wound. "You need to go home."

"We need to go home."

"No. Just you." He wouldn't meet her eyes. "Your father's security and the police can protect you. Me? I'll end up in jail or dead."

"My father will help you. He has lawyers, money—"

"And Andreev has people everywhere. One phone call and I'm dead before I make it to trial." Alex's voice hardened. "I know how to disappear. Done it before. But not with you slowing me down."

Grace felt like she'd been slapped. "Is that what I am? Dead weight?"

"You're a rich kid who's never had to survive on her own. I have." He checked the street. "We can't use phones - they're monitoring calls. Can't take transit - they're watching every station. Need to get you home without being seen."

"Fine. What's your plan?"

"Service trucks. Delivery vans. They're invisible - no one looks at them. City's full of them. We find the right one heading to your neighborhood."

"You want to steal another car?"

"Want to live?" His eyes were cold. "Then stop arguing."

Grace hugged herself, suddenly feeling very young and very alone.

Even as Alex plotted their route, she sensed him pulling away, preparing to disappear back into the shadows he knew best. She wanted to tell him he was wrong - about her father, about himself, about everything. But the words wouldn't come.

Instead, she watched the street with him, searching for their invisible ride home, each minute bringing them closer to a goodbye neither one wanted to face.

"We don't have to steal a delivery truck. We just need to hitch a ride somehow. Maybe hide in back. The tricky part is finding a van going to Connecticut."

"I might be able to help with that," said Grace.

"How?"

"My parents order stuff from Manhattan all the time, especially food. Cakes are same day delivery."

"That could work," said Alex hopeful. "Can you order a cake?"

"Sure. I've memorized my mom's credit card number and security code."

"You really are spoiled."

"I'm not spoiled. She just wanted me to have it in case I ever had an emergency."

"You mean like a cake emergency?"

"No. I—" Then she saw it. A slight smile on Alex's lips. He was playing her. She slugged him.

"Asshole."

He laughed. She joined him.

"So, where is this cake shop?" said Alex as he emerged from the loading dock. Grace followed.

Burke stepped from the shadows, knife already swinging. Alex saw it coming, shoved Grace clear. The blade caught Alex in the side, sliding between ribs. Hot pain exploded through him.

"No!" Grace screamed.

Alex tried to fight back, muscle memory from a hundred street fights taking over. He landed two solid hits, but Burke was bigger, stronger, and the knife had already done its work. The second thrust went deep. Alex felt his legs give out.

"Run," he gasped to Grace. Instead, she tried to help him, giving Volkov time to emerge from another shadow and grab her.

"Stupid boy," Burke twisted the knife, his voice almost gentle. "Playing hero. You forgot who your friends were."

Alex's vision began to fade. Grace's screams seemed to come from far away. He saw her fighting as they dragged her toward an SUV. His hand crept toward his own knife, but his fingers wouldn't work right.

"I'll kill you!" Grace screamed at Burke. "I swear I'll kill you!"

"Quite the pair you two made," Burke said, watching Alex bleed. "But play time's over."

Alex's world narrowed to pinpricks of light. The last thing he saw before passing out was Grace being dragged away, her face streaked with tears, her baseball cap falling to the filthy platform floor.

He'd failed her.

His hand fell open. The knife he'd been reaching for clattered to the ground, unused. His wounds were bad but not deadly. He wasn't dying. That would be too easy, too kind. That kind of mercy didn't exist in his world. The darkness took him. He passed out.

Burke sat next to Grace, hands tied with plastic straps, in the backseat of the SUV.

"If you hurt Alex in anyway, I swear I'll—" said Grace.

"Calm down, little lion. What happens to Alex is not up to me. The man I work for is not known to be subtle. Alex betrayed him. My best guess is that Alex's fate will not be subtle," said Burke. "You need to focus on yourself and your father. He's running out of time and so are you."

Grace fought back her tears. She knew that if Alex was tortured it was her fault. He was her friend and that was her fault too. She did her best to mask her fear. She wouldn't give Burke the satisfaction.

Special Agent Torres rubbed his eyes, the glow of his laptop screen burning spots in his vision. Numbers blurred after sixteen hours of combing through Kane's files. His fingers tapped keys, scrolling through Rubicoin blockchain transactions. A pattern emerged in the data.

"Cooper," he called. "Got something."

Cooper crossed the makeshift command center, coffee cup in hand. "What?"

"Kane's clients sold their Rubicoins to Falcon Bridge Financial Group LLC. The blockchain shows every transaction. Look at this flow - Kane's investors would get spooked, try to sell, find their was no market for the currency, then Falcon Bridge would offer to buy them out at a steep discount."

Cooper set down his coffee. "How much?"

"Over a billion US dollars. But here's the interesting part… Falcon Bridge was the only buyer of Rubicoins. There are no other transfer transactions recorded in the ledger."

"Richard must have been funneling his clients to Falcon Bridge, keeping other buyers away."

"Kinda like Falcon Bridge cornered the market on second hand Rubicoins."

"Find out who owns Falcon Bridge."

"I'm already on it."

Frank lay behind the spotting scope, watching Andreev work at his computer. The Russian stopped typing to answer his phone, speaking rapidly. Through the scope, Frank read his lips: "Good. Bring the boy through the tunnel and put him in a cell in the basement. I'll deal with him later."

Movement caught Frank's eye. Two black armored SUVs rolled down the street, turn signals blinking as they approached a worn brownstone three blocks from the compound. The vehicles disappeared into the building's underground garage.

He shifted the scope back to Andreev, who now stood at his window looking in the direction of the brownstone. Frank wrote in his notepad, adding another piece to the puzzle. Andreev had built himself a fortress, but even fortresses needed back doors.

Cooper marched into Richard's office, holding printouts. "Falcon Bridge Financial Group LLC owned by a shell corporation in Hungary, which is owned by another in Cyprus, which traces back to..." He tossed the papers on Richard's desk. "Lev Andreev."

Richard maintained his composure, but his hand trembled slightly as he reached for his water. "I told you, I don't control who buys Rubicoin on the secondary market. We just record the transfers. That's it. If other investors wanted to sell their holdings—"

"You gotta be seven kinds of stupid to be dealing with a guy like Andreev. We've got five different cases going in which Andreev is a suspect. Two of those cases involve the murder of witnesses."

"I am aware Andreev can be difficult. You can't prove any of this. The shells, the transfers - it's all technically legal."

"You were holding $157 million of Andreev's money when the Treasury Department froze your accounts. I imagine that made Andreev quite angry."

"My attorney should be present before I answer any more questions."

"Cut the bullshit, Kane. I don't care about your financial transactions with Andreev. Treasury can deal with that. I care about your daughter's safety. Did Andreev kidnap her?"

Richard thought for a long moment, then... "Probably. But I have no evidence that proves he took Grace."

"Well, that's the good thing about working with me. I've got judges that sign warrants. We can find out for ourselves."

"Get me Judge Matthews," Cooper ordered, striding out of Richard's office. Agent Sheridan fell in step beside him, already dialing.

"Sir, Andreev's compound will be a hard warrant to justify. His lawyers will fight—"

"We've got Treasury Department documents linking him to suspicious currency transactions. We've got shell companies laundering money. And now we've got a kidnapped American teenager." Cooper's voice was clipped, urgent. "Wake up every judge in the district if you have to. I want that warrant within the hour."

Sheridan pressed the phone to her ear. "Judge Matthews? Agent Sheridan, FBI. Sorry to wake you... Yes, ma'am, it's urgent. We need a no-knock warrant for Lev Andreev's Manhattan residence. We have evidence linking him to the Kane kidnapping and—"

Cooper grabbed the phone. "Judge, this is Agent Cooper. Grace Kane's life may depend on how quickly we move. I'm sending you documentation now - Treasury reports, corporate filings, bank records. The kidnapping demand matches exactly what Andreev lost when Kane's accounts were frozen by the Treasury Department."

He listened for a moment. "Yes, ma'am. Full tactical team... No, we can't wait until morning. If Andreev spooks..." Another pause. "Thank you, Your Honor. We'll have an agent with the warrant at your house in fifteen minutes for your signature."

Cooper handed the phone back to Sheridan. "Get the warrant to Judge Matthews. Then coordinate with

NYPD. I want that compound surrounded tighter than a frog's ass before we move in." His jaw tightened. "And Sheridan? If we spot the girl, we go in warrant or no warrant. I'm not losing another child to this bastard."

Frank lay prone behind the spotting scope on the warehouse roof, sweat rolling down his scarred face in the afternoon heat. Through the high-powered optics, he watched as police cruisers began to block intersections near Andreev's compound. Officers redirected traffic, creating a perimeter to keep civilians out of the line of fire.

Black FBI vehicles moved into position, surrounding the building like wolves circling prey. Through the scope, Frank saw Andreev in his office, barking orders into a phone. The Russian's agitation showed in his jerky movements. Something had spooked him. Frank adjusted the video camera's zoom, trying to read Andreev's lips.

Davis entered Andreev's office with a stack of papers. As he turned toward the window, a glint of light caught his eye - the briefest flash from Frank's camera lens being adjusted on the warehouse roof. His face betrayed nothing as he set the papers on Andreev's desk. "These need your signature," Davis said, angling himself away from the window. He touched his earpiece, speaking softly.

Frank caught the movement, saw Davis touch his ear. He glanced at his watch. He had been at his current position too long. Time to move. He broke down his equipment preparing to change position.

With everything tucked in his rucksack, Frank began his move to a new location on the opposite end of the roof. As he rounded a corner, the butt of a submachine gun slammed him in the face. Stars burst across his vision. He stumbled backward, but didn't fall. A second strike on the back of his head by another gunman drove him forward onto the gritty rooftop. Darkness swallowed him as his blood mingled with pigeon droppings and years of city grime. The last thing Frank heard was Davis's voice above him: "Secure his weapons and search him like your life depends on it."

Davis pulled out his mobile and dialed. Andreev answered. "We found Frank Kane on the rooftop of the furniture warehouse. He was watching you with surveillance equipment. You need to rid yourself of this problem."

"I agree."

"Do you want me to bring him back to compound?"

"No," said Andreev. "Deal with him off site and make it bloody. I want to send a clear message to his brother."

"We're on it," said Davis then hung up and turned to his two gunmen. "I need my pliers. Take him downstairs and get him ready. I'll be back in a few minutes."

Frank woke. Everything was a blur but slowly came back into focus. Frank's wrists ached where the handcuffs dug into his flesh, blood trickling down his massive arms and dripping onto the dusty concrete floor below him. His boots dangled inches above the cracked surface, his full weight suspended from a thick water pipe. The pipe creaked softly under his bulk.

Two guards watched him, their MP5 submachine guns held ready, their eyes wary. His KA-BAR knife hung from the shorter guard's belt, a trophy taken from a fallen giant. His Redhawk revolvers sat in their holster far from Frank's reach. Davis was nowhere in sight.

The water pipe ran along the ceiling in a straight line, secured every six feet by heavy U-bolts driven deep into concrete. Rust stains marked where water had leaked over the years, weakening the mounts. Frank lifted his legs slowly, muscles straining as he planted his feet on either side of the pipe. The guards stiffened at his movement.

"Hey, what're you—" the shorter one started, taking a step forward.

Frank pushed against the pipe with his legs, testing the mounts. Both guards moved closer, raising their weapons to strike. In one fluid motion, Frank's legs whipped down. His right boot caught the first guard's face at an angle, crushing bone and cartilage into a bloody ruin. His left boot slammed into the second guard's throat with precision, collapsing the windpipe. The man dropped his MP5, hands clawing desperately at his ruined throat, eyes bulging.

Fresh blood ran faster down Frank's arms as he pressed his feet back against the ceiling next to the pipe, pushing with his full strength. The U-bolts groaned in protest. Fine concrete dust filtered down like gray snow. One mount tore free with a screech of tortured metal, then another. The pipe sagged but held intact. Frank's boots found solid purchase on the floor and he took the weight off the handcuffs on his wrists.

He moved his right hand to his left wrist, thick fingers probing until he found the lump beneath his skin - a lockpick embedded there years ago. He pressed hard against the scar tissue. The pick's point punched through flesh, bringing a fresh flow of blood. Frank worked the bloodied pick into the handcuff's lock mechanism with practiced skill. The cuffs clicked open.

Frank knelt beside the guard with the crushed face, who lay twitching in a spreading pool of blood. He pulled his KA-BAR from the man's belt, feeling the familiar weight of the blade. The other guard still thrashed weakly on the floor, dying by inches from his collapsed throat.

"Stay where you are, Frank," said Davis standing in the doorway pointing an MP5. "You've really made a mess of things. Those were good men you just killed."

"No… they weren't," said Frank rising with the sheathed KA-BAR in his hand. He opened the leather release band dropping the sheath to the dusty floor.

"Oh, Frank. Didn't anyone ever teach you not to bring a knife to a gunfi—"

Without warning Frank threw the knife underhand. It sailed across the room and landed deep in Davis's right eye with a wet thud. Davis was shocked… and dying. He fell to the floor on his back jerking as the last moments of life left him. Frank walked over to check on him, then said looking down at the corpse, "You talk too much."

Leaving the bodies where they lay, Frank collected his weapons and rucksack, then descended the stairwell to ground level. The Imperial was parked on the street. He emptied his rucksack into the trunk and repacked it with the gear he would need including explosives and a Halligan bar that he strapped to the side of the pack. He pulled the FBI windbreaker and hat from the backseat of the vehicle. Neither fit, but he made do by leaving the jacket open.

The Compound

Frank parked the Imperial a block from the brownstone, killing the engine. The massive car settled with a creak from the aged suspension. He pulled the rucksack from the passenger seat, heavy with gear. His boots made no sound on the cracked sidewalk as he approached the garage entrance.

A security camera, its red-light blinking, covered the entrance to the garage. Frank opened his rucksack and pull out a wrist rocket with a leather bag filled with steal ball bearings. The wrist rocket has a laser sight mounted on the side of the frame. Loading one of the bearings into the pouch, he took aim with the laser as he drew back the rubber tubes. Waiting until the camera turned sideways, he let the bearing fly. The camera exploded in a shower of plastic and electronics, raining debris onto the sidewalk. It wasn't an elegant solution, but it was effective… and quiet.

In Andreev's security center, a technician's eyes flicked across two dozen monitors. Camera feeds showed every approach to the compound. He sipped cold coffee, fighting the monotony of another shift. Movement on monitor six caught his attention. Static flickered across the screen showing the brownstone garage entrance.

"What the hell?" He leaned closer, tapping keys to cycle through backup feeds. Nothing. Just snow where the camera signal should be. His finger touched his radio. Then he hesitated. False alarms were a good way to get fired. His finger moved away from the radio. He'd wait ten minutes. If the signal didn't return, then he'd call it in. On the screen, static continued to dance where the garage entrance had been.

The steel gate gleamed, new and heavy, incongruous against the brownstone's worn facade. A biometric scanner hung on the wall, its blue light pulsing. Frank ran his fingers along the gate's edge, finding the weak point where metal met concrete. He unstrapped the Halligan bar and placed its steal fork in the gap. He planted his boots, muscles tensing beneath his shirt as he gripped the bar. Metal groaned. Sweat beaded on his forehead as he pulled. The lock mechanism snapped with a sharp crack. The gate rolled sideways on its track.

Inside, fluorescent lights hummed. The two black SUVs sat empty, their armored flanks reflecting the harsh light. Frank moved past them, eyes scanning the garage. A false wall caught his attention - too smooth, too new. Another camera monitored the area in front of the wall. He loaded another bearing and let it fly. Same result – plastic and electronics exploded. He found the seam where the false wall met the foundation and muscled it open.

The tunnel entrance lay behind the wall panel, sloping down into darkness. Frank clicked on a small flashlight. Fresh boot prints marked the dusty floor. The tunnel ran straight and level, its walls lined with conduit carrying power and data cables. Several cameras lined the tunnel. Each would be taken out before Frank was seen on the security monitors. The air grew colder as he descended. After two hundred yards, he clicked off the light. A faint glow leaked from ahead - Andreev's compound. Frank moved toward it, a shadow among shadows.

Andreev stood at his office window, binoculars pressed to his eyes. Police cruisers blocked every intersection around his compound, their light bars strobing red and blue. FBI tactical teams moved into position, black body armor stark against the afternoon sun. Snipers set up on adjacent rooftops, their rifles glinting. He counted vehicles - eighteen FBI, twenty-four police units, two armored SWAT trucks. Below, agents deployed barriers, creating a hard perimeter around the main entrance to his compound.

Andreev gave particular attention to the FBI Enhanced SWAT team. The operators pulled black Nomex hoods over their faces, each movement precise from countless repetitions. Their plate carriers held titanium-ceramic composite inserts rated to stop armor-piercing rounds. Pouches bristled with thirty-round magazines for their customized HK416 carbines. The rifles wore Aimpoint T2 micro red dots paired with PEQ-15 infrared lasers, SureFire SOCOM suppressors threading their barrels.

Combat medics distributed blood type patches and QuikClot gauze. Breaching specialists checked their frame charges, det cord coiled in figure-eights around their shoulders. Ballistic shields reflected dully in the sun, the Kevlar-composite surfaces scratched and gouged from training. Radio earpieces crackled with encrypted transmissions as team members synchronized their watches.

The operators moved with measured steps under the weight of their gear - trauma plates, backup sidearms, flash-bangs, CS gas, breaching shotguns loaded with frangible copper slugs. Thermal imagers revealed heat signatures through walls. Fiber optic cameras that snaked under doors on carbon fiber poles. The gear reflected their mission - not to negotiate, but to overwhelm with precise violence.

Andreev pressed a button on his desk phone and called his helicopter pilot. "Anatoly. Land on my roof and keep the engine running."

"Seven minutes out."

Andreev took the private elevator to the second-floor data center. The room hummed with activity, his tech team working with practiced efficiency. Industrial degaussers whined as they wiped drive after drive. Screens showed progress bars as data purged from the servers.

"Time estimate?" he asked his chief technician.

"Twenty minutes for complete wipe. The degaussers need two passes to meet military specs."

Moving down to the ground floor, Andreev found his security teams at their assigned posts. These men had fought beside him in darker places than this - Chechnya, Georgia, even places that didn't officially exist. They nodded as he passed, checking weapons and equipment. No words needed to be exchanged. They knew their duty.

In the lobby, Arkadi, the team leader arranged his best men behind hardened positions. Steel barricades and sandbags transformed the marble entrance hall into a killing zone. "Like old times," Arkadi said with a grim smile.

"Hold them as long as you can," Andreev replied. "Buy time for the drives to clear. Once the drives are clean, you and your men can pull back through the tunnel and meet at the rendezvous point."

Above, he heard the helicopter's rotors as it settled onto his rooftop pad.

Dmitri watched his bank of monitors, cigarette burning forgotten between yellowed fingers. Static filled another screen. Five cameras down in ten minutes - first the lower garage levels, then the tunnel feeds one by one.

"Daniil," he said into his radio. "More cameras out. B3 East and both tunnel checkpoints dark."

Static crackled, then Daniil's voice: "Pattern?"

"Moving west to east through the tunnel. Like something's taking them offline as it moves."

"FBI maybe. Think they found the tunnel entrance." A pause. "I'll send Petrov and two men to check. Keep watching. If you see movement, call immediately." "Yes sir." Dmitri leaned closer to the screens, scanning for shapes in the static. The cigarette burned down to his fingers. He didn't notice.

Andreev returned to his office and made another call on a secured line. "Volkov, take the girl and your men to the Belomorsk and wait for my arrival."

Nearing the end of the tunnel Frank's boots scraped concrete as he approached a heavy steel door. Blue-white LEDs cast harsh shadows across the biometric panel. He wedged the Halligan bar into the doorframe, muscles bunching as he heaved against the steel. The door held. Even his massive strength couldn't overcome its reinforced hinges.

He unslung his rucksack, pulled out a brick of C4 wrapped in copper. He molded the explosive against the locking mechanism when the door's panel flashed green. Metal scraped metal as the door swung inward. Three figures filled the doorway. Petrov in front, MP5 raised. The muzzle flash lit the tunnel like lightning. Bullets tore into Frank's armored vest, the impacts driving him back two steps. His ears rang with gunfire and Russian voices. Blood ran hot down his arm where a round had found flesh.

Frank lunged through the storm of lead. His hand clamped onto Petrov's MP5, yanking the barrel up. More rounds stitched the ceiling. Frank flattened his free hand like a spade and thrust his fingers into Petrov's throat. Bone snapped. As he crumbled, Frank grabbed the MP5 still strapped around the deadman's shoulder and whipped it around, firing into the second man in the hallway. He too fell dead. The magazine emptied. Frank released the weapon letting it with Petrov's corpse fall to the floor.

The third man drew a knife that glinted in the harsh light. Frank reached for one of his pistols, but was too late. The Russian lunged at him. The blade opened Frank's forearm before he could block. As the man swung again, Frank caught his wrist. His boot shattered the Russian's knee with a wet crunch. The knife clattered away. The man backpedaled, fumbling to bring up his MP5. Frank's own blade found the man's kidney, twisted up under ribs. Hot blood poured over Frank's fist. He yanked the knife free as the body slumped. Frank stood breathing hard, fresh blood mixing with old scars. Shell casings rolled across concrete. Behind him, three bodies leaked red pools beneath the doorway's harsh light. He retrieved his rucksack and stepped over them into the compound's basement, each boot print leaving a crimson mark.

Frank moved through the basement corridor, each step silent despite his size. The fluorescent lights flickered, casting sharp shadows that danced across concrete walls. A voice rasped from behind a steel door along the corridor - young, desperate.

"Help! Someone!"

Frank paused. The voice came again, weaker this time. He found the door's hinges, tested their strength. He used the Halligan bar to pry the door open.

Inside, Alex slumped against a wall, dried blood caking his shirt where Burke's knife had caught him. His eyes went wide at Frank's size, then settled on the FBI windbreaker that wouldn't close over Frank's armored vest. Frank said nothing, just gestured toward the tunnel with a grunt.

Alex studied Frank's scarred face, the way the man filled the doorway. "You don't look like FBI."

Frank pointed toward the tunnel again, more forcefully this time.

"Yeah. Okay. I'm going." Alex started limping toward the darkness. "Thanks. For the rescue." He glanced back once, then disappeared into the shadows of the tunnel. Frank moved on, deeper into the compound.

The stairwell door yielded to Frank's boot. He began climbing past numbered landings marked in faded Cyrillic. His boots left bloody prints on concrete steps - some his, some from the men he'd killed below. Four flights up, another reinforced door blocked his path. This one heavier than the others, meant to protect Andreev's private domain. A keypad glowed red beside it, its silent warning backed by steel thick enough to stop a truck.

Frank studied the door. Beyond it lay Andreev's private quarters and office - and somewhere in those rooms, the key to finding Grace. He reached for his rucksack, for the shaped charges waiting inside. The hallway would amplify the blast, maybe bring the FBI running, but he didn't care. The time for stealth was over.

He began unpacking the explosives, his massive hands moving with practiced precision. He had little doubt the charges would breach the door.

Sheridan's Suburban skidded across the asphalt as the driver braked at the last second. She leaped out before it stopped moving, warrant clutched in her fist. "Cooper!"

Cooper snatched the warrant, already moving. Red laser dots from FBI sniper scopes painted Andreev's compound. Operators in black tactical gear crouched behind armored vehicles, weapons ready.

Cooper raised a bullhorn, his voice cutting through the chatter. "Lev Andreev! This is FBI Special Agent Cooper. We have a federal warrant to search these premises. Lay down your weapons and surrender, or we will breach with force."

Only silence answered. Cooper waited thirty seconds, then tried again. "Last chance, Andreev. Come out with your hands up. Don't make this worse than it has to be."

A single shot rang out from the compound. The bullet sparked off the armored vehicle inches from Cooper's head. His response was immediate: "All teams, execute breach! Weapons free!"

The SWAT operators surged forward in practiced formations. Frame charges detonated against three sections of the perimeter wall. The explosions lit up the sky, concrete blasting inward. Through the billowing smoke and dust, agents poured onto the compound grounds like black water.

The response was immediate and coordinated. Andreev's men had trained for this. Interlocking fields of fire caught the first wave of agents in a deadly crossfire. Muzzle flashes erupted from fortified windows and prepared fighting positions.

"Taking heavy fire!" shouted FBI Team Leader Martinez. His operators dove for cover as rounds sparked off their ballistic shields. A bullet found a gap in Agent Wilson's armor, punched through his shoulder. He went down hard. Two teammates grabbed his vest straps, dragged him behind an armored Bearcat as a medic rushed forward.

Russian voices barked commands from above. More security teams emerged from doorways and alcoves, their MP5s spraying precise bursts. They moved like special forces, using cover and suppressing fire with lethal efficiency.

The FBI answered with controlled bursts from their HK416s. Brass sparkled as it scattered across manicured grass. Blood soaked into imported soil. An

FBI marksman's .308 round caught a Russian gunman in the chest, threw him back through a second-floor window. His teammate immediately took his position, never missing a beat in their defense.

"Second floor, right window!" A spotter's voice crackled through radio headsets. A Russian appeared with an RPK light machine gun, the weapon's rounds forcing an entire FBI team into cover. Three marksmen engaged him simultaneously. The .308 rounds punched through his chest, but he managed to rake the FBI position before falling, wounding two agents.

Three SWAT operators advanced in tight formation, ballistic shields overlapped like ancient Romans. Their boots struck the ground in practiced rhythm as they approached The building's heavily defended main entrance. Behind the shields, black body armor revealed the layers of tactical efficiency.

Muzzle flashes flickered from the compound's windows. The shield bearers never broke stride as rounds sparked off hardened polymer. Standard ammunition posed little threat to their armor.

Then a steel plate slid aside above the main entrance. The massive barrel of an M2 .50 caliber machine gun emerged. The gunner aimed and squeezed the trigger.

The heavy weapon's report drowned all other sound. Teflon-coated rounds punched through ballistic shields like paper. The impacts lifted men cloaked in armored vests off their feet, throwing them backward. Even those rounds that didn't penetrate transferred enough kinetic energy to shatter ribs through body armor.

"Pull back!" Cooper shouted. "Covering fire!"

The remaining agents opened up with their rifles, forcing Andreev's men to duck behind concrete walls. But the .50 cal continued its methodical work, each burst finding gaps in the FBI's tactical formation.

SWAT operators dragged wounded comrades to cover as the machine gun swept the courtyard. Brass cases rained down from the gunport, smoking in the morning air. Cooper watched from behind a barricade as his assault team retreated, leaving equipment scattered across blood-stained pavement.

The .50 cal's barrel disappeared behind the steel plate. The message had been sent - a direct assault would only create more casualties. Cooper keyed his radio, calling for medics as he assessed his battered force. They would need another way in.

Cooper watched his teams regroup. They'd expected resistance, but not this level of military precision. "All units, adjust assault patterns. Watch your sectors."

Cooper gathered his team leaders behind an armored Bearcat. Blood still ran from the first assault's aftermath, turning puddles crimson. Medics worked on the wounded, calling out blood types and cutting away shredded body armor.

"This time we go heavy," Cooper said. "Multiple shield teams. Full spectrum of fire support." Two more tactical units arrived, their operators moving with coiled precision. Barrett .50 caliber rifles deployed on rooftops, their scopes tracking compound windows. M240 machine gun teams set up interlocking fields of fire. Grenadiers loaded 40mm launchers with high-explosive rounds. "Hit them from all sides," Cooper ordered. "Overwhelm their defenses before that .50 can target any one group."

The assault force split into four elements. Each team stacked behind multiple shield bearers - three layers of ballistic protection. The shields' edges overlapped, leaving no gaps.

"Execute!" Cooper's voice cut through radio static. The FBI's response was overwhelming. Barrett rifles cracked from above, suppressing window positions. Machine guns raked the compound's façade while grenade launchers sent concrete fragments flying.

Under the barrage, four shield teams advanced like armored phalanxes. The steel plate slid open. The M2's barrel emerged into a storm of covering fire. Concrete dust filled the air as hundreds of rounds converged on the gunport. The .50 cal opened up, its rounds punching through the first layer of shields. But the second and third layers held. The shield teams kept moving through the bullet storm.

Andreev's men added their fire from multiple positions, but the FBI's suppression forced them to shoot blind. The M2 gunner died as a Barrett round found its mark through the gunport. The massive weapon fell silent. FBI operators reached the entrance, securing the breach point. Demo charges slapped against the reinforced doors. The blast turned steel to shrapnel.

"Breach, breach, breach!" voices shouted through the chaos.

SWAT teams flowed through the smoke, carbines up and tracking. Flash-bangs burst in concrete hallways. CS gas grenades popped and hissed. The FBI's boot steps echoed like thunder as they pushed deeper into Andreev's fortress. But this was only the beginning. More of Andreev's men waited in prepared positions, ready to exact a heavy toll for every foot of ground.

Glass shattered as flash-bangs sailed through interior windows. CS gas billowed from launched canisters, its chemical stench mixing with cordite.

Andreev's men fell back, but it was an organized retreat. They fired through the gas using thermal optics, their shots still devastatingly accurate.

"Contact left!" An agent's voice shouted through static. More gunfire erupted from the eastern wing. Two of Andreev's men went down, but they'd forced the FBI team to waste precious time.

A Russian shooter caught Agent Parker in the shoulder, spun him around. Return fire nearly cut the Russian in half, but he'd bought time for his comrades to regroup and fortify their positions.

The FBI operators moved with mechanical precision, assaulting isolated defensive positions. More flash-bangs detonated inside. Gunfire echoed through marble halls, mixed with shouted commands in English and Russian. The close-quarters battle became a brutal contest.

Andreev's men used their knowledge of the building's layout to devastating effect. They'd rigged some doors with explosives, others with gas. They fell back room by room, making the FBI pay in blood for every foot of gained ground.

"Multiple contacts, north stairwell!" Static-filled voices shouted over the radio. A Russian team had flanked through a hidden passage, caught the FBI operators in a crossfire. Two agents down before they could react. The hallway became a killing ground as both sides exchanged fire at point-blank range.

Above the chaos, an FBI helicopter's spotlight cut through smoke, painting the compound in harsh light as the sun began to set. Heavy caliber rounds from Andreev's snipers traced lines across its armored hull, forcing it to back off.

On the ground, the battle devolved into a dozen smaller firefights, each side taking and losing ground in a deadly battle of will.

But something in the defense pattern caught Cooper's attention. The resistance seemed designed to slow, not stop. Like they were buying time. He keyed his radio: "All units, be advised. This could be a diversion. Watch for movement on secondary exits. Maintain perimeter security."

Inside, madness reigned as FBI teams cleared room after room. The building's pristine interior had become a war zone - bullet holes stitched across walls, blood staining imported marble, brass cartridges crunching underfoot. Both sides fought with desperate intensity, neither willing to give ground without extracting a heavy price in return.

Andreev stood before the wall of security monitors, hands clasped behind his back. On a dozen screens, the FBI's assault played out in stark black and white. His men fought well, falling back in disciplined order, making the federal agents pay for every foot of ground.

"Sir." Yuri's fingers flew across his keyboard. "Two more team members down. FBI has breached the main security station."

Andreev watched another screen where agents in tactical gear moved through smoke-filled corridors. Blood stained their black armor. His own men lay crumpled in corners, their weapons empty.

"The data wipe?" His voice remained calm despite the chaos unfolding before him.

"Six more minutes." Yuri glanced at the progress bar crawling across his screen. "Every drive will be clean. They'll find nothing."

On another monitor, flash-bangs detonated in the west wing. FBI operators advanced through the chemical haze. More of his men fell.

Frank stepped back from the reinforced door, the shaped charge molded against its locking mechanism. The C4's blast would focus inward, designed to shear steel and shatter locks. He clicked the detonator.

Andreev was fixated on the green bar showing the progress of the data wipe.

"Sir, we should move to the—" A deep boom cut off Yuri's words. The building shuddered. "What was that?"

The explosion punched through the hallway. Smoke and fragments burst outward as the door's locks disintegrated. The steel door swung drunkenly on one remaining hinge, then fell with a hollow boom that echoed through the building.

Andreev's eyes narrowed. That explosion hadn't come from the FBI teams below. It had come from inside, above, from his private floor. Someone else had breached his sanctuary. Andreev watched his empire crumble on the screens before him, counting down the seconds until his secrets burned. His inner voice screamed for him to find and kill the intruder before more secrets were revealed, but Andreev knew that the data on the drives could put him in an American prison for life. He had to stay until that risk was gone for good.

Through the smoke, Frank saw Andreev's quarters. The blast had shredded expensive furniture, turned pristine walls to rubble. Framed artwork lay scattered and torn. Blood ran from one of his ears - the confined space had amplified the explosion beyond even his expectation.

Frank stepped through the breach, boots crunching glass and splintered wood. The smoke cleared slowly, revealing the destruction his entry had wrought. Small fires burned. The room's previous elegance lay in ruins, replaced by the violent chaos Frank brought with him.

He climbed the interior stairs that spiraled to the next two levels. On the sixth floor Frank, one of his Ruger Super Redhawk revolvers drawn, carefully moved toward Andreev's office.

Surprisingly, the office seemed untouched by the explosion two floors down. Frank entered and moved to the modernist painting and swung it away from the wall on hidden hinges revealing the safe. The safe's biometric scanner glowed blue, waiting for Andreev's palm print. Frank wasn't interested. He had other plans.

He pulled bricks of C4 from his rucksack. The explosive felt warm, pliable as he molded shaped charges around the safe's edges where it met the wall. Each charge had to be precise - too much force would damage the safe's contents, too little would leave it anchored. He'd learned demolitions from the best and had plenty of practice over the years.

Frank worked fast, his huge hands surprisingly agile as he positioned the charges. He placed them in a precise pattern - the concrete would crack along predictable stress lines.

In the adjacent room, Frank repeated the process on the opposite wall for the back of the safe. More charges, each shaped to focus the explosive force inward. The room smelled of cordite and concrete dust. Multiple detonators went into each charge - redundancy born of past failures. A single failed det cord could ruin everything.

He moved in Andreev's office to the blast proof window behind the desk. The window was designed to defend against an exterior blast, not a blast from the interior. Frank placed another charge and detonator on the window.

He overturned Andreev's steel desk sending his monitors and laptop crashing to the floor. He knelt behind it for cover, unspooling det cord.

The first blast was sharp, contained. Like a giant's fist punching through the wall.

Below, Andreev felt the blast. He knew what it was. Someone was going after his safe. Maybe FBI. He could ill afford to let them have his USB hard key. But without the passcodes there was little risk of them getting access to his accounts. Then he remembered… Frank Kane had been recording him as he sat at his desk. He wondered if he had seen him enter his passcodes. Panic.

"You stay until the drives have been wiped," he ordered Yuri. "Do you understand?"

Yuri nodded knowing the consequences if he failed.

Andreev left as he headed for the stair. Four of his gunmen were fighting off the FBI agents below. He pointed to two of them, "You two with me."

They followed him up the stairwell.

Dust filled the office. Paper swirled around from the wind through the shattered window. When it cleared, Frank examined his work through the haze. The charges had blown the concrete clean away, exposing the building's skeleton. Steel reinforcement bars still held the safe in place, thick as his wrist, woven through the structure like metal veins.

Frank moved quickly. More C4 went onto the exposed rebar - smaller charges, each one positioned at key structural points. The steel would shear clean with the right application of force. Multiple detonators again, det cord trailing like surgical sutures.

In the hallway, Andreev and his gunmen advanced cautiously toward his office. Andreev could hear the wind from the blown-out window.

Frank once again took cover behind the desk, counted down. The second blast sheared through steel with a sound like violin strings snapping. The safe groaned, shifted, but didn't fall.

Frank pulled the Halligan bar from his pack and went to work on the safe. The steel fork bit into the gap between safe and wall. His massive shoulders strained as he applied leverage. Metal screamed against metal. The safe's final anchors gave way. Five hundred pounds of hardened steel crashed to the floor. Frank's hands found purchase on the safe's edges. Muscles that could bend steel bars tensed. With a grunt that started in his core, he lifted. The massive weight rose grudgingly. Frank moved toward the window he'd breached earlier, the safe balanced on the edge at waist height as he prepared to tie a rope to it.

The office door burst open. Andreev stood in the entrance, flanked by gunmen. His eyes widened at the sight of his safe perched on the window's edge, six stories above the ground. Frank met his gaze. Then his boot shot out, sending the safe tumbling into empty space.

"No!" said Andreev.

Frank dove behind the steel desk as gunfire erupted.

The safe plummeted, picking up speed. It struck the manicured lawn with the impact of a meteor, plunging two feet into soft earth. The thud echoed off surrounding buildings like thunder.

Bullets sparked off the desk. Frank drew both revolvers, waiting for his moment. Above, helicopter rotors spooled up for takeoff.

Frank knew that the gunmen shooting at him were professionals. He had little doubt they would attempt to flank him. He needed to take action before they did. Both his pistols were fully loaded.

Frank's eyes moved across the floor, calculating. Shell casings rolled with each impact. He considered jumping through the window, but six floors was a long drop and there was no guarantee that they didn't shoot him on the way out.

An MP5 clicked empty. One gunman reloaded. Frank pivoted around the desk keeping low and fired one round. The gunman's ankle exploded almost tearing his foot off. He fell screaming. Frank ducked behind the desk as the second gunmen unleashed a barrage.

Frank holstered his revolvers. His hands found the desk's edge. Frank's muscles flexed once again. Three hundred pounds of steel desk lifted. The gunman's eyes widened as Frank stood, using the desk as a shield. Bullet impacts numbed his arms, but he kept moving. Three steps. The gunman's magazine ran dry. Frank hurled the desk. It caught the man square, crushing him against the wall.

Only Frank and Andreev were still in the gunfight. Frank no longer had the desk protecting him. Drawing his revolvers he advanced on Andreev's position behind a concrete wall. Frank's revolvers belched fire as he unleashed multiple rounds taking large chunks out of the concrete wall hoping to reach Andreev.

Andreev's pistol cracked, the round catching Frank's leg. Blood sprayed. But Frank kept advancing.

Unnerved that the bullet had not slowed the giant rushing toward him, Andreev decided retreat was the better part of valor and sprinted toward the stairs leading to the roof.

Frank fired several rounds. One caught Andreev in the shoulder, crushing bone, and twirling him around. He pushed backward through the doorway to the stairwell.

Frank touched his leg. The bullet had gone clean through. Pain was good. Pain meant survival. The wound had slowed him down, but not stopped him. He moved to follow Andreev, boots crunching shell casings littering the floor.

The stairwell erupted in gunfire as Andreev's last men engaged the FBI teams pushing upward. Bullets sparked off steel railings, fragments stinging exposed skin. Muzzle flashes turned the confined space into a strobe of violence.

Andreev clutched his wounded shoulder, staying low as he climbed past the firefight. Rounds snapped past his head. A ricochet caught one of his men in the throat, blood spraying across concrete walls. The man toppled backward, his MP5 clattering down the stairs.

Flash-bangs burst below. CS gas rolled upward. Through the chemical haze, Frank's massive shape appeared. He moved through the chaos, each step calculated despite his bleeding leg. A stray round grazed his arm. He didn't flinch.

Two of Andreev's men turned to engage him. Frank's revolvers ended them before they could bring their weapons to bear. Their bodies tumbled past him as he climbed.

FBI operators pushed upward through the smoke. "Contact front!" someone shouted. More gunfire filled the stairwell. Brass shells bounced off steps, rolled into corners.

Frank shouldered past the last of Andreev's men as they fought their final battle. Bullets whined around him, seeking flesh. He kept climbing, focused only on the figure laboring up the stairs ahead.

Andreev stumbled up the stairs, blood soaking his silk shirt where Frank's bullet had torn through muscle and bone. His breath came in ragged gasps. Behind him, Frank's boots echoed in the stairwell, slowed by his own wound but still coming.

The roof access door burst open. Wind from the idling helicopter whipped at Andreev's clothes. He half-ran, half-crawled across the helipad. "Go! Now!"

Frank shouldered through the stairwell door as Andreev pulled himself into the helicopter. Both revolvers roared, their heavy rounds punching holes in the helicopter's panels and glass.

The helicopter lifted from the pad, banking away from the building. Frank planted his feet despite his wounded leg, both revolvers rising with mechanical precision and firing.

The heavy caliber rounds caught the port engine housing dead center. Metal shredded. Black smoke poured from damaged turbine blades. The pilot yanked collective, fighting to maintain control as warning lights flashed across his panel. The engine screamed. The helicopter lurched sideways, its remaining engine straining to compensate.

"Shut it down," Andreev ordered through clenched teeth. "Before it tears itself apart." The pilot killed the damaged engine. The helicopter wallowed on one turbine, its speed cut nearly in half. They limped away into darkness, vulnerable now, moving too slow.

Frank fired again, but the range was too great. His rounds fell short as the crippled aircraft disappeared between buildings.

Frank growled, the guttural noise like stones grinding together.

Six stories below, Cooper saw the helicopter rise above the building's edge. He keyed his radio and ordered the FBI pilot to pick him up before pursuing Andreev.

The FBI helicopter swooped in low, rotors cutting the night air. Cooper sprinted across the street, climbed aboard. "Do not lose visual contact."

The pilot nodded, pulling collective. They rose into the darkness, pursuing Andreev's fading running lights as they stretched their lead across the city's glowing grid.

Inside Andreev's helicopter the pilot asked, "We pick up the girl?"

"No. Get me to the Belomorsk fast," said Andreev as he used the helicopter's first aid kit to patch his shoulder wound and create a sling.

The damaged helicopter lurched between glass towers, its port engine leaving a trail of black smoke from oil residue still burning. Andreev braced against the airframe as his pilot threaded past mirrored facades, rotors seeming to slice the very air from the sky. The city spread below like a maze of steel and shadow.

Cooper's FBI helicopter closed the gap, its powerful twin engines eating the distance. Wind whipped through its open doors as the FBI sniper took position, his rifle seeking a target through the crowded airspace.

Andreev's hand found the M134 minigun's grip beneath a black canvas tarp. The weapon's weight settled against its pintle mount, six barrels dull. His pilot banked hard around the Empire State Building, G-forces crushing him against the seat. The FBI helicopter matched the turn, closing to 400 yards.

The sniper's first round punched through the damaged helicopter's tail boom. His second shattered a rear window. "Land the aircraft," Cooper's voice boomed over loudspeaker, carried away by rushing wind.

Andreev slid the door open. Frigid air blasted his face as he swung the minigun out. The electric motor spun the barrels, building to 6,000 rounds per minute. The weapon's feeder chute was thick with 7.62mm ammunition. He squeezed the trigger.

The minigun roared, its entire body vibrating as it spat out a hundred rounds per second. The recoil force pushed against Andreev's hands like a living thing.

Tracers cut through evening gloom. The sniper's chest exploded in red mist. His rifle tumbled into empty air.

Cooper reached for his sidearm but the minigun's stream walked across the FBI helicopter's cabin. Rounds shredded flesh and bone. Cooper slumped forward, blood pooling beneath his seat, finally falling to the aircraft's deck, life fading from his eyes.

The FBI pilot tried to break contact, banking away from the murderous fire. Andreev tracked him with precision, brass shells tumbling into the cabin like hot metal rain. The weapon's barrels glowed orange from sustained fire.

Bullets punctured the FBI's helicopter's cockpit. The pilot's body jerked as rounds tore through him. His hands fell from the controls.

The FBI helicopter nosed over, spinning as it fell. It struck the corner of a building, shearing off its tail rotor. The wreckage plummeted forty stories, striking pavement in a fireball of aviation fuel and twisted metal.

Andreev's pilot climbed above the smoke, banking east. The city fell away behind them, its towers casting long shadows across Manhattan's concrete canyons. Andreev wiped sweat from his face with a silk handkerchief. The minigun's barrels ticked as they cooled, the smell of burnt cordite filling the cabin. In the distance was the harbor.

The Imperial's V8 rumbled to idle at the garage entrance. Waiting outside, Richard pressed his hand on the biometric scanner. Steel gate panels rolled sideways on oiled tracks. Frank guided the massive car inside, chrome bumpers reflecting fluorescent light. The engine died with a low growl. Frank stepped out.

Richard saw Frank wounds, still bleeding.

"Jesus, Frank. You look like death dragged backwards," said Richard. "I know you're not big on hospitals, but we should at least stop the bleeding before you fall down."

Frank grunted in response, then moved to the trunk, lifted Andreev's five-hundred-pound safe covered in mud. The safe crashed onto concrete with a boom that shook the walls. He pulled a new sledgehammer from the trunk, price tag still dangling from the hickory handle. Twenty pounds of hardened steel head. A cold chisel followed.

"You're just gonna pound it open?" said Richard.

Frank nodded once. A single, economical movement.

Richard watched as his brother slammed the hammer's head against the safe's door like he was loosening it up. After several blows, Frank position the chisel against the safe's seam. "That's three inches of hardened steel. You'll break the hammer before—"

The first blow rang out like a bell, drowning his words. Frank's shoulders rolled with each strike, muscles tightening beneath his shirt. Sweat darkened the fabric. The safe shuddered but held.

Frank studied the impact point, analyzing the metal's response. The second blow landed with precise force. A third. The safe's armor began to buckle, chrome flaking away to reveal raw steel.

He found a rhythm - the sharp crack of hammer on chisel, the deeper boom of stressed metal. His arms burned but pain meant nothing. The seam widened. The garage's fluorescent tubes flickered with each impact, but offered glimpses of the safe's interior.

Frank's shadow danced on concrete, a giant caught in endless motion.

One final blow. The door gave way with a shriek of tortured metal.

"Unfucking believable," said Richard as he stared at the mangled safe.

Frank pulled the safe's door open. Andreev's USB drive sat in custom-cut foam, nestled like a jewel in a broken crown. Small. Innocent-looking. A piece of plastic and silicon worth billions in the right hands. Worth Grace's life in Frank's.

Frank retrieved it without ceremony and handed it to Richard.

"This is worthless without his passcodes," said Richard.

Frank fished the video camera out of the trunk and handed it to Richard. "Get to work, Dick. Before he moves his money."

Richard sat behind his office desk reviewing the video footage of Andreev typing on his computer's keyboard. He wrote down each passcode and each bank's log-in screen.

Frank sat on the couch using the needle and thread from his pocket to sew closed the slash in his forearm and the bullet hole in his leg. Blood dripped down onto the Persian rug.

"You could use my private bathroom to do that, you know," said Richard.

Frank ignored him, opened a bottle of hydrogen peroxide and poured it over the wounds. The wounds foamed. Blood and peroxide flowed onto the rug forming a pink puddle. Richard winced, but said nothing and went back to work plugging in the USB hard key into his computer.

The Belomorsk rose from black harbor water, six hundred feet of Soviet steel built for hauling containers across storm-wracked seas. Her hull bore scars from decades of ice and salt. Rust streaked her flanks despite constant maintenance. But her decay was a deception.

Behind weathered hatches lay a digital fortress. The forward hold housed servers and cooling systems that could run a small city. Diesel generators thrummed deep in her belly, feeding endless power to surveillance arrays hidden in cargo containers. Satellite dishes and communication domes dotted her deck like mechanical mushrooms, disguised from casual observers by stacks of empty containers.

The bridge bristled with encrypted communication gear. Radar arrays spun beneath protective covers, scanning sea and sky for threats. Steel stairs led down to the combat information center where technicians monitored wall-sized displays showing global market data, surveillance feeds, and network traffic.

The rear hold contained Andreev's private command center. Three tiers of workstations faced screens that covered the bulkhead. Blue light from dozens of displays reflected off steel walls. The space hummed with technology and conditioned air that fought the servers' endless heat.

Armed men patrolled her decks day and night. They wore civilian clothes but moved like military. Their weapons stayed hidden until needed. Sniper positions dotted the upper decks, concealed in modified containers with ballistic glass windows.

The Belomorsk was a warship dressed as a well-worn freighter. A digital castle floating on dark water. But like all castles, she had weaknesses. Points where her armor was thin. Places where a determined enemy could breach her defenses.

The helicopter settled onto the Belomorsk's deck, rotors chopping salt air. Engine wash whipped waves of heat across steel plates. Andreev moved between cargo containers. His Italian leather shoes rang hollow on metal steps as he descended into the ship's heart.

Below deck cooling fans whirred in precise rhythm, keeping the servers from dying in their own heat. The air tasted of ozone and filtered sea air.

Andreev moved past technicians who avoided his gaze. His shoulder wound throbbed where Frank's bullet had torn flesh and broken bone. Blood had dried dark on his silk shirt. He reached the far wall where a biometric safe waited behind a panel of mahogany veneer. His palm pressed against the scanner. Green light pulsed as it read his prints. The door opened with a pneumatic hiss that echoed off steel walls.

Inside, a duplicate USB hard key sat in foam padding next to stacks of bearer bonds and packets of diamonds. Emergency assets that couldn't be traced or hacked. His fingers trembled slightly as he plugged the drive into his workstation. The first login screen appeared, demanding his passcode. Andreev typed with practiced strokes, muscle memory built through thousands of transactions. Numbers filled the display - $788 million USD. He relaxed.

Then the screen flickered. Numbers changed. Zero balance. His hands flew across the keyboard, sweat beading on his forehead as he pulled up another account. Empty. Another. Nothing. Decade's worth of transfers, shell companies, hidden accounts - all stripped clean.

"Nyet." The word came out like poison. Andreev slammed his fist onto the desk, sending coffee spilling across papers. The cup shattered against a wall. His empire of ones and zeros, accumulated through decades of blood and terror, had vanished into digital wind.

Technicians hunched lower in their chairs as Andreev's rage filled the room like a physical presence. Cold. Murderous. The Kane brothers had violated something sacred. They had taken his money. For that, he would take everything they loved. Slowly. Painfully. He would make them watch as he dismantled their world piece by piece.

Then he would take their lives. But not quickly. Death would be a gift they would beg for long before he granted it.

Andreev sat in his chair, trembling with fury. On the screens above, market data scrolled past, unaware that an empire had just crumbled into digital dust.

Frank stood at the window of Richard's office, his massive frame casting a shadow across the Persian rug still stained with his blood. The city lights glinted off fresh sutures in his forearm where he'd sewn himself up. Blood had soaked through his shirt sleeve and dried black.

Richard poured another bourbon, his third since they'd emptied Andreev's accounts. The laptop screen still showed the last transfer - $788 million moved through a maze of offshore banks. Richard's fingers drummed against his glass. "He'll call."

Frank didn't move. His reflection in the glass bore little resemblance to his brother behind the desk. Where Richard's face remained smooth, wealth preserved, Frank's had been carved by violence.

Richard knocked back his bourbon. "Maybe we should call him instead. Let him know—"

Frank's grunt cut him off. It was the sound of gravel in a meat grinder.

The phone rang. Richard's hand shook as he reached for it. Frank put his hand over Richard's before he picked up the receiver. "Be strong… for Grace," said Frank.

Richard considered for a moment then nodded. The phone rang again. He put the call on speaker. "Richard Kane," he said in the most serious tone he could muster. Frank's eyes fixed on the phone like a predator studying prey.

For a moment, only static filled the air. Then Andreev's voice emerged, cold as Siberian winter: "Where is my money, you weasel?"

"Where is my daughter, you prick?"

Frank gave Richard a slight nod of approval.

"You fucked with the wrong man. I'm going to take your world apart piece by piece."

"If you harm Grace, I will donate all your money to international charities… the ones you hate."

"You always failed to understand me, Richard. You think I care about money. I can always make more money."

"You need money to pay your army."

"Their loyalty to me goes far beyond money."

"Somehow I doubt that."

"If you continue to underestimate me, I will send Grace back to you one piece at a time."

"That would be a mistake. You need to listen to me."

"No. You listen. I will send Grace back to you. Not all at once. A finger first. Then maybe an ear. You will live with each piece until there is nothing left but memories and guilt."

Frank leaned in and said, "Touch her and I will hunt you down. Then you will know real pain. You have my word."

"The monster speaks. I was wondering where you were, Frank. Now I will show you what happens when you take from me. Pray Grace dies quickly. It will be the only mercy she receives."

The line went dead. Richard stared at the phone, "He'll kill her."

"No. He won't."

"You don't know him. Andreev's a psychopath."

"I know men like Andreev. They all have reasons for their actions."

Richard exploded from his chair. "You did this! It was your idea to take his money. Now he'll kill her!" He grabbed Frank's shirt with both hands. "My daughter is going to die because of you!"

Frank looked down at his brother's hands, then met his eyes. His voice came out like steel scraping concrete: "Grace dies if you're weak."

Richard shoved him, accomplishing nothing against Frank's immovable bulk. "Weak? He's going to cut her apart while we sit here!"

"No." Frank's hands caught Richard's wrists, held them with casual strength. "Andreev keeps her alive to hurt you. Pain is his power." He released Richard's wrists. "Take his power away."

"How?" Richard's voice cracked. "How do I just stop feeling this?"

"Embrace it." Frank's eyes were cold. "Pain makes you strong. Fear makes you weak."

"How can you be so sure?"

"You're in my world now, brother. You need to trust me."

The phone rang again. Richard's eyes went wide. Unwilling to trust his brother's emotions, Frank snapped up the receiver and said, "Speak."

"I was hoping you'd answer. I will give you one chance to save your niece. Fuck it up and she's dead. Am I clear?" said Andreev.

"Keep talking," said Frank.

The Belomorsk

Frank and Richard descended rusted stairs into darkness below the old city hall subway station. Frank wore his armored vest and the shoulder holsters that held his twin Redhawk revolvers. In his right hand he carried the Barrett M82 sniper rifle with a bipod on the heavy weapon's metal stock. In his left hand he carried his rucksack. Richard carried a laptop case on his shoulder.

Their flashlight beams cut through air thick with decades of undisturbed dust. Water dripped somewhere in the gloom, each drop echoing off tile walls streaked green with age.

The station sprawled beneath stone foundations of the old city hall, a cathedral built for trains that no longer ran. Vaulted ceilings disappeared into shadow. Brass chandeliers hung like dead spiders, their crystal tears long since shattered. Ornate columns rose from platforms edge, each carved with leaves and vines now drowning in layers of grime.

Frank's boots crunched on broken tiles. Faded murals lined the walls - scenes from a city's prouder days rendered in gold leaf and ceramic. Most had crumbled, leaving ghost-shapes against the tile. Those that remained showed men in top hats boarding trains that gleamed like polished dreams.

Frank's massive frame cast strange shadows against the walls. His boots found firm ground through years of debris. He tested each step before committing his weight. The platform had rotted in places, opening holes to darker spaces below.

A newspaper scuttled across their path, driven by underground wind through the tunnel. The date was still visible: October 1957. Richard's light caught rats scurrying through ancient turnstiles, their eyes reflecting red in the beam.

The tracks lay below, rails thick with rust. Water pooled black between the ties, dripping from creases in the ceiling. The smell of wet stone and decay pressed against their faces.

The side tunnels gaped like open throats. Their lights couldn't reach the ends. A train horn sounded in the distance, but not from these abandoned rails. The sound filtered down from active tunnels somewhere above, a ghost echo from a living system that had forgotten this place existed.

Frank touched the wall, traced a finger through filth. Beneath, brass letters spelled out the station's original name in Art Deco flourishes - City Hall Station. A remnant of glory buried beneath progress and time.

"The main platform is just ahead," said Richard.

Frank nodded. His eyes scanned the platform. Extending the rifle's bipod legs, he set the Barret down beside a steel column holding up the ceiling. It was good cover. He knew he would need it. He removed a Claymore mine from his rucksack, extended the two sets of legs, and set it up facing behind him with the detonator beside the rifle.

"Don't transfer Andreev's money until Grace is safe."

"Got it."

Frank pulled a small box from his rucksack. Inside was a wireless earphone and a headset. He gave the earpiece to Richard and put the headset over his ear.

Richard placed the earpiece in his ear and said, "Are you sure your plan is gonna work?"

"No," said Frank lying down behind the steel column and shouldering the Barret. He had a clear view of most of the main platform. "Stay where I can see you."

Richard nodded, then walked toward the platform.

Frank used the rifle's scope to survey the area. He could see several of Andreev's men lurking behind columns and arches.

As Richard approached the main platform, Andreev stepped out from behind an arch and said, "Are you ready to transfer my money?"

"Where is my daughter?"

Andreev motioned to Burke. Grace appeared with Burke holding her by the scruff of the neck.

"Daddy!" she cried out.

In shock, Richard said nothing. Grace was wearing a suicide vest wired with the explosives facing inward. Andreev held the remote trigger - a deadman's switch.

Watching through his scope Frank grunted like had been expecting something like this. He placed the scope's crosshairs on Andreev's hand. He could easily blow Andreev's hand off, but not without setting off the vest.

Richard was shocked to see Grace wearing the explosive vest. "What are you doing, Andreev?"

"Ensuring your full cooperation, Richard."

"If Grace dies, so do you. My brother will make sure of that."

"I would expect nothing less. So let's keep everything on track."

Frank spoke into the headset, "Grab his hand holding the switch and hold tight. I'll do the rest."

Richard listened, unsure. He would need to move a lot closer to do what Frank wanted.

Boots moved silent through ancient dust. Two of Andreev's men crept between columns on the opposite side of the tracks, flanking behind Frank's position.

They crossed over the tracks and moved up silently behind Frank. Their MP5s raised, fingers resting light on triggers.

Frank never turned, still focused through his scope on the stand-off ahead. The gunmen took careful aim at Frank's head. They carefully squeezed the triggers on their weapons.

Without looking, Frank's hand found the Claymore's detonator. He clicked it three times in rapid succession. The blast lit up the station like daylight. Seven hundred steel balls ripped through flesh and bone at 3500 feet per second. The men were shredded before their bodies hit the ground. Blood painted the walls in swaths of red. Frank never moved, his eye still fixed to his scope, watching the deadman's switch in Andreev's hand.

Andreev held his hand up high so Frank could clearly see the deadman's switch. "Think hard about your next move, Frank," called Andreev into the dark tunnel behind Richard.

"I'll transfer the money," said Richard hoping to stop Andreev.

"Don't," said Frank in Richard's ear.

Richard ignored his brother and opened his laptop He opened the first bank website and logged in with a long passcode.

"Smart move, Richard," said Andreev. "Grace may survive this yet."

Richard suddenly stopped typing into his laptop and looked puzzled. "What the hell?"

"What's wrong?" said Andreev.

"It's gone."

"What do you mean 'it's gone'?"

"It was there an hour ago and now… This isn't my fault, Andreev. The bank has made a mistake."

Andreev stepped forward to look at the laptop's screen. Everything looked normal as if it was ready to transfer. "What the hell are you talking about, Richard?" said Andreev.

And then he saw it – Richard's eyes, frightened but determined. Andreev took a step back. Letting the laptop tumble to the floor, Richard lunged at him, grabbing his hand holding the deadman's switch. Andreev punched him hard in the ribs using his hand connecting his broken shoulder. Andreev's pain was worse than Richard's. Richard held on to Andreev's hand preventing him from releasing the trigger.

Frank smiled slightly and said, "That a boy."

He took final aim and squeezed the rifle's trigger. The weapon bucked hard.

The massive .50 Caliber bullet flew through the tunnel's thick air. It barely missed Richard's head, then hit Andreev's hand just below the wrist. Bone and flesh exploded, spraying Richard in the face. He held on tight to Andreev's hand as it was severed from his forearm. Andreev grabbed his bloody stump as crimson flowed. It took him a moment to realize what was happening, then he screamed, "Kill the girl!"

But Frank had already taken aim at Burke. Another squeeze of the trigger and Burke's head exploded covering Grace in a spray of blood.

"Daddy!" screamed Grace and ran toward her father.

"No, Grace! Run to Frank," said Richard still holding Andreev's hand.

"Who's Frank?!" said Grace, confused.

"My brother. He's in the tunnel. Run to him."

Grace nodded and said, "What about you?"

"I'll be okay. Run!"

Grace ran into the darkness. Richard held his ground shielding his daughter from any gunfire while keeping Andreev's hand on the deadman's trigger.

"Grab the girl," yelled Andreev as he moved toward the platform exit.

Two gunmen ran after Grace.

Frank took aim once again, but Grace was blocking his shot. One of the gunmen reached Grace and snatched her up into his arm. He pulled Grace back toward Andreev keeping her body between him and Frank. Frank sprang to his feet, pulled out both of his revolvers. He ran toward Grace and the gunmen.

The second gunman opened fire with his MP5 spaying the tunnel with bullets. Frank had no choice, he pivoted behind a steel column. The bullets sang as they hit the steel, chipping away the rust.

Andreev used his belt as a torniquet to stop the bleeding. The first gunman reached him and turned over Grace. Andreev grabbed her roughly. "Grab Richard. He's coming with us," said Andreev.

The gunman obeyed and moved toward Richard.

Pinned down, Frank dove to the platform and fired his revolvers. The second gunman blew into pieces as three of the Redhawk's huge bullets found their mark.

Frank regained his footing and ran toward the gunman approaching Richard. Another gunman stepped out from behind an arch and leveled his MP5. At a dead run, Frank fired his revolvers turning the gunman into a spray of red mist.

The first gunman grabbed Richard and pulled him toward the platform's exit. Richard hung onto Andreev's hand wrapped around the deadman switch.

Two more gunmen sprang from hiding and opened fire at Frank charging like an angry bull. Frank fired a barrage using the last rounds in his revolvers, killing both gunmen.

Frank pulled out his KA-BAR and kept running. Richard and the gunman reached the base of the stairs. Frank stopped, took aim, and threw his knife. It landed in the back of the first gunman's neck shattering his spine. He released Richard as he fell to the ground dead. Through all of it, Richard had held onto Andreev's hand keeping Grace alive.

"Andreev's got Grace," said Richard.

Frank pulled out a roll of tape and quickly taped Andreev's finger to the deadman's trigger freeing Richard's hands. Frank reached down and pulled out his knife from the corpse. He tossed Richard the keys to the Imperial without explanation, then sprinted up the stairs. On his way up, Frank pulled a small tracking device from his pocket and attached it on the hilt of his KA-BAR using the tracker's powerful magnet.

When he reached the top of the stairs, he watched as Andreev and his men sped off in their black SUVs with Grace in the backseat. Frank drew back his huge arm and threw his knife at the SUV carrying Andreev and Grace. Tumbling end over end, the KA-BAR's blade slammed into the tailgate burying itself deep in the sheet metal.

A few moments later, the Imperial's engine roared as Richard pulled alongside Frank, chrome gleaming under streetlights. Frank yanked open the driver's door, shoving his brother aside as he folded his massive frame behind the wheel. His boots found the pedals as Richard scrambled into the passenger seat. The ancient V8 bellowed through straight pipes as Frank slammed it into drive.

"You're bleeding again," Richard said, eyeing the wound on Frank's arm.

Frank's grunt dismissed his brother's concern. His eyes fixed on taillights ahead as Andreev's convoy of six black SUVs wove through traffic. The Imperial surged forward, its engine gulping air through four barrels. Frank's hands wrapped around the steering wheel.

A taxi cut between them and the convoy. Frank never touched the brakes. The Imperial's bumper clipped the cab's rear quarter panel, spinning it aside. The taxi driver's curse was lost in screaming metal and breaking glass.

The convoy split up. Four SUVs formed a diamond around Andreev's vehicle while the sixth brought up the rear. They cut through intersections, forcing other drivers onto sidewalks. Horns blared. Tires squealed.

A semi-truck jackknifed trying to avoid the SUVs, its trailer blocking two lanes.

Frank guided the Imperial up onto the sidewalk, brick buildings inches from the passenger side mirror. Sparks flew as the undercarriage scraped concrete. They bounced back onto the street behind the convoy.

A gunman leaned from the trailing SUV's window, MP5 chattering. Rounds sparked off the Imperial's hood. The heavy steel absorbed the impacts like mosquito bites. Frank never flinched as bullets starred the windshield.

"Jesus Christ!" Richard ducked below the dash.

Frank stomped the accelerator. The Imperial's raw power hurled them forward. Its chrome bumper struck the rear SUV's quarter panel. The modern vehicle's frame crumpled as Frank steered it into a row of parked cars. The SUV flipped, tumbling through a storefront in a shower of glass and brick.

Two escort vehicles dropped back, trying to box in the Imperial. Frank downshifted, engine screaming. More gunfire erupted as an RPK light machine gun opened up, rounds stitching across the hood. The Imperial's engine block absorbed the fire.

A fuel tanker loomed ahead, blocking the street. The convoy scattered, two SUVs going left while Andreev's vehicle and two escorts cut right. Frank cranked the wheel, the Imperial's body rolling as its momentum carried them after Andreev.

"They're going to kill us," Richard said, gripping the dashboard.

Frank's eyes narrowed. The Imperial's grille struck the nearest SUV's rear bumper. Detroit steel met modern aluminum. The SUV spun sideways, rolling twice before striking a light pole with enough force to snap the steel column. The pole crashed down across the street, forcing oncoming traffic into a chaos of locked brakes and blaring horns.

The second escort vehicle tried to ram them. Frank timed his move, letting it come. At the last second he cranked the wheel hard. The SUV clipped the Imperial's rear quarter, the sedan absorbed the blow, sending the SUV into an uncontrolled spin. It slammed into a concrete construction barrier, crumpling like paper.

The two remaining SUVs accelerated, breaking formation to protect Andreev's vehicle. Frank pushed the Imperial harder. The engine temperature climbed into the red. A gunman emptied another magazine, bullets sparking off chrome. Water pressure dropped as rounds punctured the radiator, but the massive V8 kept pulling.

Steam leaked from under the hood as they entered the warehouse district. The convoy split again. Two SUVs cut between loading docks while Andreev's vehicle continued straight. Frank kept after Andreev, engine knocking as he closed the gap.

An escort SUV's brake lights flared. Frank accelerated, tons of American steel smashing into its rear end. The impact drove both vehicles forward. Sparks showered the street as metal ground against metal. The SUV's rear tires left the ground as Frank steered it toward a row of steel cargo containers. At the last second, Frank slammed on the brakes separating the two vehicles.

The SUV struck the containers with enough force to rock them on their foundations. Metal folded. Glass shattered. The SUV accordioned, its frame collapsing as physics and momentum extracted their toll.

But Andreev's SUV gained distance, weaving between warehouses. Frank floored the accelerator. The Imperial's engine coughed, then caught. They roared through a narrow alley, side mirrors snapping off against brick walls. Steam poured from under the hood, but Frank kept pushing.

The final escort vehicle appeared from a side street, t-boning the Imperial. The impact slid them sideways. Frank fought the wheel as they scraped along a loading dock. The Imperial's steel frame groaned but held. Frank reversed, then powered forward, pushing the SUV into a support column. The modern vehicle's safety systems triggered, airbags deploying as it wrapped around the concrete pole.

Andreev's SUV was pulling away, brake lights disappearing into the maze of streets. Overheated, the Imperial's engine finally gave out, decades of Detroit muscle surrendering to physics and gunfire. Frank guided the dying car to a stop, steel ticking as it cooled. Blood ran down his arm, dripping onto the leather seat. His face remained impassive despite their failure.

"We lost them," Richard said.

Frank's grunt carried cold certainty. They hadn't lost Andreev. They still had the tracking device.

The Imperial sat wounded but unbowed, chrome scarred and engine silent. Like its driver, the car had absorbed punishment that would have destroyed anything modern, anything softer.

Andreev stared at the stump where his right hand had been, still heavily bandaged. Cold anger washed through him at the memory of Frank's bullet smashing bone and flesh.

The black SUV rolled to a stop in the harbor lot. Sodium lights cast yellow pools between stacks of shipping containers. In the harbor, the Belomorsk's bulk rose against the night sky, her running lights reflecting off dark water.

Volkov did his security sweep of the area before Andreev left the vehicle. His flashlight beam caught metal glinting from the rear quarter panel. He moved closer, light settling on the knife buried deep in the sheet metal.

"Boss." He kept his voice level, professional. Something stuck to the hilt caught his eye. "You need to see this."

Andreev stepped from the lead vehicle, waves of rage rolling off him. His shoulder wound had bled through his expensive suit. With his remaining hand, he pulled the small tracker loose from the knife.

The loss of his hand had not diminished his fury. He crushed the tracker under his heel, grinding it to fragments on the pavement.

"Get the girl to the ship," he told Volkov. "Now."

Grace stumbled as guards shoved her toward the tender boat that ferried crew and passengers to the Belomorsk. Andreev watched her board, then turned back to Volkov. "Set up a perimeter. When Kane comes - and he will come - I want him dead before he reaches the ship."

Behind them, harbor waves lapped against pilings. Something huge was coming. They could all feel it.

Frank and Richard watched the laptop screen in the Imperial. The red dot blinked steady, showing Andreev's position at the harbor.

"He's taking her to his ship," Richard said. "The Belomorsk. He brought me there once, after a business meeting at his compound. Dropped him off before flying me back to my office." Richard's fingers drummed against the laptop case. "It's not just a cargo ship. The whole thing's wired like some floating command center. Servers, surveillance gear, satellite uplinks."

The red dot vanished.

"He must have found the tracker," Richard said. His voice caught. "The ship's his fortress, Frank. Security teams, automated weapons systems. No one gets aboard without Andreev's approval."

Frank grunted his disbelief.

Steam hissed from under the Imperial's hood. Frank popped the latch and lifted it, revealing a radiator riddled with bullet holes. His huge hands traced the punctures, assessing the damage. The engine block bore similar wounds but still held compression. Oil leaked from one of the valve covers. The old V8s were built to last.

The convenience store's bell chimed as Richard burst out carrying plastic bags stuffed with water bottles. "This was all they had," he said.

Frank pulled a roll of duct tape from the glove box. He rolled pieces of tape into plugs the size of the holes in the radiator and valve cover. His fingers patched each hole, then slapped a piece of tape over the plug to keep it in place. The tape wouldn't hold forever, but it didn't need to.

Richard twisted off bottle caps and poured water into the radiator. The liquid dripped through some of the patched holes, but most held. Frank kept working, sealing leaks until the radiator took fluid.

Jumping behind the wheel, Frank turned the key. The Imperial's starter groaned, then caught. The engine coughed clouds of steam but settled into a rough idle. Oil pressure was low and the temperature gauge climbed, but the massive V8 refused to die.

Like the man behind the wheel, the Imperial absorbed punishment that would destroy anything modern. Both man and machine were relics of an age when things were built to endure. To survive. To keep fighting long past when they should have failed.

Frank dropped the transmission into drive. The engine's knock grew louder but power still flowed through the drivetrain. They pulled away from the curb, leaving puddles of water and oil on the cracked asphalt.

"You're going to need more than those revolvers," Richard said. "He's got an army on that ship."

Frank's face remained impassive as he guided the car toward the harbor.

The doctor's iron hissed against raw flesh. Andreev's jaw clenched, but he made no sound as smoke rose from the stump where his hand had been.

Volkov entered Andreev's cabin, his face carefully neutral. "The men are asking questions, sir. About their pay."

Andreev's eyes opened. "Are they?"

"With your bank accounts being emptied..." Volkov let the words hang.

Andreev waved the doctor away with his good hand. He crossed to a wall safe set behind a panel of polished teak. His remaining palm pressed against the biometric scanner. The lock clicked.

Inside, bricks of hundred dollar bills lay stacked in precise rows. Andreev grabbed several bundles one-handed, tossed them to Volkov. American currency hit the deck with solid thwaps.

"Pay them," Andreev said. "We'll operate on cash until the banking situation is resolved."

Volkov hefted the money. "And when might that be?"

"Soon." Andreev's eyes drifted to the cauterized stump. "Very soon."

Outside the cabin, waves slapped against steel hull plates. The money would keep his men loyal for now. But Andreev knew time was running short. He needed to finish this.

He gestured for the doctor to continue. The iron descended again, filling the air with the stench of burning flesh.

The Imperial's engine died with a low rumble as Frank cut the lights. The yacht club's gate gleamed under sodium lamps, its heavy padlock taking only seconds to yield to Frank's picks. The tumblers clicked open with familiar precision.

Inside, boats bobbed at their moorings, hulls creaking against weathered docks. Frank moved between them, his boots silent on wet planks. The waterproof bag slung across his massive shoulders held his tools - shaped charges, detonators, his Redhawk revolvers and plenty of extra ammunition. Diving fins protruded from the top, alongside a black tactical mask and snorkel.

Richard followed, trying to match his brother's quiet stride. Frank stopped at a black cigarette boat. Forty feet of raw horsepower built for running fast and deep. Its low profile and dark hull would blend with harbor shadows. His found the hatch lock, made quick work of it. The engine compartment yielded to the same treatment.

Richard watched his brother's fingers dance across wires beneath the console. "A cigarette boat is a bit ostentatious, isn't it?"

"I like to get out of trouble as fast as I get into it," said Frank.

"I guess that makes sense."

"Can you pilot this thing?"

"I can manage."

The twin Mercury engines caught with a muted growl.

Salt air whipped at their faces as Richard eased them away from the dock, keeping the throttle low until they cleared the marina. Once in open water, Richard opened the engines up. The bow lifted as they cut through harbor chop, throwing white spray. Behind them, the city's lights faded to a distant glow. Ahead, the Belomorsk's bulk rose from darkness like a steel mountain. Following Frank's instructions, Richard kept them in the shipping channel's shadows, running without lights.

Water slapped against the hull as they sliced through waves. Frank gripped the gunwale, his eyes fixed on the darkness ahead where Grace waited. The cigarette boat ate distance in engine thunder and salt spray.

Richard watched his brother's profile, understanding for the first time why the world needed men like Frank. He had spent years despising his brother's violence, his separation from civilized life. Now that same darkness was their only hope. Richard's fingers tightened on the wheel as shame and gratitude warred in his gut.

The cigarette boat's engines died to an idle 300 yards off the Belomorsk's stern. Richard cut power completely. Frank shrugged off his shirt, revealing a torso mapped with scars - knife wounds, bullet holes, burns. Violence written in flesh. He pulled on the mask and fins, checked his waterproof bag one final time. The weight of the revolvers and explosives inside felt right.

Without a word, Frank slipped into black harbor water. The cold hit like a fist but he barely noticed. He adjusted his snorkel and submerged, kicking deeper where the water grew colder. His powerful strokes ate up the distance, arms pulling against resistance. The ship's running lights cast wavering columns through murky depths. Fish scattered at his approach.

The anchor chain appeared, thick links vanishing up into darkness. Frank followed it, conserving air, staying in shadow. His lungs began to burn, but he ignored them. Near the surface, voices filtered down - guards speaking Russian, their words distorted by water. Frank hung motionless, listening to their boot steps move away across steel deck plates.

He surfaced in the anchor chain's shadow, pulled off his mask. Saltwater ran in rivulets down his face. The guards' voices grew fainter. Frank began to climb, massive arms hauling his weight up chain link by link. The iron was slippery with green slime. The wet bag dragged at his shoulder. Halfway up, boot steps returned. Frank froze, hanging by one arm. A guard appeared at the rail above, rifle slung across his chest.

Smoke curled from his cigarette. Frank remained motionless. The guard finished his smoke, flicked it into the harbor. The ember traced a red arc through darkness. Boot steps receded. Frank resumed climbing.

He mounted the rail silent, water streaming from his legs. The guard had vanished around a corner. As jumped down onto the deck, Frank pulled his twin Ruger Super Redhawk revolvers and holster from the wet bag. He did a quick check to ensure they were operational by rolling each of the cylinders and checking the hammers. Harbor water dripped from his clothes, seeping around the shoulder holster. He fished out the derringer from the wet bag and placed it in his wet pants pocket.

The orange and white lifeboats hung outboard on steel davits, their fiberglass shells reflecting dim harbor light. Frank tested the sealed door of the nearest one. The latch yielded to his muscles.

Inside lay darkness and the sharp smell of fiberglass resin. He slipped the wet bag beneath a molded bench, fingers checking that his spare ammunition rode secure. A radio crackled somewhere above. Frank eased the door closed and moved toward the steel containers stacked on the ship's deck, leaving the lifeboat and its cargo suspended in night air. His bare feet made no sound as he began to hunt through the freighter's steel maze. The revolvers pressed cold against his ribs, ready. The weapons in the bag could wait. For now, three guns and his hands would be enough.

He moved toward the superstructure, bare feet silent on steel deck. Somewhere above, Grace waited. Frank felt nothing but cold purpose as he began to hunt.

The superstructure loomed five stories above deck, its steel flanks scarred by salt and time. Frank found a maintenance ladder bolted to the hull, rungs slick with ocean spray. He climbed one-handed, one revolver ready, massive shoulders rolling with each pull. His wet clothes clung like a second skin.

The first hatch yielded to his massive hand, hinges oiled against sea air. Inside, fluorescent lights hummed in empty corridors that smelled of diesel and sweat.

Frank rounded the corner and froze. A guard stood three feet away, his eyes widening at Frank's sudden appearance. Before the man could reach for his slung MP5, Frank's fist caught him square in the face. Bone and cartilage collapsed under Frank's knuckles. With Frank's help the guard dropped without a sound, blood pooling beneath his head.

Frank dragged him toward a maintenance room. Tools hung on steel walls, their shadows sharp in dim light. The guard's boots scraped deck plates. Frank couldn't tell if he still breathed. Couldn't risk it. The man had made his choice. Frank's massive hands found the guard's jaw and crown. One sharp twist. The neck broke with a wet crack. Frank eased the body behind shelves of cleaning supplies, shut the door. He moved back into the corridor, continuing his search.

Frank moved through shadows, water still dripping. His feet left wet prints on steel steps but the darkness hid them. Red emergency lights cast bloody shadows across bulkheads riveted with thick steel.

A guard's voice echoed through metal corridors ahead. Frank pressed against a bulkhead. Boot steps passed within inches. The guard's radio squawked, Russian words distorted by static. Frank didn't move until the steps faded.

The corridors twisted like a maze. Frank struggled to keep a mental map of where he had searched. The ship groaned around him, steel flexing against harbor swells. Frank checked rooms methodically - crew quarters with narrow bunks still warm from sleeping bodies, storage compartments filled with crates stenciled in Cyrillic, a galley that smelled of fried fish and cigarettes. No Grace. His revolver stayed ready, trained on every shadow.

Voices approached. Frank ducked into a side passage as three guards rounded the corner, MP5s slung across tactical vests. Their whispered Russian carried through recycled air. One paused, head cocked. Something had caught his attention. Frank's finger settled on the Redhawk's trigger. The guard shrugged, moved on. Frank waited until their steps faded before continuing his search.

A ladder led up to the next deck. Frank climbed silently despite his size, keeping to shadows. Water dripped from his clothes, each drop echoing in the confined space. At the top, light spilled from an open hatch.

Inside, a guard sat watching security feeds, cigarette smoke curling around his head. His boot tapped against the chair leg in a slow rhythm. Frank eased past, the guard never turning from his screens.

More corridors branched like veins through the ship's steel heart. Each empty room increased the cold knot in Frank's gut. They'd moved her off the ship. The thought settled like ice in his chest. A door creaked somewhere ahead. Frank froze. Boots on metal - multiple guards approaching from both directions. Their voices bounced off walls, growing louder.

Frank tried a hatch. Locked. Another. Also locked. The steps grew closer, echoing through steel passages. A third hatch opened and Frank slipped inside, easing it shut as guards passed. He stood in darkness, surrounded by paint and supplies that reeked of industrial chemicals. Voices stopped outside. Keys jingled. The hatch began to open. Frank raised his revolver.

A radio crackled. Words Frank couldn't understand. The guards moved away, boots ringing on steel. Frank waited two full minutes before emerging. The ship's guts seemed to swallow him as he pushed deeper into the maze of corridors. But Grace wasn't there. Which meant only one possible place remained - the bridge. Frank's jaw clenched. They wanted him to come up. He'd oblige them.

The ladder to the bridge deck waited, rising into shadow. Frank touched the first rung, steel cold against his palm. Above, Grace waited… hopefully. Frank began to climb, each step carrying him closer to violence. His scars ached with old memories, but pain was welcome now. Pain meant he was still alive and there was still a chance at success.

Frank moved through shadow, water still dripping from his wet clothes, making puddles on the steel floor plates. The corridor ahead opened into a wider passage.

Boot steps approached. He pressed against a bulkhead as Kolkov strode past, Frank's KA-BAR jutting from the back of his web belt. The knife's blade caught dim light from overhead fixtures. Frank's eyes fixed on the weapon. He'd carried that knife through war zones and on covert missions. The leather grip bore the imprints of his fingers from dozens of kills.

The blood of better men than Kolkov had stained its steel.

Frank followed, keeping to darkness. Kolkov's boots rang against deck plates as he moved deeper into the ship's maze. The Russian paused, lit a cigarette. Smoke curled toward pipes that ran along the ceiling. Frank closed the distance, each step silent despite his size.

Kolkov never saw what grabbed him. Frank's arm locked around his throat, cutting off air and blood. The Russian thrashed but Frank's grip was iron. Kolkov's feet left the deck as Frank lifted him, muscles bulging beneath his skin. The cigarette fell, ember spinning across steel. Darkness took Kolkov.

Frank lowered the unconscious body, retrieved his knife. The familiar weight settled in his palm like coming home. He pressed the blade against Kolkov's throat. One cut and arterial blood would paint the deck. The Russian's pulse beat against cold steel.

Boot steps echoed from around the corner. Voices speaking rapid Russian grew closer. Frank melted into shadow, leaving Kolkov sprawled on deck plates. The knife disappeared beneath Frank's wet clothes as two guards rounded the corner. They shouted in alarm at finding Kolkov. Frank was already gone, moving deeper into the ship's steel heart. The knife rode against his ribs, ready for whatever was coming.

Frank shouldered through the bridge door, both revolvers ready. The helmsman spun, reaching for his sidearm. Frank's first shot took him in the chest blowing a hole the size of a child's fist through his body. The navigator died trying to key his radio, his head exploding. The captain charged with a knife.

Frank caught his wrist, twisted. Bone snapped. The captain's scream cut short as Frank's shot ended him.

Blood ran between deck plates. Shell casings rolled with the ship's motion. Frank moved to the helm, his hands finding throttles. The electrical panel caught his eye. Switches controlled both bow and stern anchors. He threw them. Chain rumbled through hawse pipes. The ship shuddered as anchors broke free from the sea floor.

The alarm screamed through steel corridors. They'd found Kolkov or heard the shots from his guns. It didn't matter. There was an intruder on board.

Frank advanced the throttles. Diesel engines roared deep in the ship's belly. The massive vessel lurched forward, straining against inertia. Water churned white against the bow. The harbor's night traffic lay dead ahead.

The ship's sudden lurch caught Andreev off balance. He stumbled, his handless arm flailing against a bulkhead. The wound felt like fire as it thumped against steel.

Steel groaned as the stern anchor chain dragged across the harbor floor. The deck pitched beneath his feet. His shoulder wound screamed as he caught himself on the edge of a desk. Instruments tumbled. Papers scattered like leaves. Andreev snatched up the bridge phone with his remaining hand. Static answered. He slammed it down, snatched his radio instead. "Bridge, report." Nothing. "Bridge!" His voice cracked with fury.

The ship's engines roared louder, pushing the massive vessel faster through dark water. Kane. The name burned in his mind. Blood dripped from his bandaged stump as his fist clenched. He keyed his radio again. "All units. Find Kane. Now. Shoot on sight, $100,000 to the man that kills him."

The response came fast - acknowledgments in Russian, boots already moving through steel corridors. "He's hunting for the girl. Check every deck, every corner, every hatchway." Andreev steadied himself as the ship heeled into a turn. "Find him before he finds her." The radio crackled with orders as his men spread through the ship. Andreev stared at his ruined wrist. Soon Kane would learn that some things were worse than death. Much worse.

Frank searched the bridge's storage compartments. Nothing. A hatch led down to the radio room. Empty. The chart room held only maps and instruments. No Grace. Each dead end twisted the knot in his gut tighter. The ship's motion grew stronger as it gained speed.

He found the captain's quarters behind a teak door. The bed was still made, brass fittings gleaming. The head showed signs of recent use - a wet towel, steam on the mirror. Frank pulled open the closet. Uniforms swayed with the ship's roll. He checked under the bed, behind chairs. Grace's absence felt like a physical thing.

The ship's alarm wailed through every compartment. Boots pounded on steel stairs as guards rushed to respond. Frank moved back into shadow as a fire team passed below, weapons ready. Their shouts echoed off bulkheads. The deck plates thrummed beneath his feet as the engines pushed 300,000 tons of steel through dark water.

Somewhere in the ship's guts, Grace waited. The vessel's motion would work in his favor - guards trying to maintain balance would be slower to react. Frank touched the KA-BAR riding against his ribs as he descended into the depths. Ahead, more corridors branched like veins through the ship's heart. He chose one and moved forward, staying in darkness. The hunt continued. And then it hit him…

Frank moved outside the superstructure onto a balcony. Wind whipped at his clothes, still wet from the harbor. The truth hit him like a physical blow. He'd been hunting through empty rooms while Grace sat trapped in a steel box. His hands gripped the rail as he stared out at the containers - a maze of metal stretching the length of the ship. They rose from the deck like a metal mountain range, thousands of boxes stacked four high. Different colors, different shipping lines. Some fresh-painted, others corroded by years of salt spray.

The ship plowed deeper into harbor waters, containers creaking against their lashings. Waves broke white against the bow. An impossible task. Grace could be in any of them, sealed away behind steel doors. No sounds would escape. No signs would show. Frank scanned the rows. Too many places to hide someone. Too many possibilities.

Guards shouted in Russian from below, their voices thin in the wind. They'd retake the bridge soon. Frank touched the KA-BAR at his ribs, its familiar weight offering no comfort. Grace was down there somewhere, trapped in a steel cell. But which one?

The containers blurred together in the sodium lights, a rhythm of metal edges and sharp corners that seemed to mock him. Frank's scars ached with old memories as he studied the maze below. He'd fought his way through the ship for nothing. The real challenge lay in those silent boxes stretching into darkness.

Andreev stormed onto the bridge, guards spreading out behind him, weapons ready. Blood from dead crewmen still ran between deck plates. He moved to the helm with his remaining hand, eased back the throttle. The massive ship shuddered as the engines slowed. Harbor traffic lay scattered in their wake, horns blaring in protest.

"Get this mess cleaned up," he snapped, gesturing at the bodies with his bandaged stump. His radio crackled. "Still no sign of Kane." Andreev's jaw clenched. "Boris, Matvey - reinforce the girl's container. Now." The guards nodded, rushed out.

Frank watched from shadow as two guards sprinted across the deck toward the container stacks. Their boots rang against steel as they wound through the maze of boxes. His eyes narrowed. The men moved with purpose, knowing exactly where they were going.

Frank followed, staying low, letting the guards lead him to Grace. The KA-BAR seemed to pulse against his ribs as he stalked them through the metal canyon. Wind whipped between containers, masking his steps. The guards disappeared around a corner. Frank gave them ten seconds, then moved after them.

The guards stood before a rust-streaked container, MP5s cradled against their tactical vests. Their breath caught silver in sodium light. The new arrivals took positions beside the original guards, four men total forming a box around the container door. Wind moaned between steel walls. Frank moved from shadows.

The first guard never saw what hit him. Frank's hands caught his head, one on jaw, one on crown. The wet crack of breaking bone was lost in the wind. As the body crumpled, Frank was already moving. The second guard's eyes went wide as the KA-BAR slashed across his throat. Blood sprayed black in dim light.

The third guard managed to bring up his MP5. Two shots cracked out. One round grazed Frank's arm, tearing flesh. Frank didn't feel it. His boot caught the guard's knee, shattering it sideways. As the man fell screaming, Frank's massive hands found his throat. Cartilage collapsed under brutal fingers.

The fourth guard backpedaled, fumbling for his radio. Frank closed the distance in two steps. His fist caught the man's temple, a hammer blow that caved in his skull. The guard dropped without a sound, radio clattering away across steel deck plates.

Blood flowed hot down Frank's arm, but the pain was distant, unimportant. The bodies leaked red pools around his boots. He pulled out his lock picks and went to work on the container lock. It was open in less than ten seconds until the lock sprang open. Hinges shrieked. The door swung wide.

Grace huddled in the corner, knees pulled tight to her chest. Terror filled her eyes as she stared at Frank's giant silhouette in the spilled light. Then recognition slowly dawned. The face was her father's but twisted by violence, like looking at Richard through broken glass.

"Uncle Frank?"

Frank's grunt was lost in the wind. He crossed the container in two steps, bloody arm leaving prints on steel walls. Grace yelped as he scooped her up, throwing her over his shoulder like she weighed nothing. Her world tilted sideways as Frank ran.

His boots rang sharp against the deck as he wound through the metal maze. Grace bounced against his back, saltwater from his clothes soaking into her shirt. Shouts erupted behind them, voices sharp with alarm. Gunfire cracked out. Rounds sparked off containers, throwing blue metal fragments. Frank fired back, the heavy rounds thundering against the containers' metal walls. Guards ducked for cover as the bullets from Frank's gun punched through steel.

Frank ran faster, Grace clinging to his wet shirt. More guards would come, drawn by the shots. But they'd have to be faster than Frank to catch him. In all his years of covert missions, few men were. Once Frank got moving, he was like a freight train. Unstoppable.

Frank ducked into the enclosed lifeboat where he had stashed his rucksack, the fiberglass shell glowing orange and white in the glare of searchlights. He lifted Grace up and pulled her inside. He shut the heavy hatch behind them, sealing off the wind and spray.

Grace huddled in the cramped space as Frank's bulk filled the narrow aisle between bench seats. His blood left dark streaks on white fiberglass where his wounded arm brushed against the vessel's wall.

Boot stomped across steel deck plates above them. Frank's hand found Grace's shoulder, urging her lower. She curled beneath a bench as voices shouted in Russian. Frank's fingers traced the hatch seal, checking it. He quietly reloaded his pistols with speed loaders from the rucksack.

Searchlight beams pierced the small windows, casting harsh shadows inside the capsule. Grace watched her uncle's ravaged face, seeing her father's features reshaped by violence into something harder.

Finished reloading, Frank pointed both barrels at the door. Frank remained motionless except for the slow rise and fall of his massive chest. Blood dripped onto the textured floor, spreading in thin tendrils. His eyes stayed fixed on the hatch, watching through the small window. Pain from his wounded arm meant nothing. Pain was focus.

Grace's words tumbled out in excited whispers. "I never even knew my dad had a brother."

"Quiet," Frank rasped, his ruined voice barely audible above waves slapping against the hull.

"But you'll kill the bad guys if they come, right?" Grace whispered. Her eyes found the fresh wound on his arm where blood still flowed. "You're bleeding."

The wound was on the back of his arm making it hard to reach. Frank pulled needle and thread from his wet bag, fingers thick as he tried to guide the thin metal through torn flesh. The thread tangled, refusing to cooperate with hands better suited to violence than delicate work.

Grace watched him struggle for a moment before reaching out. "Let me." She took the needle from his calloused fingers. Frank's eyes narrowed, but he offered his arm.

Her small hands worked with surprising skill, each stitch neat and precise as she closed the ragged gash. Blood stained her fingers, but she never hesitated, pulling the wound edges together with careful tension.

Frank studied her work without expression.

"Birthday cards would have been nice. Maybe a fifty tucked inside," she whispered. "I'm just saying…"

"I didn't know you existed," said Frank.

"Oh, well… I guess that makes us even."

She tied off the last stitch. Frank cut the suture with the KA-BAR. Grace wiped her bloody hands on her shirt. "Mom made me take a first aid course last summer. Said it would look good on college applications." She gave a quiet laugh. "Guess it came in handy."

Frank shushed her.

Grace found the lifeboat's first aid kit and opened it. Fishing through the medical supplies she found a large bandage. She opened the package and placed the bandage on Frank's arm covering the wound. "Good as new," said whispered.

Frank grunted.

Voices carried across the deck above - guards searching methodically through the night. Grace fell silent, pressing closer to her uncle's massive frame as boots passed nearby. For now, the darkness held them safe.

"I need to end this," said Frank.

"You're not going to leave me?!" said Grace panicking.

"I'll be back soon."

"Let me go with you."

"No. You'll be safer here."

"Unless they find me."

"They won't. I'll lead them away."

Frank pulled out the derringer. "Ever fire a gun?"

"Just paintball at Mallory's birthday party."

"You get two shots. Pull the hammer back until it clicks, then pull the trigger. Pull the hammer back a second time and pull the trigger. Let 'em get close and aim for their head."

"Okay. I can do that."

Frank nodded, then handed her the derringer.

"And don't shoot me."

"Right. Don't shoot Uncle Frank. Got it."

Frank grunted unsure.

"If I am not back in twenty minutes, there's a flare gun in the lifeboat's emergency box," he said pointing. "Fire a flare into the sky and your dad will come get you."

"What about you?"

"Don't worry about me. I'll be dead."

"That's not fair. We just met. You can't die."

"I'll do my best not to."

"Thanks."

Grabbing the rucksack, Frank looked out through the lifeboat's windows, then climbed out through the doorway shutting the door behind him.

Grace sat in the darkness staring at the derringer going over what her uncle had said. She mustered her confidence. "Two shots. Aim for the head," she said quietly to herself. She believed she could shoot a bad guy, but really hoped it wouldn't be necessary.

Frank climbed the steel stairs in the superstructure's stairwell, pausing on each landing to listen. The superstructure was a labyrinth of offices and crew quarters.

The first brick of C4 went behind a fuse panel near a steel support column. Frank's sausage-sized fingers molded the explosive precisely, his movements mechanical. The ship's rolling made the work difficult, but his hands never wavered. He inserted the timed detonator, checked the connections twice.

A guard's voice echoed up the stairwell. Frank lifted his bulk over the railing, hanging by one arm as the guard's boots passed inches from his fingers. The guard's keys jingled with each step. Frank waited until the sound faded before pulling himself back up.

More charges went into key structural points - junctions where support beams met bulkheads, corners that bore the most weight. Frank worked methodically upward through the decks. Each charge had to be perfect. The superstructure's collapse would seal off escape routes, trap men in steel coffins, and most of all... kill Andreev.

On the fourth deck, Frank froze as a door opened. Two officers rushed past, discussing the search for the intruder in Russian. Their polished shoes clicked on steel plates. Frank pressed into an alcove. One officer stopped, lit a cigarette. The ember glowed inches from Frank's hiding spot before they moved on.

The fifth deck housed navigation equipment and radio gear. Frank placed charges where they would do the most damage - near load-bearing walls, beside critical electronics. His fingers traced wiring paths, finding nodes where systems intersected. The bridge lay directly above. Its destruction would blind the ship.

Voices approached - a work crew coming to check communications equipment. Frank slipped into a maintenance shaft as boots rang on metal. Tools scraped against deck plates. The workers' conversation echoed off steel walls. Frank held motionless until they passed, then resumed his work. He checked his watch. The timed detonators were counting down. Time was running short.

Frank moved silently down the fifth deck corridor toward Andreev's quarters. The oligarch's private domain sprawled across the ship's top level - a series of interconnected rooms protected by steel doors and electronic locks. Frank pulled more C4 from his rucksack. This charge would be larger than the others. No chances.

His fingers shaped the explosive against the wall where it joined Andreev's bedroom. The blast would collapse the outer wall, turning the room into a tomb of twisted metal. Frank's fingers traced connections in the dark, checking each wire. A timed detonator went into this charge, meant for breaching armor.

Boot steps echoed from around the corner. Frank pressed under stairs as two guards passed, speaking low Russian. Their weapons caught red light from emergency fixtures. He waited until they turned the corner before finishing his work. The timer would synchronize with his other charges - detonating as one.

He set the detonator, checked the connections one last time.

Hearing steps on steel plates, Frank retrieved his KA-BAR as he moved back toward the stairs. A guard emerged from a side passage. The knife caught him under the chin, its blade angled up into the brain. Frank lowered the body without a sound and continued his sabotage.

The charges went in near the bridge access. Frank could hear movement above - officers coordinating the search, radio static, urgent voices in Russian.

Setting the detonator, Frank started down through the steel maze he had wired to explode. His boots made no sound on metal steps. A guard rounded the corner, MP5 raised. The man's neck broke before he could squeeze the trigger. Frank caught the body, lowered it quietly to the deck.

He passed the fourth deck as shouts erupted above. They'd found the dead guard. Boots thundered on steel stairs. Frank pressed into shadow as men rushed past, weapons ready. Their radios crackled with orders. The hunt intensified.

Frank descended past crew quarters, staying close to the walls. A door opened ahead. He grabbed the crewman's throat before he could cry out, dragged him into darkness. The body slumped to the deck with a soft thud.

The second deck bustled with activity - search teams mustering, officers barking orders. Frank waited in a maintenance closet as boots passed. Sweat ran down his face despite the cold.

Frank moved through shadow toward the engine room access, each step calculated. A guard walked the catwalk above, boots ringing on steel. Frank pressed against a bulkhead. The guard's radio crackled. Frank caught fragments of Russian - teams sweeping the forward decks, others searching the stern. The man's cigarette ember traced lazy arcs in darkness before he moved on.

The engine room hatch yielded silently to Frank's massive hands. Heat billowed up from below, carrying the reek of diesel fuel and hot metal. He began his descent. The massive engines grew louder, their synchronized rumble filling the space like mechanical thunder.

Three decks down, Frank entered the engine room proper. Twin V16 diesels towered over him, their cylinder heads disappearing into shadows above. Turbos the size of oil drums fed pressurized air into manifolds thick as a man's torso. The engines' combined 14,000 horsepower sent vibrations through the deck plates that Frank felt in his bones. The engines generated energy for the ship's instruments and the energy hungry electronics used by Andreev's hackers and communication technicians.

He moved between the huge machines, staying low. A technician in orange coveralls checked gauge readings on a clipboard twenty feet ahead. Frank waited as the technician made notes, sweat gleaming on his balding head in the harsh light. The clipboard clattered to the deck. As the technician bent to retrieve it, Frank slipped past unseen.

Deeper in the mechanical space, catwalks crisscrossed overhead. Frank caught movement - two guards patrolling the upper level. Their boots struck metal in perfect rhythm. He tracked their pattern, noting the thirty-second gap between passes. The fuel tanks lay on the far side of their patrol route.

Frank pressed into an alcove as boots approached. A guard descended the ladder, his back to Frank. The man's neck broke with a wet crack before he could turn. Frank caught the body, eased it behind a fuel purifier. Blood flowing from the man's nostrils spread across the deck in thin streams.

More voices echoed from above - a work crew coming to check the port engine's injector timing. Frank moved quickly through the mechanical maze, counting seconds between the guards' passes overhead. Sweat ran down his face from the engine room heat.

The main fuel tanks rose before him, three stories of steel containing thousands of gallons of marine diesel. Frank pulled the last bricks of C4 from his rucksack. The first charge went against the forward tank's base, where the blast would rupture both the tank and the ship's hull. His fingers moved with practiced efficiency, molding the explosive and inserting the detonator. Setting the timer he realized how little time was left. He picked up his pace.

A wrench clattered on the catwalk above. Frank froze, explosives in hand. A technician cursed in Russian. Tools scraped on metal as the man searched in darkness. Frank remained motionless until the boots moved away. Two more charges to place. Each had to be precise.

He worked methodically, setting charges at structural weak points.

Frank set the final charge as boots rang on the ladder behind him. He pressed against the fuel tank's warm steel as two guards descended, speaking rapid Russian. Their lights swept the space. Frank stood motionless. The beams passed over him once, twice, before the guards moved on.

He checked the charges one final time. Everything had to be perfect - the timing, the placement, the delayed fuses.

A technician looked up from his gauges, mouth opening in surprise. Frank's fist caught his throat before he could shout. The body slumped quietly behind a generator.

He climbed past heat exchangers and purifiers. Three guards rushed past below, responding to movement on the cargo deck. Their boots rang sharp against steel. Frank counted his breaths, waiting for them to pass. He checked his watch, unsure he could make it back to Grace.

He reached the upper engine room access. Voices carried from the next compartment. Frank pressed into darkness as the watertight door opened. Light spilled across the deck. Two engineers entered, discussing valve timing in Russian. Frank's muscles coiled, but the men turned away, heading deeper into the engine room. They had just saved their own lives.

Frank moved through the passageway, staying low. He reached the weather deck, wind whipping at his clothes. Searchlights swept the container stacks. Frank counted his steps through the metal maze, marking his path back to Grace. Three minutes remained as the lifeboat's orange hull appeared ahead. He checked his surroundings before opening the hatch.

Hearing the hatch opening, Grace raised the derringer and cocked the hammer back. Then she saw Frank's disfigured face appear through the doorway. "You came back," Grace said with a grin.

Frank took the derringer from her small hands and uncocked the hammer. She looked disappointed that it had been taken away. "I wasn't going to shoot you. Really," she said.

He handed the weapon back. "It's time to go. Hand me the flare gun and a flare," he said.

She grabbed both and handed them to him. "Let's go," he said helping her out the doorway.

Frank fired the flare into the night sky. Next, he released the lifeboat. It lowered into the harbor. He turned to Grace and said, "Can you swim?"

"Yes… in a pool," she said with confidence.

Frank nodded, then picked her and threw her over the side. She screamed until she plunged into the cold water.

Frank watched as her head bobbed up and she began treading water.

Frank reached for the railing to vault over when movement caught his eye. Six gunmen emerged from behind containers, MP5s raised. The first burst caught the railing near his head, throwing blue sparks into the night. Frank drew his revolvers. The heavy weapons boomed, their muzzle flashes painting Frank's ravaged face in stark light.

Two gunmen fell, their bodies tumbling across steel deck. More rounds snapped past as Frank fired again, the massive revolvers' recoil like nothing in his grip. His eyes found his watch - no time left.

He jumped over the side, plunging into black harbor water. The cold hit like a fist. Grace treaded water nearby, her face pale in the darkness. Frank grabbed her with one massive arm. "Hold your breath," he rasped. She nodded, sucking in air before he pulled her under wrapping her arms around his neck and pushing her onto his back.

The gunmen ran to the railing and looked over seeing the lifeboat in the water. Believing Frank and Grace were inside, they opened fire.

Frank and Grace sank into murky depths as gunfire erupted above. Through the water, Frank watched tracers tear into the lifeboat. The MP5s' rounds shredded fiberglass, sending fragments spinning through darkness. Water rushed in through the holes flooding the vessel. The orange hull disappeared beneath waves.

Frank kicked deeper, Grace clinging to his neck. His powerful strokes carried them toward the stern anchor chain. They surfaced in its shadow, Grace gasping quietly. The guards leaned over the rail, their weapons trained on the lifeboat's last position. Satisfied with their kill, they moved back toward the superstructure. Frank heard them radio Andreev in rapid Russian - targets eliminated.

Frank touched Grace's arm, pointed toward Richard piloting the cigarette boat approaching in darkness. She nodded, understanding. Still hanging on to his neck, Grace took another deep breath as Frank began swimming away from the Belomorsk's steel flanks.

They popped up next to the cigarette boat, its engines idling. Richard reached down and hauled Grace from the freezing harbor, crushing her against his chest. "My baby," he sobbed, running trembling hands over her face as if to make sure she was real. "Are you okay?"

"Yeah. Uncle Frank saved me."

"He's good at that."

"He sure is."

Water ran from her hair but neither noticed. Grace clung to him, her small fingers digging into his shirt, then pushed away with exciting news… "Uncle Frank gave me a gun."

"He what?!" said Richard.

"To kill bad guys."

"You need to give it back to him."

"Okay, but it's just a small one."

"You're not keeping the gun, Gracie."

"Right. No guns, Dad."

Frank's bulk landed beside them, like a wet bear. "Go, now," said Frank.

"I'm on it," said Richard jumping back behind the boat's control and gunning the engines.

As the boat picked up speed, Richard opened the throttles wide. The cigarette boat's twin Mercury engines roared as the bow lifted, its hull throwing white spray.

Behind them thunder erupted from the Belomorsk's depths. The first blast turned night to day. Flames roared through ruptured steel, consuming everything in their path. Men's screams carried across the water as fire chased them through corridors. The superstructure charges detonated in sequence, each explosion more violent than the last. Steel groaned as decks pancaked downward, burying men alive in tombs of twisting metal.

"Dear God," Richard whispered, shielding Grace's face against his chest. But she pulled away, wanting to see. Her eyes reflected the inferno as the bridge erupted.

Through walls of flame, they saw Andreev stagger onto the wing. His clothes had become his funeral pyre. He flailed with his remaining hand, flesh blackening, melting from his bones. His screams rose above the explosions - the sound of a demon discovering Hell was real. Then he fell, trailing fire through darkness until the harbor swallowed him.

When the fuel tanks detonated, the Belomorsk's spine shattered with a sound like mountains breaking. Her bow lifted toward stars now hidden by smoke. Containers crashed into the sea, each impact sending waves across the harbor. Burning men jumped from her decks, their bodies small against the massive ship's death throes. Some screamed until they hit the water. Others fell silent, accepting their fate.

Grace pressed against Frank's massive side, shaking with cold and horror and relief. His huge hand found her shoulder, steadying her. She felt the coiled strength in his grip - the same strength that had carried her through darkness to safety. They watched the Belomorsk sink beneath black water.

Fireboats and a Coast Guard ship raced toward the wreckage. The harbor churned with burning fuel and dying men. Grace looked up at her uncle's ravaged face, seeing the flames dance in his eyes. "Is it over?" she whispered.

Frank's grunt was soft, almost gentle. His grip tightened slightly on her shoulder - not to hurt, but to reassure. They watched until the last giant bubbles broke the surface, until only floating debris marked the Belomorsk's grave. The water went black as oil, reflecting the fires still burning on its surface. Grace felt the tension finally leave Frank's massive frame.

Cookies

The Imperial battered but not bowed sat in the Kane driveway leaking oil on the pristine concreate. It had made it back home... barely.

Through the pool house windows, Frank watched Richard and Vivian embrace Grace in the mansion's bright living room, their shadows cast against silk curtains. Grace was chattering about what had happened. Richard and Vivian just listened grateful to hear her voice. A family whole again.

Frank turned away from their reunion. As grateful as Richard and Vivian were for what he had done, he didn't belong. He never would. He had chosen a path in life and it didn't include a family. His was a world of violence and that was not what he wanted for Grace. She needed to be teenager again, if that were even possible.

He lifted the footlocker onto the bed. The steel latches clicked open beneath his fingers. His hands moved with mechanical precision, unloading, then returning each weapon to its foam cutout. The twin Ruger Super Redhawks settled into their slots. The

Barrett's components separated smoothly, each piece finding its place in the hidden compartment. His armored vest folded in its tray. The explosives had all been used. He made a mental note to replace them.

Bare feet padded on tile. Grace stood in the doorway, the derringer cradled in her small hands. Her hair and clothes stiff with sea salt from the harbor. She watched her uncle's methodical movements, the way his massive frame filled the space between bed and wall. "I brought back your gun," she said. Her voice was steady, but her fingers trembled slightly as she held out the weapon.

Frank took the derringer, checked it with practiced efficiency, removing the unused bullets. No ceremony. No explanation.

Grace lingered, shifting her weight from foot to foot. "Thank you," she said finally. "For saving me." Frank grunted.

"That's it? A grunt. I'm kinda pouring my heart out here."

"I did what was needed," said Frank not looking up from the footlocker.

"So, what happens now?"

"I go back."

"Why? I mean my dad still needs a bodyguard. You could be it."

"No."

"So, you just go back and forget about us?"

"Yes."

"That's pretty sucky."

"Yes."

"It doesn't have to be that way. We're your family and family is important."

Frank grunted.

"I still need you."

Frank grunted again.

"What if I have nightmares?"

Frank turned to face her, his ravaged features catching light from the bedside lamp and said, "You will."

"So, that's it? I'm just supposed to suffer? How do I make them stop?"

Frank considers for a moment, then "You don't. You think about something else."

Grace's brow furrowed. "Yeah, like that's easy."

"Most things worth doing aren't easy."

"Great advice. I don't see how that helps me in the middle of the night?"

"Even in dreams, your mind is yours. You decide what to think." Frank's voice scraped like stones in his ruined throat.

"I'm not a child. I know what's possible and what's not. I cannot control my dreams."

"What's your favorite cookie?"

The question caught her off guard. "What?"

"Your favorite cookie. What is it?"

"White chocolate macadamia nut," she said slowly. "Why?"

"Cause they're really yummy. Even my dad thinks so. Our chef taught me how to make them. You have to melt the white chocolate just right or it gets grainy. And the macadamia nuts need to be fresh or they taste bitter. The secret is browning the butter first. It makes them smell like toffee when they're baking."

Frank nodded once. "Next time the bad dreams come, think about those cookies. Every detail. The smell. The taste. How the chocolate melts."

"That's it? Just think about cookies?"

"Your mind. Your choice. Cookies are a good choice."

Grace considered this, her head tilted slightly. "That's way too simple."

"Simple is good."

"How do you know it'll work?"

"I'm an expert on nightmares."

"Cuz you've killed a lot of people?"

"Yes. You can't kill someone with paying a price. The dead come to me in my dreams."

"Does the cookie thing work for you?"

Frank's face remained impassive, but something flickered in his eyes. "I think about when Richard and me were kids. Before everything changed. Playing baseball in the backyard. Building a treehouse that collapsed soon as we climbed in it. Racing our bikes down Miller's Hill. Back when we were the same."

Grace stepped closer, close enough to see the web of scars across his knuckles, the way his massive hands could cradle the tiny derringer with surprising gentleness. "I'll try the cookie thing," she said. "But if it's a really bad nightmare, maybe I'll think about my Uncle Frank instead."

Frank's grunt might have been agreement. Or maybe just acknowledgment.

A man's voice cut through the night from the mansion. "Where is he? Where's Frank?" The words carried rage and desperation.

Dropping the derringer and cartridges on the bed, Frank's hands found his revolvers and two speed loaders as his mind registered the threat. "Stay here," he told Grace.

"But—"

"Stay." The word held no room for argument. Grace pressed herself against the wall as Frank moved to the door. Through the windows, shadows moved across the mansion's bright interior. "Tell me where he is or I'll kill Vivian," said the voice.

He opened each revolver's cylinder. He used the speed loaders to load each weapon and slammed the cylinders shut with a flick of both wrists. His fingers wrapped tight around the revolvers' grips as he slipped into darkness, leaving Grace alone with the scent of gun oil and violence.

Frank moved closer and saw Andreev standing in the mansion's living room, his skin a mask of burned flesh. His remaining hand gripped a pistol. The other arm ended in a bandaged stump. His face had melted, features twisted into something demonic.

"I'll transfer the money back into your accounts," said Richard desperate.

"You had your chance. No more deals, Richard. I'm taking everything you love," said Andreev.

Frank aimed and fired both revolvers. The .44 magnum rounds shattered the window, missing Andreev's head by inches. Glass rained onto marble floors.

Before Frank could fire again, Andreev's pistol cracked. The round caught Richard in the gut. He collapsed, blood spreading across his white silk shirt. Vivian screamed as Andreev grabbed her by the hair, pressing the pistol under her sculpted chin. Her perfume mixed with the stench of his burned flesh.

"Drop the guns, Frank, or she dies next." Andreev's voice rasped through charred vocal cords. His melted lips pulled back in what might have been a smile. "We have unfinished business."

"We trade," said Frank.

"Sounds fair. Come out where I can see you. I want to see what I am trading for."

Frank had no choice as he stepped through the shattered window, glass crunching beneath his boots, revolvers up and aiming.

Andreev's pistol cracked in the enclosed space, the sound deafening. The round punched through Frank's chest with brutal force, nearly lifting him off his feet. His massive frame twisted as he fell. The revolvers slipped from his fingers, steel ringing against marble. Each breath brought pink foam to his lips, the bullet having torn through lung.

Andreev released Vivian no longer needing her as a shield. She ran to Richard, her hands pressing against the spreading red stain on his shirt. His skin had gone grey, breath coming in shallow gasps. Wine from a shattered crystal glass seeped into the Persian rug, mixing with his blood until it was impossible to tell which was which.

Andreev moved toward Frank with the slow deliberation of an executioner, burned flesh cracking with each step. The pistol's barrel looked massive as he leveled it at Frank's head. His finger tightened on the trigger.

The derringer's report was sharp, unexpected. A spray of arterial blood erupted from Andreev's neck, painting the white walls. He made a wet gurgle of surprise and fury, spinning toward Grace with unnatural speed, smoke curling up from the derringer's bottom barrel in both her hands. Andreev's pistol came up, his remaining hand rock-steady despite his wounds.

Seemingly helpless, Frank watched from the floor, another nightmare. Frank's boot caught Andreev's knee from behind with a crack of shattering bone and tearing ligaments. Andreev's shot went high, the round punching through silk curtains inches from Grace's head. He collapsed, howling in pain and rage.

Grace walked forward through broken glass and blood, the tiny derringer never wavering. She pulled the hammer back with a click. Andreev looked up at her, his ruined face a mask of hatred and disbelief. His mouth opened to speak or scream. Grace's second shot took him between the eyes. His body spasmed once, then went limp. The pistol rolled from his dead fingers, coming to rest in a pool of mingled blood and wine.

The derringer slipped from Grace's trembling fingers, clattering to the marble floor. She stared at Andreev's body, at what she had done, her face draining of color. Her eyes went wide with something beyond fear - the realization that she had crossed a line that could never be uncrossed.

Frank saw it happen, saw the moment childhood innocence died in her eyes. His chest ached with more than just the bullet wound.

Grace turned and ran to her father, falling to her knees beside him in the spreading pool of blood and wine. She grabbed his hand, tears streaming down her face. The sobs came then, deep and raw, shaking her small frame as the full weight of everything crashed down.

"Don't die, Daddy. Please don't die," she pleaded.

Frank laid back starring at the ceiling, his breathing shallow, sporadic. It was all too painful to watch. He closed his eyes.

A rack of greeting cards slowly spun. Frank reached for one – a birthday card with a pile of cookies each with a candle. He opened it, read the writing inside, and grunted unamused. It would have to do.

Fully recovered from his wounds, Frank moved to the store's counter, paid for the card and a postage stamp, then borrowed a pen and scribbled his signature – Uncle Frank. He placed a twenty inside and sealed the envelope addressed to Gracie.

Outside the store Frank slipped the envelope into a well-worn post office box. Climbing down the stairs, he moved to the restored Imperial sitting in the parking lot. Richard's money had brought the metal beast back to life and then some. It looked like new. Frank didn't like the polished paint and chrome. It drew too much attention. He took solace in the fact that it would tarnish with time and abuse.

The feral cat watched from shadows as Frank worked on the lighthouse, its yellow eyes gleaming. The animal had grown fat in recent months, its matted fur filling out. It no longer hissed when Frank passed, though it still kept its distance. They had once again reached an understanding and left each other alone.

Fresh paint covered most of the lighthouse now, white against slate sky. New windows caught afternoon light. The rusted spiral staircase had been replaced, steel treads rising in a perfect helix. Frank's sweat had washed away the salt, his blood had mixed with the mortar. The tower stood straighter, prouder, though work remained.

The rental car's engine echoed across the water. Frank looked down from his perch near the top of the lighthouse. A man in a worn sport coat stepped out of the car. His shoulders were broad beneath the jacket as he walked the weathered boards of the pier. His gate had a military rhythm. At the end, he stopped and stood facing the lighthouse.

Frank returned to his work, trowel scraping against old brick as he repointed another section. The man could wait. Or leave. Frank didn't care which. He wasn't in the mood for visitors.

Hours passed. The sun sank into the ocean, painting the waves copper and gold. Still the man stood, motionless as the granite blocks that formed the breakwater. His shadow stretched longer until it merged with evening darkness.

Climbing the newly rebuilt stairs, Frank checked the light, wound the clockwork mechanism that would keep it turning through the night. He flipped the switch turning the light on. It began to turn sending its beam across the waves. When he looked again, the man was a silhouette against stars.

Dawn broke grey and cool. Frank's boots echoed on the stairs as he climbed to check the light. His fingers found the switch, mechanical and certain. He turned the light off. It spun to a stop.

He looked toward shore through salt-streaked glass. The man still stood at the pier's edge. His sport coat rippled in the morning breeze. He might have been a statue, might have been there forever. Might never have moved at all.

Curiosity gnawed at Frank like an old wound. The boat's engine growled as he guided it toward the pier, salt spray stinging his scars. He cut power, letting momentum carry him to the weathered pilings. The man hadn't moved. Frank tied off the boat, his huge hands making the rope look like thread.

"Who are you?" Frank's voice scraped through his ruined throat.

"My name is Culper."

Frank went still. The name settled in his mind like a stone in deep water. "You're Culper?"

The man nodded once.

"What do you want?" Frank's words carried caution.

"You," Culper said simply.

The waves lapped at wooden pilings. Seabirds wheeled overhead. And somewhere in the depths of Frank's memory, doors long sealed began to open.

Letter to Reader

Dear Reader:

I hope you enjoyed *The Unwanted*. Frank Kane was far from your normal hero. It was a lot of fun to write.

The next book in The Frank Kane Series is *The Defiant*. Frank's back and meaner than ever. You'll finally learn who the enigmatic Culper is. Sorry to keep you hanging (I'm really not sorry.)

Sharing my books with your friends and reviews are always welcome. Thank you for supporting my work.

Regards,

David Lee Corley, Author

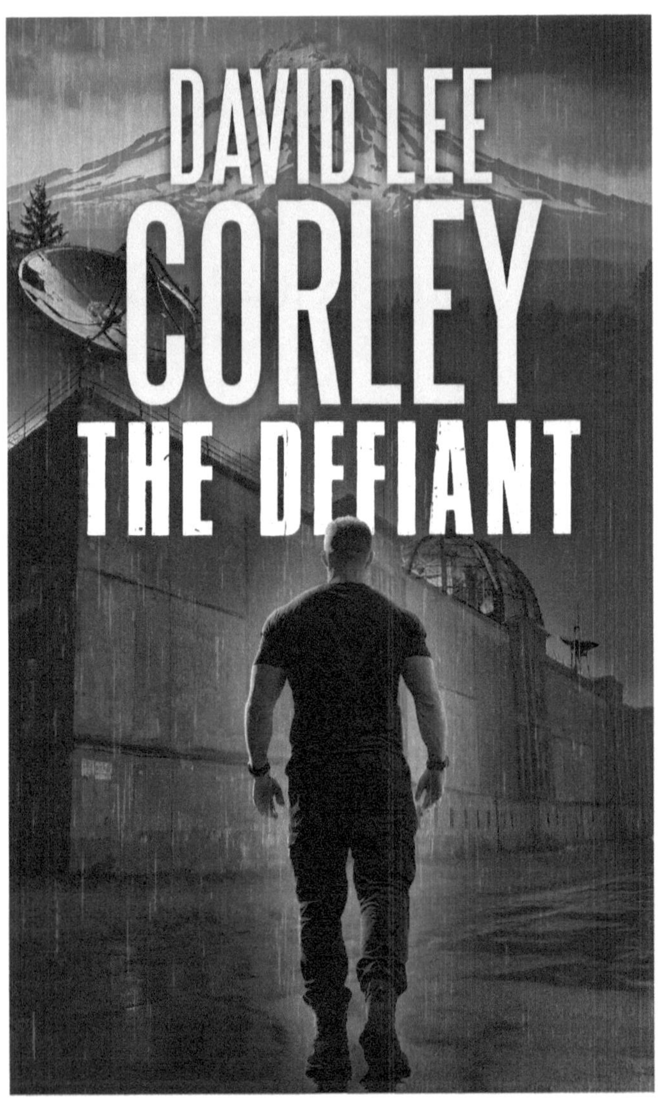

DAVID LEE
CORLEY
THE DEFIANT

Author's Biography

Born in 1958, David grew up on a horse ranch in Northern California, breeding and training appaloosas. He has had all his toes broken at least once and survived numerous falls and kicks from ornery colts and fillies. David started writing professionally as a copywriter in his early 20's. At thirty-two, he packed up his family and moved to Malibu, California, to live his dream of writing and directing motion pictures. He has four motion picture screenwriting credits and two directing credits. His movies have been viewed by over fifty million movie-goers worldwide and won a multitude of awards, including the Malibu, Palm Springs, and San Jose Film Festivals. In addition to his twenty-four screenplays, he has written twenty-nine novels. He developed his simplistic writing style after rereading his two favorite books, Ernest Hemingway's *The Old Man and the Sea* and Cormac McCarthy's *No Country For Old Men*. An avid student of world culture, David lived as an expat in both Thailand and Mexico. At fifty-six, he sold all his possessions and became a nomad for four years. He circumnavigated the globe three times and visited fifty-six countries. Known for his detailed descriptions, his stories often include actual experiences and characters from his journeys.

www.ingramcontent.com/pod-product-compliance
Lightning Source LLC
Chambersburg PA
CBHW031026310726
48969CB00007B/1877